TITUS OF ROME

Books by Alice Curtis Desmond

FAR HORIZONS

SOUTH AMERICAN ADVENTURES

LUCKY LLAMA

FEATHERS

JORGE'S JOURNEY

SOLDIER OF THE SUN

FOR CROSS AND KING

MARTHA WASHINGTON—OUR FIRST LADY

THE SEA CATS

GLAMOROUS DOLLY MADISON

THE TALKING TREE

ALEXANDER HAMILTON'S WIFE

BARNUM PRESENTS: GENERAL TOM THUMB

BEWITCHING BETSY BONAPARTE

YOUR FLAG AND MINE

GEORGE WASHINGTON'S MOTHER

TEDDY KOALA: MASCOT OF THE MARINES

SWORD AND PEN FOR GEORGE WASHINGTON

MARIE ANTOINETTE'S DAUGHTER

CLEOPATRA'S CHILDREN

TITUS OF ROME

Alice Curtis Desmond

ILLUSTRATED WITH PHOTOGRAPHS
AND MAPS

DODD, MEAD & COMPANY
NEW YORK

The maps and the Herod geneological chart
are by Donald T. Pitcher

Printed in the United States of America
by The Cornwall Press, Inc., Cornwall, N.Y.

Library of Congress Cataloging in Publication Data

Desmond, Alice Curtis, Date
Titus of Rome.

Bibliography: p.
Includes index.
SUMMARY: A biography of the second Flavian emperor who was noted for his generosity and regard for the people's welfare.
1. Titus, Emperor of Rome, 40–81—Juvenile literature. [1. Titus, Emperor of Rome, 40–81. 2. Kings and rulers. 3. Rome–History–Flavians, 69–96] I. Title.
DG290.D47 937'.07'0924 [B] [92] 75–38353
ISBN 0–396–07299–2

CONTENTS

ILLUSTRATIONS

Following page 84

Following page 180

MAPS AND CHART

TITUS OF ROME

1

THE EAGLE LEGIONS FLY THE CHANNEL

On a July day in A.D. 43 at Lyn-din, a Celtic hamlet the Romans were to rename Londinium, young Titus sat on the east bank of the Walbrook, a small stream that here flowed into the river Thames, waiting for his father. The boy was the son of T. Flavius Vespasianus (Vespasian), the legatus (commanding general) of the Second Augusta, one of the four legions the Emperor Claudius of Rome had sent to conquer Britain.

Being second-in-command of the expedition, Vespasian lived in the army camp on the west side of the Walbrook. The families of the legionaries were not allowed to live in the soldiers' camp. So Titus and his mother, Domitilla, occupied one of the round, thatched-roofed huts on the east bank of the stream that had been abandoned by the Trinovantes, a tribe of Britons who fled at the approach of the invading Romans. But as often as Vespasian could, ever since his family had arrived on the first supply ship to cross the Channel from Gessoriacum (Boulogne) in Gaul (France and Belgium), he had ridden over from camp to see them. Today, Domitilla had said to her son, his father would surely come, for he expected shortly to go off with the army and attack Camulodunum.

Titus was only four, but being a precocious boy, he had understood when his mother told him how the Romans had landed on the southeast coast of Britain and marched inland to the river Thames, only to find the tiny settlement of Lyn-din there deserted, its inhabitants having fled to their tribal center of Camulodunum.

While Titus waited that day by the Walbrook for his father, inside the beehive-shaped hut behind him, his mother was preparing Vespasian's favorite dish. As she placed the meat pie in the hot embers to bake, Domitilla sang to herself, for she was happy (even in barbaric Britain) so long as she was with her husband. Their marriage was a love match. It had taken place in spite of the opposition of Vespasian's grandmother Tertulla and that of his brother Sabinus, who had objected for what they considered to be a good reason—Domitilla was a slave girl.

She had been born in North Africa, the daughter of Liberalis, a slave owned by Statilius Capella, who was a centurion in the Third Legion stationed at Sabrata. Domitilla's parents died from abuse; and Capella, on retiring from the army, had brought their daughter back to Italy with him. There the girl labored with his other slaves on land he bought in the Sabine hills in a village named Falacrina, located by the river Velinus, a tributary of the Tiber.

On a small farm nearby lived an old lady, Tertulla Flavius by name, with her grandsons, Sabinus and Vespasian. Their father, Titus Flavius Petro, a tax collector, died young, as did their mother, Vespasia Polla. The two boys were brought up by Tertulla, their father's mother. When Domitilla came to Falacrina to work in the Capella olive orchards, Tertulla's eldest grandson, Sabinus, had gone to Rome to make his fortune; the younger one, Vespasian, was away in the army.

Domitilla became acquainted with the Flavian family when Tertulla, wanting a household slave, persuaded Capella to sell her the eighteen-year-old Domitilla. A better life now began for the poor girl. She worked in Tertulla's kitchen and tried hard to please her mistress. And Domitilla did. That is, until the twenty-nine-year-old Vespasian came home from his duties in Thrace as a centurion in the army, saw his grandmother's pretty new kitchen maid, and fell in love with her.

Meeting Domitilla by Tertulla's pigpen one day, Vespasian spoke the words the humble slave girl had never expected to hear. "I love you. I want to marry you!"

"How can you?" She stared at him in disbelief. "It's forbidden by law for a Roman citizen to marry a slave."

"I'll buy you from my grandmother and set you free."

Domitilla's beautiful eyes shone with delight. "But I haven't even a name."

"I'll give you not one but two. Flavia Domitilla. Do you like them? They are our family names."

Still, the slave girl refused to let Vespasian kiss her. There was something first the young master must know. She blushed with shame.

"What is it, my darling?" he asked.

"I've been . . . branded!" Domitilla lifted her skirts to let him see the large C that Capella had burned on her thigh with a hot iron, the same mark that he put on his cattle.

"Oh, is that all?" Vespasian exclaimed, taking her in his arms.

That had been five years ago and Domitilla sang happily today as she bustled about the one-room hut that was her home while Vespasian helped Aulus Plautius, the leader of the expedition, conquer Britain. Domitilla had followed her husband here, as she had gone with him to Crete and Germany, where Vespasian had been stationed since their marriage, and not for a moment had he regretted making her his wife. Although Grandmother Tertulla had refused to allow the wedding to be performed in her house, and Domitilla had never learned to read or write, she made up to Vespasian for her lack of education in other ways. When, on December 30, A.D. 39, she gave birth to little Titus, their happiness was complete.

From the first, there had been a close bond between father and son. So now Titus jumped excitedly to his feet, for he saw the general, on his horse Gilder, fording the shallow Walbrook. Ajax had seen him, too. The tan spaniel, barking shrilly, was running to greet him.

"Father!" shouted Titus. "Father!"

Vespasian reined in Gilder. A stocky man of thirty-four, wearing a bronze helmet and a metal cuirass, he dismounted. As his aide took Gilder's bridle, Titus ran into his father's arms. Then, taking his son by the hand, the general walked into the thatched hut and tenderly embraced his wife.

Everyone was hungry, so the Vespasian family sat right down to eat. Domitilla brought the meat pie from the hearth and placed it on the table beside some dark bread and two mugs of beer. There was a cup of milk for Titus, and Ajax, lying under the table, received his share of the pie and bread, which the spaniel swallowed at a gulp and was back begging for more before anyone could chew a mouthful.

Domitilla looked up lovingly from her plate at her husband. "Dear one, I wish you didn't have to go and attack

Camulodunum. Do you think there will be much fighting?"

"Possibly," he replied. "But not until Camulodunum is taken will Britain be conquered. And we've been waiting here in Lyn-din, by the Thames, too long. We should have pushed on after the Trinovantes immediately, while we still had the Britons on the run. Why hasn't Plautius given us the order to march? I cannot understand it–"

Vespasian never finished that sentence, for just then a soldier came hurrying into the hut. He saluted. "Vespasianus, Plautius wishes to see you at once."

The second-in-command sprang to his feet and snatched up his helmet. "Are we finally advancing on Camulodunum?" he exclaimed. "By Jupiter, it's about time!"

2

WHEN ELEPHANTS CAME TO BRITAIN

BRITAIN WAS KNOWN only vaguely to the ancient world before the time of Julius Caesar. He invaded the island in 55 and 54 B.C. and, after advancing only a short distance beyond the river Thames, was forced to hurry back to Rome and fight Pompey for the supreme power. Almost a century passed before the Romans returned to Britain, but their expedition under Claudius in the summer of A.D. 43, unlike Caesar's, came to stay.

The time was right for an invasion. The most powerful British king in Caesar's time, Cunobelin of the Trinovantes, had died and his domain had been divided between his sons, Togodumnus and Caratacus. It was these two kings, ruling southeast Britain, who tried to stop the invading Romans.

The troops selected for the conquest, led by Aulus Plautius, a cousin of the Emperor Claudius' first wife, Urgulanilla, consisted of four legions–the Ninth Hispana from the Danube, and the Second Augusta, the Fourteenth Gemina, and the Twentieth Valeria from the Rhine, with some Bavarian auxiliaries. Their start was not auspicious. When the soldiers assembled at Gessoriacum (Boulogne) to cross the Channel, they refused to board the transports and serve in Britain "outside the known world," for it was believed by most people that the earth ended beyond the shores of Gaul. Only Vespasian's pleas calmed the legionaries' superstitious fears and induced them to sail after a month of rebellion.

Luckily for the Romans, the delay helped them. Thinking that the invasion had been given up, the native Britons retreated inland and Plautius landed his troops early in July, 43, on the southeast coast of Britain, without meeting any opposition. At the river Medway, the Romans caught up with the fleeing Trinovantes tribesman, and Vespasian's Second Augusta legion led the attack across the stream. During the fighting on the opposite bank, Togodumnus was killed; his brother Caratacus, left to carry on the fight alone, fled with his forces to the far side of the Thames.

Plautius pursued the retreating Britons to a cluster of wooden huts with pointed, thatched roofs inside a stockade situated on the north bank of the stream. It was named Lyn-din (meaning in Celtic, Fort-on-the-Lake), for the native village was located at the widest part of the river, at the junction where the tiny Walbrook flowed into the Thames.

Arriving there in mid-July, the Romans found Lyn-din deserted. Caratacus and its few inhabitants had fled once more, fifty miles north, to the Trinovantes' chief town of Camulodunum. That was over a week ago. Impatiently, Vespasian and the other officers on Plautius' staff wondered why in all that time their commander had not given his legions the order to hurry on in hot pursuit of the fleeing Britons. What was he waiting for?

As Vespasian sat in his commanding officer's tent that afternoon, the reason for their delay by the Thames became clear to him.

"We're not leaving for Camulodunum for some days. Possibly not for several weeks," Plautius informed his staff. "The Emperor wishes to lead the march beyond the Thames. We must wait for his arrival." It seemed that Plautius had left Rome with secret instructions. He was to make a landing in Britain and, after advancing as far inland as seemed safe, send for Claudius.

Vespasian, a simple Etruscan peasant, knew his place, but being usually an outspoken man, he now ventured an opinion. "The Emperor will be six weeks getting here from Rome. Meanwhile, Caratacus will have time to strengthen his defenses. Why does Claudius wish to join us? He's no soldier."

"That's just the reason why the Emperor is coming to Britain," Plautius explained. "His advisers, Narcissus and Pallas, think that he should project a more warlike image. The Romans admire a military man. So Claudius is to witness the capture of Camulodunum. Then, when Britain is ours, he will get the credit for having added a new province to the Empire."

"Well, it won't be a victory for Rome but for the Britons, if we linger by the Thames much longer–" Vespasian broke off. He wanted to say more, but being of plebian birth, he knew better than to argue with a superior officer–especially one who was the Emperor's cousin. So Vespasian rose, picked up his helmet, and said, "Very good, sir. There will be no march on Camulodunum until the Emperor arrives. I will so inform the troops."

"And, Vespasianus, you can also tell the men that, while we wait for Claudius, I don't intend for them to be idle. We must build a more substantial bridge over the Thames. That pontoon affair our engineers made out of rafts won't be strong enough to hold the elephants."

"The *what?*" gasped Vespasian. Had he heard correctly? "You can't mean it! The Emperor is bringing elephants . . . why?"

"Because he is a student of Carthaginian history, and Hannibal took a herd of elephants with him when he went to conquer Rome." Plautius spoke casually, as though bringing elephants to Britain was the most natural thing in the world to do. "Narcissus, the Emperor's secretary, writes that Claudius will also have camels with him. For pack purposes, I suppose."

"I can't believe it!"

"Nor can I, but that's what the Emperor is bringing—thirty elephants, fifteen camels, and a troop of Nubian spearsmen." Plautius tossed a roll of papyrus across the table. "Here, read Narcissus' letter—" But Vespasian had heard enough. Snatching up his helmet, he stormed out of the tent, wishing that he had never come to Britain.

At Gessoriacum in Gaul, the first beacon was lighted, and the summons that Claudius had been waiting for crossed the Alps to Italy by means of a relay of smoke signals. It reached Rome late in July and the Emperor prepared to leave at once. The elephants and camels were loaded aboard a ship that Caligula had originally built to transport an eighty-foot-long obelisk from Egypt to Rome, and escorted by galleys containing the infantry and cavalry, the expedition sailed from Ostia, chief port of Italy, across the Mediterranean to Massilia (Marseilles), where they disembarked. Then by the roads and rivers of Gaul, Claudius' strange entourage reached the Channel and crossed by barge to Britain, where, for over six weeks, Plautius' troops had been dutifully waiting.

The long delay, which nearly drove Vespasian frantic, had been an exciting time for his young son. His father took Titus to see the first permanent bridge over the Thames being built and a stockade being erected for the elephants. They were from Ceylon and, since coming from India, had been working on the docks at Ostia. An elephant! Titus had never seen one, and it seemed to the boy that the day would never come when Claudius of Rome was due to arrive in Lyn-din with these strange beasts—like another Hannibal, as Plautius had said to Vespasian.

Others in Lyn-din were as excited as Titus, and on the morning of September 5, 43, everyone in the little settlement, young and old, was out of their huts to greet the Emperor. Holding tightly to his mother's hand, Titus stood in the crowd, watching the procession approaching along the trail beside the Thames. Some mounted soldiers came first. "Those are the Praetorians, the Emperor's bodyguard," Domitilla said to her son. "He must be right behind them. Oh, there he is!"

As Titus and his mother, who had Ajax on a leash, stood gaping at an ornate traveling coach rumbling by, the curtains at a window parted and Claudius looked out. Titus waved his hand. The Emperor waved back.

Next, the black Nubian spearsmen from Africa passed, wearing little else but leopard skins slung over their shoulders. Behind them came fifteen camels, walking with necks outstretched, wagging their jaws. Then followed thirty elephants, each with a turbaned Indian mahout astride his neck, the trunk of one elephant clinging to the tail of the elephant ahead.

In the lead strode Raja, and Ajax, never having seen such a huge beast, began to bark. A dog! Raja's little eyes glittered with hatred. "*Wurrumpt!*" he trumpeted. Instantly, the long line of elephants behind him stopped too, screaming with fear.

Titus snatched Ajax up in his arms and, by putting a hand over the dog's mouth, managed to stop his barking. But for a few bad moments it looked as though the parade of huge animals might all of them bolt, spilling their loads. Only the firm voice of the mahout Saba, astride Raja's back, finally calmed his angry snortings. Looking back over his shoulder, the big tusker commanded the other elephants. "*Harrum!*" he ordered.

As the great beasts swung into step behind their leader, and Raja led them off down the path, a voice shouted at Titus, "You wretched boy, what are you trying to do? Start a stampede? Get that dog away from here!" Titus turned. A handsome man in a plumed helmet was looking down at him from the back of a chestnut horse, an angry look in his eyes. "Don't you know that elephants hate dogs?" he demanded.

"No, I didn't, sir," Titus replied, holding Ajax tight in his arms. But the Emperor's secretary, Narcissus, without another word, galloped on.

That evening, Narcissus bathed in a tin traveling tub and shaved. Then, wearing an immaculate white toga, he joined Claudius and his Greek physician, C. Stertinius Xenophon, at dinner in the big leather tent with the Imperial standard before it that had been erected for the Emperor. His valet,

Lars, had unpacked Claudius' belongings. There were Persian rugs on the floor, silk pillows on the couches, a feather mattress and wool blankets had been unrolled, and beside the Emperor's bed, stood a painting of the Empress Messalina and their two children.

The elephants and camels had also carried war equipment on their backs, but getting all of this personal paraphernalia of the Emperor's into Britain had been Narcissus' chief reason for bringing along these exotic beasts. Still, in every army camp, hadn't Julius Caesar insisted upon having mosaic floors laid down? And hadn't Mark Antony, Claudius' grandfather, carried a gold dinner service all over Asia Minor on his military campaigns?

When Narcissus entered the Imperial tent, the tall, ungainly Emperor (a man of fifty-three, with a limp and a stammer) was asking his doctor, "Xenophon, where can I find some good pearls?" It seemed that Julius Caesar had brought Cleopatra two huge fresh-water pearls from Britain, and Messalina wanted her husband to bring her some—larger than Cleopatra's.

Halfway through dinner, the Emperor exclaimed, "Narcissus, can you imagine what Lars has laid out for me to wear tomorrow? A helmet and cuirass!"

"We will all of us have to get into armor tomorrow," his secretary replied. "You, especially, my dear Claudius, since you're leading the troops to capture Caratacus."

"Who says I am? Do you expect me to mount a horse? You know I can't. Riding gives me a backache."

Xenophon spoke up anxiously. "How far is Camulodunum? Fifty miles! I wouldn't want the Emperor to ride that distance."

Tears of self-pity rushed to Claudius' eyes. "What are you trying to do, Narcissus? Make a warrior out of me overnight? Come now, do I really have to go to Camulodunum? Couldn't Plautius capture Caratacus for me? Or that other fellow . . . what's his name? Vespasianus? I refuse to ride to Camulodŭnum with the troops and endanger my health. Do I have to, Xenophon?"

Since his physician was paid a colossal sum per year to agree to whatever the Emperor said, his secretary dropped the subject.

Narcissus, already heartily disgusted with the invasion of Britain, bade the others good-night as soon as the meal ended and went off to his tent. He knew by now why Claudius had consented to come to Britain. It wasn't to lead the troops in capturing Caratacus, but to get Messalina her pearls.

3

LONDON'S FIRST BIRTHDAY

TWO DAYS LATER, Titus and his mother stood among the crowd gathered by the Thames to see the Roman troops leave to attack Camulodunum. And it was Vespasian, not Plautius, who was to be in charge of the men going to capture Caratacus. On arriving in Lyn-din, Narcissus had quickly appraised the inept, elderly Plautius and replaced him.

It had not been difficult to get Aulus Plautius to step aside. Not a military man but the governor of Pannonia, a Roman province on the Danube, Plautius had been selected by the Emperor on a whim to lead the invasion. Secretly, he was only too glad to remain in Lyn-din with his "dear Cousin Claudius," for the Emperor, ill with a sore throat—as the army was told—could not lead his legions to capture Camulodunum as he had hoped to do.

"Claudius wants to parade Caratacus, the most important of the Celtic tribal kings of Britain, in chains through the streets of Rome," Narcissus had informed Vespasian. "So you must bring him back alive. If you do, we will reward you well. What do you want?"

There was no doubt in Vespasian's mind. "The surname of Britannicus," he replied.

A Roman's names meant a great deal to him. He had three—a *praenomen*, the given name, put first, and usually designated by one letter; a *nomen*, showing to what family (*gens*) he belonged; and a *cognomen*, indicating the branch of that family. Besides these, a fourth name, called a *cognomen ex virtute*, was sometimes given to a victorious general. For example, P. Cornelius Scipio, for having destroyed Carthage, became known as Scipio Africanus.

Hadn't Vespasian the right to ask for such a title of honor? At the Channel, hadn't he persuaded Plautius' legions to sail off into the unknown? Hadn't his Second Augusta won for the Romans at the Medway, their first battle in Britain? So T. Flavius Vespasianus was leaving Lyn-din today to earn for himself a fourth name—one of which he could be proud. Who had ever heard of the Flavian family of Falacrina?

But to win the surname of Britannicus, Vespasian must capture Caratacus alive. Could he do this with such a small force? He was starting north with only the Second Augusta (his own legion), the Nubian spearsmen and, as pack animals, the elephants and camels. Vespasian could have done without those exotic beasts. But Narcissus was determined to be rid of them. The elephants' snoring and the groans of the camels kept him awake at night.

More serious to Vespasian, though, was his concern about what Caratacus had been up to during the six weeks that they had been forced to wait for Claudius. The Britons had last been seen by the Romans when they fled before them at Lyn-din.

The nominal leader of the third Roman Conquest of Britain, Claudius of Rome, was the second son of Drusus and

Antonia. The latter was the daughter of Mark Antony and Octavia, the sister of the Emperor Augustus. Born at Lugdunum (Lyons) while his father was stationed in Gaul, little Claudius suffered from a defect in speech. He was lame and had palsy. A physical weaking, as a boy he devoted most of his time to study, and his tutor, the Roman historian Livy, had interested the sickly youth in the Carthaginians and the Etruscans.

In A.D. 41, Claudius was fifty-one and living quietly in Campania, writing books on the Etruscans that few people read, when Caligula's assassination changed his entire life. He happened to be in Rome visiting his nephew on January 24, the night that tyranical emperor was murdered by the Praetorians, his bodyguard. Claudius hid behind a curtain, thinking that he, too, would be killed. But the soldiers spied the trembling man and dragged him out.

"Our next Caesar!" their captain exclaimed, partly in fun.

Claudius pleaded that he didn't want to be emperor, but the Praetorians insisted. Wasn't he the son of Rome's great war hero, Drusus? And the younger brother of Germanicus, another popular general, who had died fighting in Asia Minor? Claudius was the only male member of the Imperial family left. So, much against his will, two years before his journey to Britain, this stuttering, limping, aging man became the fourth emperor of Rome.

"Poor Claudius," as the Romans called him, made a sad ruler. But did it matter? His secretary, Narcissus, and his finance minister, Pallas, ran the government for him.

Both were high-born Greeks, well educated, and former slaves of Claudius' mother. At her death, Narcissus and Pallas had received their freedom, but, as freedmen, continued to live with Claudius and run his affairs, first in Campania, and after he became emperor, on Palatine Hill.

The invasion of Britain had been hatched at Rome in Narcissus' fertile brain, and since coming to Lyn-din, he had not been idle. While Claudius amused himself rolling dice with Plautius, his able secretary was busy consolidating the Romans' foothold in Britain. Plautius had made the initial landing, but the twelve native kings must now be turned into vassal chieftains, subject to Rome. Otherwise, as soon as the legions left, they would declare themselves free again. Of course, Caratacus of the Trinovantes was included in the list of prisoners, because everyone in Lyn-din felt sure that Vespasian would capture him without any trouble.

"We'll summon the twelve captive kings to Lyn-din and give a banquet for them," Narcissus said.

Claudius was delighted with the idea. Calling in his head cook, he began to plan the feast.

But, as the days passed and Vespasian did not return, the Emperor grew increasingly restless. "Narcissus, I've been in Britain nearly a fortnight and I'm sick of the place," he complained. "When can I go back to Rome?"

"As soon as Vespasianus returns with Caratacus. You want to parade him in chains through the Forum, don't you?"

Claudius' face brightened. "Indeed, I do, and it will be the proudest day of my life. Narcissus, I'm going to have the finest triumph Rome has ever seen. I've earned it. Just think, I've done what Julius Caesar failed to do. I've conquered Britain!"

But, eventually, the Emperor grew weary of the long wait in this dull place, and bending over the mounds of pearls being brought in daily for him to examine, he kept saying fretfully, "As soon as I find some large enough to please Messalina, I'm going home."

Knowing that Claudius' departure would have a bad effect upon the morale of his troops, Narcissus, to keep the Emperor in Britain, said to him one morning, "Caesar, help me to lay out a city here. Lyn-din is an ideal spot for the capital of Rome's new province of Britannia. It is located as high up the Thames as ships can go, and as near its mouth as the river can be bridged. Come along, a walk will do you good. We'll cross over the Walbrook into Lyn-din. From there, we can get a better view of the terrain."

Claudius protested, but being a weak-willed man, his secretary, as usual, had his way. The two men set out from the Imperial tent, located in the army camp on the left bank of the Walbrook, to wade the shallow stream. It was hard going for a handicapped man. On reaching a hilltop in Lyn-din, the lame Emperor, whose leg always pained him, sank down exhausted on a boulder.

"Narcissus, what do I do now," he complained.

"Sit here and tell me where we should put the forum, the basilica, and the baths."

So Claudius pointed out to Narcissus a slope down to the Thames, and he was explaining to him why this would be a good place for the forum, when a small boy and a dog came along.

"Who are you, child?" the Emperor asked.

"Titus."

"He's Vespasian's son," Narcissus explained. Then glaring sternly down at Titus' little spaniel, he added, "And this, I believe, is the dog that barked and frightened our elephants."

"I'm sorry, sir. Ajax didn't mean to. He's a good dog," Titus hastened to say. "I've taught Ajax to do tricks. Would you like to see him roll over?"

The tan spaniel rolled over. Then he stood up on his hind legs and walked. Claudius, who was a simple and kindly man at heart, as well as a scholarly one, clapped his hands in approval. "You've a clever dog there, little Titus," he said, genially. "I'm laying out a city. Do you want to help me?"

So, when the boy had sat down beside him, the Emperor pointed out to Narcissus a spot down by the river, below the bridge across the Thames, where a house for the Roman governor might be built some day. And, further up the hill on which they were seated, a fort. Narcissus went to put markers on the places Claudius indicated.

That is how on a day in September, 43, an emperor and a boy came to survey the site for the town the Romans called Londinium, which later became London. Neither of them imagined that it would grow into the largest city on earth, in a small country that would, in time, rule over lands four times the size of the Roman Empire.

4

ROMAN WOLVES AND BRITISH FOXES

Next day, Vespasian's army came marching out of the wolf-infested oak forest that surrounded Lyn-din and covered most of Britain. As the standard of the Second Augusta—a gilt eagle carried on a pole—emerged from the woods across the Thames, the sentinels on the bridge shouted, "Vespasian is back!" and everyone in Lyn-din rushed out to welcome him. But it was at the long line of British prisoners trudging along, hands tied, behind the columns of soldiers, that the excited Romans were looking.

"That must be Caratacus," a woman said to Domitilla, standing with her son Titus in the crowd, as a long-haired giant of a man went by, glaring defiantly at his captors.

But was it he? The Roman garrison was still in doubt when an hour later, with his prisoners safely locked up, Vespasian sat in the Imperial tent telling the Emperor, Narcissus, and Plautius about his journey. "We came upon the Britons the second evening," he said. "Doubling back from Camulodunum, Caratacus and his warriors were waiting to ambush us."

Ordering his soldiers to halt, Vespasian rode up alone, close to the enemy. Caratacus and his men were asleep in their tents. And, at last, Vespasian could see some use for his elephants, other than to use them to pull chariots out of the mud. Returning to his legionaries, Vespasian said to them, "The elephants are to lead the attack. Then will come the camels and the blacks from Africa. A wall of huge beasts looming up suddenly on top of the Trinovantes, out of the darkness, may panic them. Remember, these people have never seen an elephant, a camel, or a dark-skinned man."

Elephants, for all their huge size, move noiselessly, so the Romans were able to slip up quietly on the Britons. Beyond their tents, in a field, were Caratacus' war chariots and horses. *Horses.* Even more than dogs, elephants hate horses. Catching their scent, Vespasian's herd of thirty elephants came crashing through the forest, knocking down everything in their path, to get at the hated beasts.

Caratacus and his warriors came running from their tents to see what was the matter. The long-necked camels ran at them, spraying the Britons with their bad-smelling spit; the half-naked Nubians from the Nile added to the confusion by leaping about, whooping savage war cries and brandishing their spears. Staring in disbelief at the elephants, the camels, and the black men they thought to be evil spirits, the Britons fled. A few of the Trinovantes managed to escape, but the majority of them were killed by the Romans, trampled to death by the elephants, or taken captive, and Vespasian started back to Lyn-din with his prisoners.

"Which one of them is Caratacus?" Claudius asked eagerly. Vespasian hung his head. "I'm sorry, but on the way back he escaped."

"Escaped? Oh, no! You're . . . joking?" The Emperor began to stutter, as he always did when upset. "Vespasianus, you know that Caratacus was the prisoner . . . I wanted most. He was to have been the high point of my triumph. Oh, this is dreadful! How could you have let him . . . get away?"

As Claudius and the others listened in shocked silence, the unhappy Vespasian told them how the King of the Trinovantes had managed to loosen the ropes that bound his feet by gnawing at them with his teeth. A short while later, as the Romans milled excitedly about their camp searching for him, Caratacus appeared on a cliff above their heads, his hands still manacled.

Javelins in their hands, the Romans started up after him. "Surrender, you fool!" Vespasian called out. "Don't you know that you can only drink? You cannot catch food or eat, for you can't untie your hands. Alone in the forest, you will starve."

To show his contempt of the invaders, Caratacus spat down on them. Then he disappeared. The Romans searched everywhere, but never found him.

"You had a throwing spear," Narcissus reminded Vespasian. "Why didn't you hurl it at Caratacus and wound him, so he couldn't escape?"

"I had a weapon, he had none, and his hands were tied behind his back. Could I harm a helpless man?"

Narcissus burst out. "By Jupiter, this is war! When you have an enemy cornered, Vespasianus, you show him no mercy. I'm surprised at you."

"And why didn't you go on to Camulodunum?" demanded Plautius.

"It was now an open town. All of Caratacus' warriors had accompanied him back on the trail."

"Nevertheless, you should have pushed on and burned the Trinovantes' tribal center to the ground."

"With no one left in it but old men, women, and children?"

"Certainly!" exclaimed the Emperor. "Vespasianus, you handled the expedition badly." And that was the general opinion in camp. Jealous of his second-in-command, Plautius told everyone that had he been in charge of the march to Camulodunum, Caratacus would never have gotten away.

Vespasian was in disgrace when, the following day, the Celtic kings of Britain began to arrive in Lyn-din. For years, these tribal chieftains had been fighting among themselves. Now each of them wanted to make the best possible terms with Rome.

Like the Gauls across the Channel from where they had come, the Britons were tall, long-haired Celts, moustached, blue-eyed, and blond. They wore horned helmets, tunics and long trousers, and tattooed their bodies with the blue dye of the woad plant to look more frightening in battle—a custom the Romans thought loathsome and barbaric. They were practical people, and although fierce fighters, knew when they were beaten. So it was a friendly enough gathering of men who crowded into the Imperial tent that night and sat down to the lavish feast that Narcissus had ordered prepared for them.

When Claudius' guests had all consumed great quantities of wine and beer, enough to be feeling mellow, there were speeches. Cogidubnus, King of the Regnenses, rose to say that he would willingly send hostages and pay tribute to Rome. Other tribal heads then proclaimed their friendship. Among them, Prasutagus of the Iceni announced that he would gladly lead the delegation of British kings that was to march in the Emperor's Roman triumph.

Seated at the head of the table, Claudius had been drinking steadily as he listened to the speeches. His bloodshot eyes went from king to king. "There are only eleven of you," he suddenly exclaimed. "There should be twelve. Who is missing? Oh, I remember, it's Caratacus. Where . . . is he?"

There was a painful silence. No one dared to speak.

"Oh, it was *you* . . . who let him escape!" The Emperor glared down the table at the unhappy Vespasian, who sat, head bent, his cheeks scarlet. "Caratacus won't be in my triumph. You've ruined the whole affair. It was to have been . . . the proudest day of my life. . . ." Claudius saw the frightened, averted faces. No one knew where to look or what to say. "Vespasianus, I'll have you thrown to the lions!" the Emperor shouted. Then the crash came. The drunken monarch fell forward over the table.

Next morning, Claudius had a hangover; not that there was anything ususual about that. But the Emperor felt somewhat better when he was brought two enormous pearls. "Lars," he called excitedly to his valet. "I've two perfect ones—large enough to please even the Empress. At last, I can go home!"

With less than half the island conquered, Claudius declared it to be Rome's new province of Britannia. He made his cousin, Aulus Plautius, its first governor, and the preparations for his journey back to Italy began at once. That afternoon, having spent only sixteen days in Britain—but long enough to justify what he craved for, the glory of a triumph—the Emperor was ready to return to Rome with his elephants, camels, and Nubian spearsmen, leaving it to the army to consolidate their gains.

Titus had made friends with Raja's driver Saba, a wrinkled old East Indian in a turban and sarong. So Saba lifted the boy onto Raja's back and he rode proudly before the mahout,

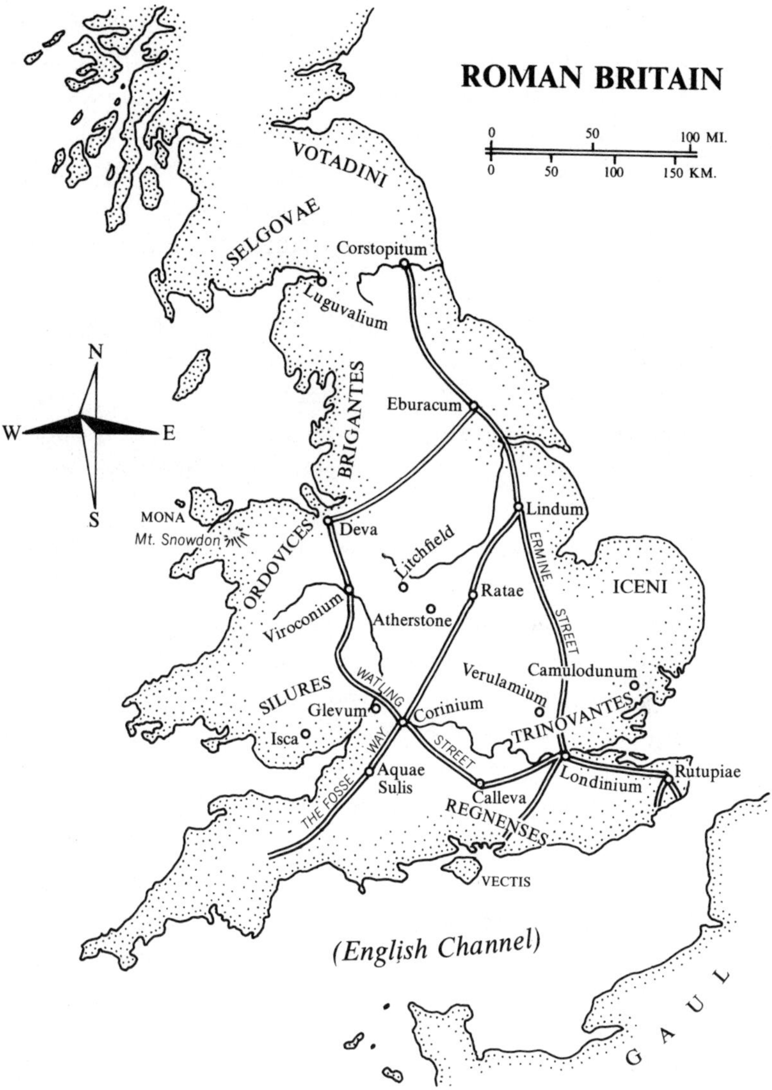
ROMAN BRITAIN
0
50
100 MI.
0
50
100
150 KM.
N
S
W
E
VOTADINI
SELGOVAE
Corstopitum
Luguvalium
BRIGANTES
Eburacum
MONA
Mt. Snowdon
Deva
Lindum
ORDOVICES
Litchfield
ERMINE
STREET
ICENI
Ratae
Viroconium
Atherstone
WATLING
STREET
Verulamium
Camulodunum
SILURES
Glevum
Corinium
TRINOVANTES
Isca
Aquae
Sulis
THE FOSSE
WAY
Calleva
Londinium
Rutupiae
REGNENSES
VECTIS
(English Channel)
GAUL

astride the neck of the largest bull in the herd, down to the Roman transports anchored on the Thames. Behind Raja followed the other twenty-nine elephants, each one carefully putting his big feet in the tracks of the elephant ahead.

The Emperor had already gone aboard the Imperial galley, and on the wharf Narcissus and Vespasian stood watching to see the fifteen camels, with their haughty, supercilious expressions, safely up the gangplank.

"I'm sorry, Vespasianus," Narcissus said. "Claudius gave you a hard time the other night. He gets that way when he's been drinking."

Vespasian spoke bitterly. "I regret that I had to disappoint the Emperor, but in fairness to Caratacus, I don't see how I could have acted otherwise."

"Well, catch him for us, and all will be forgiven. Where do you think he went?"

"To Wales, I imagine, and I'll bring him to Rome in chains, if it takes me the rest of my life."

"Good for you! Well, Vespasianus, I'll keep my end of the bargain. I'll see to it that the Emperor gives you the surname of Britannicus if you bring us Caratacus."

Neither of them imagined that it would take Vespasian four years to do it. His Second Augusta first added Vectis (the Isle of Wight) to the Empire, and it was two years before he was free to go after Caratacus, who, meanwhile, had taken refuge among the Ordovices of North Wales. In that wild mountainous terrain, the Romans finally caught up with him. The King of the Trinovantes and his Welsh allies were beaten, but Caratacus managed to escape again and fled to the Brigantes, a tribe in northern Britain.

It was a fatal mistake. Queen Cartimandua of the Brigantes

had once wanted Caratacus to marry her. He preferred a younger and prettier woman. So now she had her revenge.

"If you want the King of the Trinovantes, he is my prisoner," Queen Cartimandua sent word to Vespasian. "Come and get him."

5

HOW GOOD IS A PROMISE?

IN DECEMBER OF 47, T. Flavius Vespasianus was to be given an ovation in Rome for finally capturing Caratacus, and his wife was unhappy. Why? It was because she must go to the Forum and sit with the guests of honor. Could Domitilla do it? Sit there, with everyone staring at her, when she was nine months pregnant.

On his return from Britain four years ago, the Emperor had erected a lighthouse to mark the spot where he crossed the Channel. He had minted a gold coin and staged the triumph he longed for, but what Claudius most wanted to see—Caratacus in chains being led through the streets of Rome—was lacking in his triumph of 43. That was why people were so excited today. Everyone was hurrying to the Forum to gloat over the humiliation of the British king who had held out longest against the Romans.

Domitilla wondered how she could get through the crowd to the reviewing stand, even with Titus to help her. He was a big boy now, eight years old, and sturdy like his father. What had she to fear? Yet Domitilla, feeling the child stir within her, was frightened as to what might happen as, leaning on her son's arm, she left for the Forum.

They finally reached their seats. But, after that, there was a long wait in the hot sun for the procession that was forming outside the city walls. Vespasian's elder brother, Sabinus, and his wife, Paulita, catching sight of Domitilla, came over. Since returning from Britain with Vespasian, Domitilla had seen little of her in-laws, although they lived next door to her in Rome, but today she was the wife of the hero of the occasion. Sabinus and Paulita wanted to be seen talking with her.

A sly-looking little man dominated by his big, hard-eyed wife, Sabinus arranged his mouth into a patronizing smile and said, "Too bad Grandmother Tertulla isn't alive to be here today." Yes, thought Domitilla, what would the old lady have said to see the Emperor honoring the grandson whom she considered had disgraced the Flavian family by marrying her slave girl?

Sabinus had been Tertulla's favorite. She was proud when he went to Rome, married above him (the daughter of a goldsmith), and grew rich by furnishing supplies to the army at outragous prices. And today Paulita had news to impart. She could hardly wait to gloat over her sister-in-law. "Have you heard, Domitilla? Sabinus is to be governor of Moesia!"

It was a rich province on the lower Danube. Domitilla murmured congratulations. Sabinus would return to Rome a millionaire. The provinces were gold mines for corrupt officials.

She wanted to tell him that his brother had also been promised a governorship (of a province richer, possibly, even than Moesia) and also the surname of Britannicus. But trumpets sounded, heralding the arrival of the Imperial party, and Sabinus and Paulita hurried off to their seats.

First into the reviewing stand came the ladies and gentlemen of the court. Then appeared the lame Emperor with his foolish smile, accompanied by the Empress. She was beautiful. Her blonde hair hung down about her shoulders, like a mantle of gold, and from Messalina's ears hung the two huge pearls Claudius had brought her from Britain.

Now down the Via Sacra, the main street of the Forum, came Vespasian's triumphal procession, but Domitilla was never to see it. The faces about her began to blur. She fainted.

"Mother . . . Mother!" Titus cried in alarm.

Domitilla had slipped off her seat. She lay on the floor of the reviewing stand, in danger of being trampled on by the curious people pressing around her.

"Stand back! All of you! A woman has fainted. Give her air." It was a bossy voice that spoke; and Titus, bending over his mother, lifted grateful eyes to a large, homely woman who helped him lift Domitilla back onto a seat.

"It's the heat," said the woman. Then she noticed Domitilla's figure. "My boy, your mother is pregnant! Why did she come out on such a hot day?"

"To see my father's ovation."

"Then you're Vespasian's wife and son. What is your name?"

"Titus."

"Well, Titus, we must get your mother home. Where do you live?"

"On the Via Malum Punicum."

"That's not far. I'll go with you. How could a boy like you look after a woman about to have a child any minute? See, your mother is coming to . . . You fainted, my good woman, but you'll be all right. Titus and I are going to take you home."

"Oh, no!" Domitilla protested, faintly. "I must see my husband ride by!"

"Well, you can't. Do you want your baby to be born in the Forum?"

The woman shouted angrily at everyone in their way. Her manner was so commanding that people scattered. Before long, the three of them reached a shabby *insula* on Quirinal Hill and, with some difficulty, the boy and the strange woman got Domitilla up the tenement's steep stairs to the third floor.

They were no sooner inside a small, dark room than Antonia Caenis (for that was her name) turned to Titus. "Boy, heat some water. Quick! Because you're going to have to help me deliver a baby."

So another event took place that day which seemed to the Vespasian family fully as important as his ovation. When the commander of the Second Augusta legion returned home, he found that he had a daughter.

They named the frail child Domitilla after her mother. But, from the first, the Vespasians knew that she would not live long. The baby died in two weeks. And what would they have done but for Antonia Caenis! She came every day and, in her bossy but kindly way, took over the household.

In contrast to Vespasian's still-pretty wife, Antonia Caenis was a masculine-looking woman in her forties, with the suggestion of a mustache on her plain face. She, too, was a freedwoman. But while Domitilla had been sold as a girl in Africa, forced to strip naked and be examined by the crowd like an animal, Antonia had known nothing but kindness. Born of

Greek slaves in the household of the Emperor Claudius' highly respected mother, Antonia, she was well educated and, being a bright girl, had become her secretary.

Antonia's will freed Antonia Caenis, as it had Narcissus and Pallas. She was left a small pension and the name of her former mistress, for Roman slaves had no more right to names of their own than they had to marry or own property.

Having grown up with the Imperial family, there was little that Antonia Caenis didn't know about them. Narcissus was "tricky"; Pallas, a former slave, had become so rich and haughty on becoming the Emperor's finance minister that he no longer deigned to speak to his servants, but issued his orders to them in writing. As for Claudius, how the poor stupid fool was ruled by "that harlot of a Messalina!"

"Antonia! Don't speak so disrespectfully of the Imperial family!" Vespasian would exclaim, but Domitilla enjoyed listening to Antonia's gossip. It made her forget the loss of her baby.

Ovations were all very well, but when would Vespasian get his real reward for capturing Caratacus, his family wondered. Where would he be sent as governor? So when Narcissus summoned the general to the Imperial palace one day, they watched Vespasian ride off to the Palatine with anxious eyes. What would he have to tell them on his return?

Through marble halls and richly furnished rooms, Vespasian was ushered by African slaves into Narcissus' private study. "To show his gratitude for your services in Britain, Claudius intends to send you to one of our provinces as governor," the Emperor's secretary said to him. "Have you any preference?"

"I'd like Britain. My wife and I were happy there."

"No, Britain is impossible. Scapula, who succeeded Plautius there as governor, is doing too well to be replaced. How about Africa?"

Tears of disappointment rushed to Vespasian's eyes. To be given Africa, the smallest, most unhealthy, of the Roman provinces—hardly more than a strip of desert between Numidia and Libya—after all his years of military service in Britain, when Sabinus was being sent to rich Moesia! What, he thought bitterly, had his brother ever done for the Empire?

Vespasian wanted to protest angrily, but he didn't dare. Even his moment of hesitation had turned Narcissus' smiles to frowns. "Don't you like the appointment?" the Emperor's secretary demanded.

Vespasian forced himself to express his thanks. But, at the door, he was bold enough to say, "How about the name of Britannicus? You promised me that, you know."

"I'm sorry. I know how much a title of honor means to you." Narcissus, averting his eyes, tried to dismiss the matter lightly. "But, unfortunately, Claudius wants the name of Britannicus for his son. He wishes the whole world to know that he conquered Britain."

Vespasian's legs grew weak under him from the shock. He had to clutch at a table to keep from falling. To confer the name of Britannicus on a boy of six, who had never so much as stepped foot in Britain, when it was thanks to him, T. Flavius Vespasianus, that the legions had sailed from Gaul and there was any invasion at all. Yet before he left Narcissus that day, a worse blow befell him, such a calamity that it put all previous disappointments out of his mind.

* * *

Vespasian rode back to the Quirinal that day, heartbroken, wishing with all his soul that he did not have to face his family. "Domitilla! Titus!" he called, on entering the small, dark rooms that were his home in the shabby tenement. They rushed to greet him. As usual, Antonia was there too. Looking at Vespasian's face, they knew. It wasn't good.

"Where?" asked Antonia.

"Africa."

"Oh, no!" cried Domitilla. To live again in that frightful place, where her slave-father was forced by Capella to wear an iron collar riveted about his neck day and night for having tried to escape! In an instant, Antonia was beside her. "Sit down, dear." She forced the hysterical woman down onto a stool and put her arms about her. Sobbing bitterly, Domitilla wept on her friend's broad shoulder.

After a while, Antonia asked, "Surely, Vespasianus, they gave you what you wanted so badly . . . the surname of Britannicus?"

"No, not even that . . ." Tears in his eyes, her husband tried to tell Domitilla as gently as he could, "And when we go to Africa, Narcissus says that we must leave Titus behind. The Emperor wants him as a companion for his son."

She stared at him in shocked disbelief. "We're to be separated from our child? Why?"

"The heir to the throne is timid. In Londinium, the Emperor saw Titus ride Raja, the largest of our elephants, down to the boats. He wants Titus to teach his son to be like that, not afraid."

"Oh, no! I couldn't give him up!" Domitilla was sobbing again in Antonia's arms. "It would kill me!"

"I know. It breaks my heart, too," her husband said, sadly.

"But we have no choice. Those are the Emperor's orders."

"Domitilla, stop crying!" Antonia came to Vespasian's aid. "You must not be selfish and stand in your son's way. Don't you see how splendid it will be for him? Titus will live at court. He's a bright boy. There are no schools in Africa. He would have grown up there to be a dunce. Now your son will be educated with the Imperial children. Aren't you thrilled?"

Antonia promised to see that no harm came to the boy. She would have Titus visit her every week and would write his parents about him. So Domitilla finally agreed to go to Rome's province of Africa with Vespasian; and in March, A.D. 48, Titus, age nine, came to live on Palatine Hill as the *paedagogus* of the heir to the throne.

6

THE NAUGHTY EMPRESS

As *paedagogus* (boy companion) to the seven-year-old Britannicus, as Germanicus was now called, Titus slept in a big room in the Imperial palace where the page boys lived. Mornings, the freedman in charge of them pounded loudly on his gong, and the dormitory was full of arms and legs as fifty boys jumped, rolled, or were dragged out of bed.

After breakfast, Titus left for the schoolroom to have his lessons with the Imperial children, Britannicus and Octavia, while the other boys went about their duties elsewhere in the palace. Nine-year-old Titus Flavius Vespasianus was the son of T. Flavius Vespasianus, governor of the province of Africa. That made him outrank his dormitory mates, but the other boys forgave him. They liked Titus because he was curly-headed, snub-nosed, and square-jawed, because his brown eyes were honest and twinkling, and although he was the *paedagogus* of the heir to the throne, he wasn't haughty about it.

Separated from his parents in Africa, Titus had three things to comfort him: his lyre, his dog Ajax, and his weekly visits to Aunt Antonia. In the pages' dormitory, Titus kept his small Greek harp on the shelf above his bed. Ajax slept under the cot. But the friendly little spaniel came out from under the bed to wag his tail at everybody.

When Titus first introduced his pet to the heir to the throne of the Caesars—a thin, pale boy with sad eyes—Britannicus drew back frightened when Ajax jumped up on him. "He won't bite you. He only wants to lick your face," Titus explained. "Let Ajax show you how he can walk." So the spaniel stood on his hind legs and walked. He rolled over and played dead. "What a smart dog!" exclaimed Britannicus' sister Octavia, a pretty, dark-haired girl, but very shy.

One day, when the children were at the blackboard, translating into Greek the words that Sosibius, their tutor, recited to them in Latin, the door opened and the Emperor entered. With him was the loveliest lady Titus had ever seen.

"I hear you're making my son very happy," the Empress said to him. "Britannicus tells me that he never had a real friend until you came to the Palatine. And the Emperor says you sing to the lyre. Will you play for me sometime?"

A few days later, Messalina sent for Titus. He hung his harp over his shoulder, and a page boy led him through the palace to the Empress' sitting room where she and her ladies were seated. "We're bored. Sing for us," Messalina sighed.

Titus plucked the strings of his harp. But he had forgotten to tune it. "Quank, guang—" his lyre sounded, sourly. The women laughed. And Titus blushed to the roots of his brown hair. "That will do, little boy, run along now. Come again, when your harp is behaving better," said the Empress. Titus was nine years old. He hated to be called "little boy." He almost ran from the room.

It was a week before he was invited to sing for the Empress and her ladies again. This time, Titus had tuned his lyre in advance, and when he ran his fingers over the strings, he could create lovely ripples of sound.

Messalina was twenty-five, too young, people said, for a man of fifty-seven. Why had the gay, beautiful Messalina consented to marry tiresome, aging Claudius? All of Rome wondered, but the reason was simple. At sixteen, a wild girl who chased after sing-song boys, actors, and grooms, she had become pregnant by a handsome Macedonian slave of her father's, the rich Senator Barbatus, and must be married off at once. But her mother, Domita Lepida, was the granddaughter of Mark Antony and Octavia, the Emperor Augustus' sister, so Messalina could only marry into the Imperial family. And who was there among them of suitable age? Or unattached, except foolish old Claudius?

So it was arranged. Messalina was sent by her parents to visit in the hills of Campania, where the Emperor Caligula's middle-aged uncle lived quietly as a scholar and recluse. Claudius had been married three times. Livia Medulla had died on their wedding night. His next two marriages, to Plautia Urgulanilla and Aelia Paetina, ended in divorce. Bad luck with women, Claudius said, discouraged him from wanting to marry again, but that was before he saw Messalina. Soon Claudius found it hard to take his eyes off the girl. "Why don't you marry her?" Narcissus suggested.

"I'm forty-eight. Messalina is sixteen, young enough to be my granddaughter. She would want a younger man."

"Messalina tells me that young men bore her. She likes mature men, like you."

Messalina had never said any such thing. But Claudius was

eager to believe every word. "Then, as a husband, she wouldn't consider me too old?"

"Ask her and see," urged Narcissus.

Senator Barbatus and his wife were greatly relieved when Claudius married their daughter. Now there would be no scandal. Messalina's baby would have a father. Claudius was too old for the girl, thirty-two years her senior, but otherwise he was not such a bad catch. Being the grandson of Mark Antony, and the uncle of the ruling emperor, Caligula, made Claudius a member of the Imperial family, if not a very important one.

Six months after her marriage, Messalina gave birth to a little girl. People were told that Octavia was a premature child. They smiled, but Claudius didn't care. Messalina's elderly husband was madly in love with her.

Poor Messalina! The passionate, teen-age girl found out what it was like to have married a tired old man. Three endless, boring years passed. Then, on January 24, 41, a wonderful thing happened—Caligula was murdered! Claudius, discovered trembling behind a curtain, was named Emperor by the Praetorian Guard and Messalina, at nineteen, became Empress. The Romans loved her. Never had they had such a young and beautiful empress. Even boring, dottering Claudius seemed to improve. His head wobbled, his hands shook, but he was now the Emperor, so people overlooked these defects.

Then, a miracle happened. At fifty-one, Claudius had never expected to have a baby, but a month after he was crowned, the Empress gave birth to a boy they named Germanicus, after the Emperor's older brother who had died winning his surname-of-honor fighting in Germany. Claudius was beside himself with joy, for no one could say that little Germanicus was not his own son. The sickly infant was obviously the child of an old man. He had even inherited his father's palsy.

Titus was too innocent a boy to believe these skeletons in the past of the Imperial couple to be true, although it was common gossip about the palace. He only knew that when he was summoned with his harp to entertain Messalina and her guests in the Empress' private apartments, if the Emperor was present, "poor Claudius" was treated with little respect. He usually drank too much, and when he fell asleep at the table and snored, the Empress and her ladies threw olive stones at his nodding head, to the amusement of the young men present.

There were always many male guests. Messalina, too young and frivolous to appreciate her husband's virtues, had only contempt for the scholarly old man. Having fulfilled her wifely duty by giving Claudius an heir, she was finding romance elsewhere with gladiators, actors, and dancers, even with Calpurnianus, the captain of the Emperor's bodyguard.

All of this went on, surprisingly, under the unsuspecting eyes of Messalina's doting old husband, for who would dare tell him?

7

NEWCOMERS TO THE PALATINE

AGRIPPINA, one of the eight children of Rome's great military hero Germanicus, who was Claudius' older brother, had been born while her father was stationed on the Rhine at Colonia Agrippinensis (Cologne), a German frontier town named after herself. She was only four when the gallant Germanicus died out in Syria, and her mother returned to Italy with her husband's ashes to accuse Tiberius of having had his nephew poisoned out of jealousy. The Emperor was furious. He had Agrippina's mother and two of her brothers imprisoned on the island of Ponza where they died, and the fourteen-year-old girl was married off to Cnaeus Domitius, a dissolute member of the rich Ahenobarbus family, nicknamed the Red Heads because they all of them had red hair.

In 37, Agrippina's brother, Caligula, became emperor, but that did not make life any easier for the poor girl. Cnaeus Domitius Ahenobarbus died and Caligula, insane and suspicious of everyone, accused his sister Agrippina of plotting against him and exiled her to Ponza, the same prison where their mother, to end her miseries, had starved herself to death. Had not Caligula been murdered, Agrippina would still be locked up there in jail; but now, with her Uncle Claudius on the throne, she was set free and married again—a man named Crispus Passienus—only, after a few years, to find herself a widow once more, burdened with a child by Ahenobarbus and with neither good looks or money to help her. While she was in prison, Caligula had confiscated her first husband's large estate.

In despair, Agrippina came to the elegant villa of Pallas, the Imperial treasurer, on the Esquiline. "Is there a small room at the palace I could have?" she pleaded. "Uncle Claudius once said that he would always give me a home. I need one, badly. Some place where I can have my boy with me, for while I was in jail I was forced to board Nero with strangers, and I never want to be separated from him again."

Agrippina looked so drab and forlorn that Pallas felt sorry for her. "I think it can be arranged," replied the Imperial treasurer. "Come to the Palatine tomorrow, you and your son. We will find a place for you."

So, a week later, when Britannicus and Octavia came into the schoolroom on a September morning in 48, they had a red-haired boy with them. "Nero has come to the palace to live," Britannicus announced to their Greek tutor, Sosibius. "He is to have his lessons with us."

Lucius Domitius Ahenobarbus, commonly called Nero, was a tough-looking boy of eleven with hard blue eyes, a thick neck, and a disdainful expression. Titus wasn't sure that he was going to like him. But he came forward with a friendly smile and said, "I'm Titus, the son of T. Flavius Vespasianus."

"Vespasianus? Never heard of him," Nero replied, loftily. "Well, I'm the great-grandson of Drusus, and the grandson of Germanicus—how's that for ancestry, son-of-Vespasianus?"

Titus flushed. He had been put in his place. Of course his father's achievements in Britain, proud as Titus was of them, were not to be compared with those of Drusus (brother of the Emperor Tiberius) and his son Germanicus, who had added Germany to the Empire.

It was several weeks before Titus grew to like Nero any better. His tough, coarse manners were due in part, Titus discovered, to the hard life that the big redhead had been forced to live while his mother was in prison. Boarded for two years in squalid conditions with a male actor, the impressionable boy had grown to love the sordid world of the theater. Singing, lyre playing, and acting became, and remained, the chief interests in Nero's life.

It was their mutual love of music that now made the two boys congenial, if not actually friends. Nero would sit by the hour, listening to Titus perform on his harp. "If I could only play like that!" he sighed.

"Get yourself a harp," Titus said, "and I'll teach you."

No one ever tried harder to learn to play it. But Nero, unfortunately, did not have Titus' talent for music or his fine voice. In fact, there was little that Vespasian's son could not do and do well.

Meanwhile, Nero's widowed mother was making herself well-liked around the palace. Agrippina was so humble, so eager to please. Hardly had she and her son been settled into two small rooms in the kitchen wing, before Claudius' niece came to thank him for giving them a home.

"How can I ever show my gratitude?" Agrippina exclaimed, covering the Emperor's hand with kisses. She thanked him again and again. Finally she said, "I've a favor to ask, Uncle."

"What is it, my dear?"

"I'm distressed that you're having trouble with your eyes and need a secretary to read to you. May I sometimes take his place?"

"My darling!" Claudius replied, greatly touched. "Would you come, afternoons, and cheer up a lonely old man? You'll find me an awful bore."

"You? A bore!" Agrippina laughed at such an absurd idea.

It was not long before Messalina heard about these visits. At first, she thought of putting a stop to them. But who could be jealous of Agrippina? "How meek she is!" the Empress said to her ladies, after the two women finally met. "Really, I wonder why I thought her worth removing. She's an ideal companion for the Emperor." So Agrippina began going daily to Claudius' apartment, with the full approval of his wife. A plain, dumpy widow of thirty-three seemed harmless enough to the lovely, twenty-six-year-old Messalina.

One afternoon, when Agrippina left the Emperor's suite, she found the Imperial treasurer waiting for her. "Claudius has grown very fond of you," Pallas said. "In return for my getting you a home in the palace, will you do me a favor?"

"Gladly," Agrippina replied.

"Then try to open her husband's eyes to the Empress' scandalous goings-on. It was Narcissus who persuaded Claudius to marry her, so Messalina will do anything for him. And, since Narcissus and I are rivals, she hates me. I would welcome her downfall. Agrippina, will you help me?"

"I'll try," she murmured.

As Pallas looked into Agrippina's expressionless, thin-lipped face, a strange thought occurred to him. Was this quiet young widow the colorless, meek little person she seemed? After her second husband made a will leaving Agrippina all of his fortune, Crispus Passienus had mysteriously died. His family insisted that he was poisoned. But then, had not the death of Agrippina's first husband, Cn. Domitius Ahenobarbus, presumably of dropsy, also been sudden, convenient and odd—since Ahenobarbus's great wealth passed entirely into his widow's hands?

"Could it be that Agrippina is not pathetic at all," Pallas said to himself, "but a murderess, clever and cunning?" However, he quickly dismissed such a ridiculous thought from his mind, for who could think such a shocking thing of the daughter of Rome's great hero, Germanicus?

Messalina, weary of waiting for her tiresome, old husband to die, decided to divorce him and promised her handsome young lover, Gaius Silius, the throne if he would marry her. So on a December day in 48, when the Emperor was away in Ostia inspecting some docks, his wife moved Silius into the palace and the lovers went through a mock marriage.

Narcissus had ignored Messalina's previous love affairs. Her succession of gladiators and actors were no menace to Claudius or to his own power. But Gaius Silius was different, an able young consul, well-born and ambitious. Afraid of not being able to handle Silius as he did Claudius, Narcissus hurried to Ostia to inform the Emperor of his wife's adultery.

Claudius was horrified. He ordered his traveling coach, and the two men set off immediately on the fifteen-mile drive back to Rome, where the "bridal couple" was still celebrating their bigamous marriage.

Warned of the Emperor's approach, the wedding guests fled; Silius found that he had urgent business to attend to in the Forum and Messalina was left alone. Regretting her rash act, the Empress panicked. What should she do? Only one thing could now save her. She must fetch her children, go and meet her husband, and pretend that nothing had happened.

Titus was in his room, reading Greek poetry, when the Empress entered. "We're going to meet the Emperor, who is returning from Ostia," she said to him. "Britannicus and Octavia refuse to go without you. So come along!"

The streets of Rome being narrow and congested, wheeled vehicles were not allowed on them during the daytime, so Messalina and the three young people had to walk clear across town to the city gate and some ways out along the road to Ostia, before they could hitchhike a ride on a passing cart. When the Emperor's carriage came in sight, they jumped down from it and stood by the roadside.

The Imperial coach slowed down in front of them, and then rolled on, for Narcissus had quickly pulled down the shade over the window beside Claudius. He must not see his family, for Narcissus knew that if Britannicus and Octavia ran into their father's arms and kissed him, he would forgive their mother everything.

"Hurry! Get going!" Narcissus shouted at the coachman, and the horses were whipped into a gallop, leaving the Empress, her children, and Titus behind in the dust.

On reaching Rome, the Emperor signed the death warrant for Silius but, his anger cooling, he decided to consider his wife's punishment on the following day. Knowing that if she were permitted to see her husband, Messalina could make silly old Claudius believe anything she pleased, and the life of the man who had informed on her—his own—would be in great danger, Narcissus hurried to summon the guards and told them, "The Emperor has ordered that the Empress be killed immediately."

They found her at her parents' home, where Messalina had taken refuge, nervously awaiting her fate. Told of the Emperor's decision, she burst into hysterics and tried to stab herself, but hadn't the courage. So one of the soldiers sent by Narcissus plunged his sword into her breast and ended the young Empress' dissolute life.

Claudius was informed of his wife's death the next day while at dinner. He calmly went on eating. The mind of the senile old man was so confused that for some time the Emperor kept asking where the Empress was. But, finally, Claudius was made to realize that Messalina was dead, he was a widower, and "for the good the Empire" he should remarry. Pallas urged him to consider Agrippina.

"Marry my niece?" protested the old Emperor, but feebly, for he desired nothing more. Wasn't good, kindly Agrippina, who mothered him and watched over his health, just the person? But wouldn't marriage with his niece be incest?

"Don't worry! That can be arranged," Pallas assured him. He had the Senate pass a law making such a union legal, and in A.D. 49, Agrippina became Claudius' fifth wife and the sixth Empress of Rome.

8

BEWARE OF MUSHROOMS

AGRIPPINA, on becoming empress, dropped all pretense of being meek and self-effacing. Utterly heartless in all but her love for her son, she set out to rule in the name of her bleary-eyed old husband.

Her first act was to purge the government of all but her own friends. Narcissus, who had made the mistake of backing a rival candidate for Claudius' fifth wife, was forced to commit suicide; and Pallas, who had helped Agrippina become empress, ruled supreme. Sextus Afranius Burrus became prefect (commander) of the Praetorian Guard, and taking Sosibius' place in the schoolroom was the Spanish-born Lucius Annaeus Seneca. Some eight years ago, for displeasing Messalina, Claudius had banished the Stoic philosopher to Corsica. Agrippina recalled him from exile and made Seneca, now in his fifties, the tutor of the Imperial children.

The Empress had but one ambition, to win the throne for her Nero, and as a first step to achieving this aim, she forced Claudius in February, 50, to inform the Senate that he was adopting his stepson. What Agrippina really wanted done was to have her husband make Nero his heir instead of his own Britannicus, born of his marriage with Messalina. This the Emperor refused to do. Dominated by his strong-willed wife as he was, the feeble old man still had spirit enough to rebel occasionally.

But, three years later, Agrippina was able to take another step toward the realization of her ambition. Titus was a member of the wedding party when Nero, sixteen, was married to the Emperor's fifteen-year-old daughter. Octavia and Nero had always disliked each other, but their marriage, which Agrippina arranged, was a great triumph for her. Nero became Claudius' son-in-law as well as his adopted son. He had moved a step nearer the throne.

But how much good would it do him? Claudius was talking of presenting Messalina's twelve-year-old Britannicus to the Roman people as their future emperor. Agrippina knew she could wait no longer. The time to act had come.

Locusta was a middle-aged widow, always extremely polite to the fashionable ladies of Rome who came to buy her cosmetics. There was nothing about her shop to suggest what she secretly was, a notorious poisoner.

The quiet little woman had begun in an amateur way by stirring up a mixture on her kitchen stove to do away with a husband who beat her, and becoming interested in the study of poisonous herbs and powders, she now mixed deadly concoctions for a few people she could trust. Locusta charged high prices, but only to the rich. She was kind to the poor, and if in the right mood, would poison for very little.

Locusta kept her ingredients hidden in the back of her shop, and her customers were equally discreet. If they asked for something that would produce a quick death, it was usually to do away with some ailing animal. If they wanted a poison that caused a death that was slow and had the appearance of being due to natural causes, Locusta knew that they had come to her for a more sinister reason.

The Empress Agrippina was in Locusta's shop one day, and after buying some face powder, she said casually, "I'm told you're quite a chemist and make your own perfumes. Also that you mix poisons. I have an old dog, who is crippled with rheumatism. Can you give me something to end his miseries?"

Agrippina had the hard face of a murderess. Locusta felt she could trust her. "Come this way, please . . ." she murmured, taking the Empress into a tiny room behind a curtain. It was a white powder, the one that caused a slow death not easily detected, that Agrippina bought. Locusta knew that it wasn't to poison any dog.

On the night of October 11, 54, in the banquet hall of the Imperial palace on the Palatine, the main course at dinner was mushrooms of which the Emperor was extremely fond. The Empress nibbled at a few of the smaller ones, then pushed the platter over before Claudius. "Here, darling, try some of these." She indicated the larger, more succulent mushrooms. "You'll find them delicious."

He ate them with relish.

Locusta had said the white powder that Agrippina had sprinkled on the bigger mushrooms would act slowly. She watched the Emperor, anxiously. It was not until the end of the meal that the Empress saw him holding his stomach with both hands, an agonizing look of pain on his face.

Springing to her feet, Agrippina bent lovingly over her husband. "The Emperor is ill! Get the doctor!" she cried.

But by the time that Xenophon arrived, Claudius had stopped groaning. "It's only a digestive upset," declared Rome's leading physician. He ordered the old man to be given the usual remedy—his throat was tickled with a feather. The Emperor vomited and said he felt better, but the cramps in his stomach returned, and he was carried off to his bedroom.

It took him a long time to die. Until he did, Agrippina never left the sickroom, and allowed no one else near his bed, for fear that Claudius might recover, suspect and denounce her. Oh, why had she chosen such a slow poison! But soon the Empress had nothing more to fear. Her husband grew too weak to utter a word against her; and at dawn on the second morning, he passed away.

Now Agrippina moved swiftly, for she must secure the succession for her son Nero before Claudius' death became known. So she kept it a secret. The Roman people were told that the Emperor was ill, but getting better.

To keep up this pretense, the dead man was propped up on pillows. Comedians, acrobats, and jugglers were brought in. They cracked jokes and did tumbling tricks before the lifeless body whose eyes stared at them vacantly. From time to time, Agrippina would go over to the bed and ask solicitiously, "Claudius dear, are you enjoying the entertainment?"

The deception went on all the day of the Emperor's death and that night. By the next morning, Agrippina had the stage set. At noon on October 14, 54, with the square before the Imperial palace filled with people, the Praetorian Guard was assembled to pronounce Nero the next emperor of Rome, as they had proclaimed Claudius to be after Caligula's murder.

Nero was about to step out onto the balcony of the palace to announce the death of the old Emperor, when, to Agrippina's dismay, Britannicus and Titus rushed into the room, for they had heard that Claudius was dying.

"No, your father is already dead!" Agrippina flung her arms about Britannicus, as though beside herself with grief. "Dear boy, have you come to comfort me?"

His stepmother clung to Britannicus so tightly, that the frail boy could not possibly escape from her. Nero was able to slip by them out onto the balcony, and the Praetorians, on the square below, hailed the eighteen-year-old youth with a loud shout. Their commander, Sex. Afranius Burrus, lifted his hand in salute and barked, "*Ave, Caesar Imperator!*" Someone yelled, "Long live the Emperor Nero!" When the young man returned the salute, there was such a wild burst of cheering from the crowd that their repeated cries of "Hail Caesar!" could be heard, even inside the palace, where Titus was trying to pull Agrippina and her stepson apart.

Beside himself with anger and frustration, Titus pleaded, "Britannicus, break away from her! Don't you see what she's doing? Get out onto that balcony with Nero. Don't let him take the throne away from you!" But Messalina's son was too small and weak to be able to escape from Agrippina's iron grasp.

9

MURDER IS EASY

PEOPLE SAID that Agrippina had poisoned her husband to get the throne for her son. But who regretted old Claudius? Nero was certainly an improvement on his stepfather. Pallas ran the government for the eighteen-year-old Emperor, and Seneca wrote his speeches, which left the young man free to devote himself to the arts.

Nero sculptured, painted, took singing lessons, and wrote poetry. But his great love was the theater. He especially liked to award prizes for poetry writing and harp playing—competitions the Emperor entered himself—for it was as an artist that he longed to be recognized. Unfortunately, Nero had little talent. That made him envious of anyone who performed better than he did.

One night after dinner the Emperor suggested that Britannicus sing for them, hoping that the fourteen-year-old boy would make a fool of himself. Instead, at the conclusion of his song, the audience broke into applause. Nero remained silent and scowling, for he hated to be outdone. Envy boiled up in him at the praise his young brother-in-law was getting, and he was furious with Titus, who had taught Britannicus to sing and play so well.

That night the Emperor came to a decision. He would kill the two of them. His mother had shown him how.

Titus' dog, Ajax, didn't like Nero. He teased him.

One afternoon, Titus was reading when his spaniel came running down the hall and into the room, to cower trembling against him. A few minutes later, the young Emperor sauntered in and Ajax, whimpering, tried to hide behind his master's legs.

"He ran away from me," Nero said. "Come here, Ajax."

Titus knew that the Emperor liked to maltreat helpless animals. "Go and torment your own dogs, but leave my Ajax alone!" he warned him. And Nero left, slamming the door.

As Titus hugged his pet's silky body against his leg, neither of them knew that they were saying good-by forever to the other. But when Titus woke the next morning and hung over the side of his bed and called, "Ajax," no loving spaniel with adoring brown eyes was there. Jumping out of bed, he ran out into the hall. "Ajax!" he called. Then, having scrambled into his clothes, he rushed frantically through the palace.

Nobody had seen his dog. Titus could not believe that his spaniel had run away. Ajax had been kidnapped. And he knew by whom. Striding past the guards at the door, Titus burst into the Emperor's suite and accused him, "You stole Ajax! Where is he?"

"How should I know? I haven't seen him."

Titus was sure that Nero was lying. He searched everywhere for poor Ajax, and several days later, found his dead body thrown on a garbage heap. It had stiffened, but the legs were contorted, and Titus knew his pet had been killed by a deadly poison that had caused the little spaniel long and frightful suffering. Sinking in anguish to his knees, he noticed on the dog's body ugly black spots.

Tears streamed down Titus' cheeks. It was the first great sorrow of his life. He would have other dogs, but never one that he would love as he had Ajax.

The next night, Nero was celebrating his mother's fortieth birthday. Agrippina lay on a dining couch to the right of the Emperor, the place of honor, with his wife, Octavia, on his left. At another table, Britannicus and Titus were placed with other guests. Slaves served wine and platters of delicious food, but Britannicus refused to touch a mouthful. He had not eaten all day because, for two days now, he had been ill with diarrhea and nausea.

Urged to do so, Britannicus finally accepted a bowl of soup. His taster, Measa, had sampled it, but Britannicus found the drink too hot and refused it. Some cold water was added. As he lifted the bowl to his lips, Titus called out a warning. "Don't! Make Measa taste it again." But the man having moved some distance away in the crowded room, Titus took a sip of the drink himself. The soup seemed to him all right, so he returned it to Britannicus as harmless.

A few minutes later, a cry of horror filled the room, as the heir to the throne, writhing in pain, sank to the floor. Agrippina looked on, in alarm. She knew who had done this and she was terrified, for she had taught her son that murder was easy. Would Nero do away with her someday, with the same cool deliberation?

Britannicus' body was carried off, and Octavia, seeing her brother poisoned in cold blood before her eyes, did not dare to utter a word. The Emperor lay back unconcerned on his dining couch and said, "It's nothing, my friends, my brother-in-law often has these epileptic fits." After a horrified silence, the banquet continued; most of the guests, too frightened to run away, remained rooted in their places, staring at Nero.

Only a few people managed to flee. Among them was Titus. He started off at a run for Britannicus' apartment, but he never reached there. Having taken a sip of the deadly poison, he doubled up with excruciating pains out in the hallway. Everything swam before Titus' eyes, but he managed to stagger to the front door of the palace. If he could only live to get to his Aunt Antonia! "To the Via Tiuta, on the Aventina . . . Quick!" Titus gasped and, climbing into a litter, collapsed.

Thinking that he was one of the usual drunks they carried home nightly from Nero's parties, the litter bearers started off for Antonia Caenis' house. Titus never remembered arriving there. When he came to, he was undressed and lying in bed. He raised his head to call to his adopted aunt, but the room spun so around him that he fell back weakly on the pillow and shut his eyes. Gradually the dizziness passed, and he vomited into a basin by the bed until he was exhausted.

Some time later, Titus heard the door open. A man and a woman came in. "He's awake," said Antonia. She and the man came and stood by the bed. Looking up, Titus saw the lean, gray-bearded L. Annaeus Seneca standing beside Antonia, who had a bowl in her hand. Drawing up a stool, she sat down and asked, "Dear, could you swallow a little gruel?"

Titus opened his mouth, and Antonia poked into it several spoonfuls of bread softened in milk. She watched him, anxiously. "Good!" Antonia turned to Seneca. "He managed to keep it down. He's going to be all right."

"He'll live, but it was a close call," the Spaniard replied.

"You were wise, Titus. Always eat a hearty meal before going to Nero's. Otherwise, you would be dead like poor Britannicus. The poison took effect quickly on his empty stomach."

"Britannicus is dead?"

"Yes. His body was cremated the same night, so people wouldn't see the black spots that broke out all over Britannicus' body, caused by Locusta's poison."

Titus lay remembering those black spots on Ajax.

"I'm told that Locusta's first poison had little effect." Antonia scraped a spoon around the sides of the bowl to get the last of the gruel. "It only made Britannicus sick for a few days."

Titus raised himself on an elbow. "So that was why he was ill! But how could Britannicus have been poisoned? Measa first tasted everything he ate and drank."

"Measa was bribed. He gave Britannicus the first concoction," Seneca explained. "When Britannicus became ill but the mixture failed to kill him, Nero had Locusta prepare more deadly poisons and tried them out on several unfortunate animals—"

"I know," Titus groaned. "My poor Ajax!"

"By the night of Agrippina's birthday party, Nero had found the deadly dose he wanted," Seneca went on to say. "Britannicus disliked warm drinks. So the soup was purposely served to him too hot. The poison was in the cold water they added to it. Why do you suppose, Titus, Measa wasn't there to taste that second drink? That you had to do it? Of course, because Nero wanted to kill you, too. . . ?" His tutor rose and pushed back his chair. "Now, young man, we've talked long enough. Try to get some sleep."

It was several days, though, before Titus could sit up without vomiting. One morning Seneca came to see him again. "Do you feel well enough to travel?" he asked. "I hope so, because you're leaving for Germany."

Titus looked at him aghast.

"Burrus has a cohort of soldiers bound for the Rhine, and you're going with them," Seneca explained. "Titus, it isn't safe for you to remain here. You were Britannicus' best friend, so Nero has it in for you. My advice to you is–go with the legions, as far from Rome as you possibly can, and never come back!"

10

BOW YOUR HEADS TO THE EAGLES

On a morning in A.D. 61 Titus Flavius Vespasianus stood again by the Walbrook, having arrived in Britain the day before from Germany where he had been stationed for six years. The twenty-two-year-old centurion could scarcely believe the changes he saw before him. In the eighteen years since the Conquest, the hamlet of Lyn-din had spread westward across the Walbrook. There was a temple to the goddess Diana where the army encampment had been; and the Thames was crowded with ships, for Londinium, as Lyn-din was called by the Romans, had become the chief city of their northernmost province.

Titus remembered the thatched hut in Lyn-din where he had lived with his mother. His heart ached to think that he would never see Domitilla again. She had died two years ago, and Vespasian had sent their son Domitian, born to them in Africa, back to Italy to be brought up by Antonia Caenis on the Sabine farm he had inherited from Grandmother Tertulla.

What was his brother like, Titus wondered, as he walked back to the Gallic Horseman where he had spent the night.

He found the inn crowded with merchants, who had come over from Gaul to sell their goods to the people of Londinium (London), Verulamium (St. Albans), and Camulodunum (Colchester), the three large towns of Roman Britain.

A portly man sat down at the table with Titus and, after ordering breakfast, began to talk. "I've just come up Watling Street from the coast. Now I'm going on to Camulodunum. There's a fair there. Opens today."

"I'd like to see Camulodunum," Titus said. "I remember my father telling me about Caratacus' old stronghold."

"Then why don't you come with me?" suggested the merchant. "I've an extra horse you can ride."

It seemed like a good idea. Before reporting to Legatus C. Suetonius Paulinus, commander of the Roman army of occupation in Britain, at his headquarters with the Twentieth Legion in Deva (Chester), why not see something of the province? So Titus set off with the merchant Blandus, who came from the hamlet of Lutetia Parisiorum (Paris) in Gaul, on a road that ran north out of Londinium. They rode through the dense oak forest single file—Blandus first, then the merchant's servant leading a string of mules with bulging saddle bags, and Titus following.

At Caratacus' old tribal center, the Romans had built a fort, a theater, baths, and a temple dedicated to the worship of Claudius—like all Roman emperors, deified after his death—but on the day that Titus arrived in Camulodunum, the great sight there was the fair. The plain by the river Colne was laid out in streets lined with booths and tents, and the town was jammed with traders. From all over Gaul and Germany they had brought their metal mirrors, glassware, and red Samian pottery across the Channel to sell them to the Roman veterans of the Conquest, who had been settled in Camulodunum to keep an eye on the hostile Trinovantes.

There was also unrest to the north, the merchant Blandus told Titus as they dined at the tavern that evening on oysters from the Colne. It seemed that Prasutagus of the Iceni, one of the British tribal kings to pay allegiance to Claudius, had died and left his kingdom partly to Nero and partly to his widow, Queen Boudicca. But Catus Decianus, Nero's tax collector in Londinium, claimed that Prasutagus had only been granted the life-use of his land, so his entire domain should now revert to Rome.

"Britain isn't conquered, Titus, not even a corner of it," declared Blandus. "Someday, if the Trinovantes and the Iceni can forget their differences enough to unite, they'll hurl you Romans back across the Channel."

But in Deva (Chester), the Fourteenth Gemina and the Twentieth Valeria were stationed; the Second Augusta was at Glevum (Gloucester), and the Ninth Hispana at Lindum (Lincoln) among the Iceni. How could Britain's tribes, which had never been able to act together, dream of revolting against the best-trained army in the world?

After three days of hard riding, as Centurion T. Flavius Vespasianus reached the western terminus of Watling Street, the most important of the military roads that the Romans only eighteen years after the Conquest had built in Britain, he was surprised to find the fort of Castra Deva there nearly empty. "The Valeria and Gemina have left for Caernarvon Bay," a guard at the gate explained. "Only Suetonius is here. And the Legatus and his staff go to join them today."

"Going off to North Wales?" Titus exclaimed. "When

every Roman soldier may be urgently needed in the east of Britain!"

Ushered into the general's headquarters, he found Suetonius Paulinus and his officers planning their route to North Wales on a map spread out before them. The Romans' troubles in Britain had not ended with the capture of Caratacus. The powerful Druid priesthood continued to stir up the Ordovices of Wales to rebellion. And now that they were assembled on the island of Mona, holding a religious festival in a sacred grove of oak trees believed to be the dwelling place of their gods, Suetonius intended to round the Druids up and eradicate them once and for all.

He looked up when Titus entered the room. "What is it?" the general snapped.

"I'm Centurion Vespasianus, transferred from Germany, here to report." The handsome young officer in a plumed helmet and long military cape saluted. "But first, sir, I must speak with you personally. I've just come from Camulodunum. The Trinovantes and the Iceni are about to revolt. If you go off to North Wales, they certainly will."

"Really? What do you want me to do?"

"Call off your attack on the Ordovices."

Suetonius and a young Gaul on his staff, the twenty-eight-year-old Gnaeus Julius Agricola, exchanged looks. "What did I tell you, Suetonius?" Agricola exclaimed. "The East Anglia tribes are only waiting for us to turn our backs on them to create trouble."

"Ridiculous! There isn't a thing to fear," retorted Suetonius, a hard-faced man in his fifties. "Haven't we veterans from Claudius' invasion, who haven't forgotten how to fight, settled in Camulodunum to watch any hostile move the Trinovantes make? Isn't the Ninth Hispana stationed at Lindum, among the Iceni, capable of handling any trouble there? Enough of this! It's time we were off to Wales."

At the door, Suetonius remembered Titus. "You're Vespasianus' son, I gather. Come along with us and see where your father fought Caratacus."

So when the commander of the Roman army of occupation left for Wales, in the cavalcade of horses with Suetonius rode an unhappy centurion, wishing with all his heart that they were not going west, but east. But what could Titus do about it?

By forced marches the Romans reached North Wales, where the Twentieth and Fourteenth legions were waiting. Out in the Irish Sea lay the island of Anglesey, known to the Romans as Mona. To capture the Druids' sacred isle and put an end to their power forever, Suetonius had to ferry his infantry across Menai Strait, his cavalry swimming their horses. But this was done, and arriving on Mona, the Fourteenth's standard-bearer leaped into the surf and waded ashore, calling on his comrades to follow.

In vain the white-robed Driud priests, standing before their altars, raised hands in prayer to their gods for help. They and their congregations were massacred, their sacred oak trees and mistletoe chopped down. But in the midst of the Roman victory, a dispatch rider who had galloped across Britain from Londinium thrust into Suetonius' hand a confirmation of Titus' warning to him of possible danger to his rear.

It seemed that when Catus Decianus, Nero's tax collector in Londinium, had seized her land, Queen Boudicca of the Iceni violently objected; and the Roman official, to teach Prasutagus' proud, red-haired widow a lesson, had her publicly whipped. In retaliation the Iceni rose as one man to avenge their queen and, with the Trinovantes to the south, who had their own grievances, swooped down upon Camulodunum and sacked it. The temple of Claudius, hated by the Britons, was burned; the Roman colonists, who had taken refuge in it, were slaughtered; and the Ninth Legion, which hurried down from Lindum to the rescue of Camulodunum, was ambushed on the way and practically wiped out.

What a situation! And Suetonius could not have been in a worse place to meet this crisis. With him in North Wales were two-thirds of his army. The only troops he had left to police eastern Britain–the Ninth Legion–were now crippled and out of action. And Catus Decianus, Nero's tax collector who caused the uprising, had fled to Gaul, leaving Londinium unprotected.

The cavalry was sent galloping ahead, and Suetonius set off with his infantry on the 250-mile journey back to Londinium. But halfway there, Suetonius and the infantry, coming on the double from Wales, were met by his cavalry, under Agricola, riding forlornly back from Londinium.

"Boudicca beat us to it," Agricola told him bitterly. "By the time we reached Londinium, the town was in flames."

Having burned Verulamium and the little, unwalled Londinium to the ground, the British warrior queen and her tribesmen came after the Romans. The two forces met in the Midland forests. Drunk with success, the overconfident Britons arrived to do battle accompanied by their women and children in oxcarts, and rashly drew up too close to the enemy. The result was that when the Romans attacked, Boudicca's forces, trapped in their own wagon-lines, were slaughtered–men, women, and children.

Next day, the jubilant Romans lined up to watch the defeated Britons "sent under the yoke." Two spears were set upright in the ground, and a third fastened across the top, forming something like a yoke worn by oxen. Beneath this low arch, the conquered British were forced to walk with heads bowed. To be thus humiliated was a terrible disgrace, and it would be a proud moment for Suetonius when the haughty, red-haired Queen of the Iceni was forced to bow humbly before him. He stood watching, a whip in his hand. His brutal face flushed with annoyance when Boudicca sank to the ground, holding up the line of prisoners. "Get up!" the Roman shouted at her, raising his whip.

This was too much for Titus, who had come to despise Suetonius for the many cruel things he had seen him do. "Stop that! You brute!" the young centurion cried, and wrenching the whip from the legatus' hand, flung it into the bushes.

What happened after that Titus never knew. Arms grabbed him from behind, his helmet was knocked off, and someone hit him a hard blow on the head. Several hours later Titus recovered consciousness, lying on a cot in the hospital tent, with Agricola seated beside him. "What happened to me?" he asked.

"You were roughly removed from the battlefield by Suetonius' bodyguard," his friend said. "Titus, don't you know better than to humiliate a general before his troops? When you wrenched the whip from his hand, the legionaries burst into cheers. Suetonius is furious."

"Am I under arrest?"

"No, I pleaded for you, but take my advice, and get transferred to another legion. Suetonius has it in for you."

"I'll do better than that. I'll resign from the army. I've had enough of it," Titus replied. "I want to return to Rome and become a lawyer." But could he? He remembered how Nero had tried to poison him and Seneca had said, "Go off with the legions, as far from Rome as you possibly can, and never come back."

The Roman doctors were experts at trepanning (repairing cracked skulls), and by the time his bandages were off, Titus had decided to risk it. "I'm going back to Italy and take my chances with Nero," he informed Agricola. "Surely Rome is big enough for both of us."

Was it? Titus would have to find out.

11

BEWARE OF NERO

AT FALACRINA, a village forty miles northeast of Rome, Antonia Caenis knelt in a field beside the modest Flavian farmhouse, wearing a big straw hat to keep off the sun. Leaping from his horse, Titus hurried to the vegetable patch and, crouching down before the homely, middle-aged woman, gave her a hearty kiss.

"Titus! Why didn't you let me know you were coming?" Antonia snapped in her harsh voice. But as they walked to the house, arm in arm, she said, "Forgive my nasty tongue, dear. I was angry because you took me by surprise and saw me like this, ugly and dirty from farm work."

They went into the thatched, white house that smelled of smoke, herbs, and good cooking. Antonia sat down and, looking fondly at Titus' square face which showed his Etruscan peasant ancestry, as did his father's, she asked, "Are you in Italy on furlough?"

"No, I'm out of the army."

"Good. I need your help with Domitianus! I find him to be quite a problem. Oh, there he is . . ." Going to the door, Antonia called to a boy who was driving some calves into the yard. "Domitianus, come and meet your brother."

A handsome, sullen-faced youth came into the house. "My, you're tall, how old are you? Ten?" was all that Titus could think to say to him. He was twenty-two. There was twelve years difference between their ages.

"Oh, Titus, it's good to have you safely home!" Antonia was saying. "When we heard about those savage Britons murdering every Roman they could lay their hands on, your father was sick with worry. Oh, didn't you know? He is back from Africa and also out of the army. Vespasianus will tell you about it. It's suppertime, he should be here any minute."

A short while later the former general came into the yard, driving a cart of manure. He tied up his oxen and entered the house. "Titus!" Vespasian exclaimed in surprise, clasping his eldest son in his arms. He was fifty-two. He had aged and grown bald. Titus hardly recognized his father out of uniform, dressed in the sweat-drenched tunic and muddy boots of a Sabine peasant. What had happened?

"I came home from Africa to report and was told by Nero that I was not to go back," Vespasian explained, as they sat down to a frugal meal. "So I'm a farmer now, raising mules for the Roman market."

Antonia burst out, "Titus, your father has no one to blame for his dismissal from the army but himself! As you know, the Emperor has no interest in ruling. He only wants to win acclaim as an actor or singer, so he likes to entertain his guests by performing for them. And Vespasianus insulted him. What do you think your father did? While Nero was singing, he went to sleep."

The old man burst into hearty laughter. "I not only went to sleep, but I snored!"

Nor had the honest Vespasian made himself rich in Africa,

as most Roman governors did. Talking with him the next day, Titus was shocked to learn that his father was so deeply in debt that he had been forced to mortgage the Flavian ancestral acres to his brother, Sabinus, in order to stock the farm with mules. Yet Vespasian cheerfully accepted his reverses. "It's not a bad life," he insisted, "I always was a farmer at heart."

The Flavians were desperately poor. They lived, like most Sabine peasants did, on black bread and vegetable stew, from dawn to dark they worked hard, and at sundown, went to bed to save lamp oil. It was only thanks to Antonia Caenis' thrift and industry that conditions on the farm were not worse.

On his last day in Falacrina, she reminded Titus how Nero had tried to poison him and, but for her nursing, he would have died. "Is it safe for you to return to Rome?" Antonia asked, anxiously. "Anyone who could murder his mother will do anything!"

Titus had heard in Britain of Agrippina's death. Also, the ugly rumors concerning it. Nero first tried to make it look as though Agrippina had met with an accident, people said; he invited his mother out on a boat and had it sunk, but she managed to swim ashore. So Nero made a second and, this time, successful attempt on her life. He had men go to the Dowager Empress' villa at Baiae and assassinate her.

"The Emperor got rid of his mother because she tried to dominate him, as she had Claudius, and also to please Poppaea," Antonia was saying. "Poppaea knew that so long as Agrippina lived she would never allow Nero to marry her. One of them had to go."

Having been absent from Rome for six years, Titus was

not conversant with court gossip. "Who is Poppaea?" he asked.

"You haven't heard of the Emperor's current mistress?" Antonia exclaimed. "Well, Poppaea was the wife of Marcus Salvius Otho, Nero's best friend. When the Emperor fell in love with her, it was all agreeably arranged between them. Otho was sent off to Lusitania as governor, leaving the beautiful Poppaea behind in Rome, of course. The Emperor wants to marry her, they say, and he's murdered his mother and tried several times to strangle his wife Octavia so he can. Nero's a killer, Titus. Do keep away from him! And, dear, before you leave for Rome, I wish you'd have a talk with Domitianus."

Antonia was trying hard to fill Domitilla's place and be a good mother to Vespasian's younger son, but there was a cruel streak in him that worried her. "Titus, Domitianus spends hours in his room, catching flies and pulling off their wings. And he's so quick-tempered, so brutal, with the farm animals . . ."

He would have a talk with Domitian, Titus promised, and the two ill-matched brothers took a walk together.

"Titus, I hate it here on the farm," Domitian cried, resentfully. "Why can't I go to Rome with you?"

"Because I must earn my living there as a lawyer. What would I do with a boy of ten?"

His brother was an unhappy, mixed-up youth, Titus found, who hated living on a remote farm in the Sabine hills, and talked incessantly of running away to Rome and becoming a chariot driver or an actor. Like Nero, Domitian longed for the crowd's acclaim. To compensate for his feelings of self-hatred and wretched insecurity, he boasted about his exploits, mostly imaginary, and made up incredible stories of adventures he had never had—anything, to attract attention to himself.

Titus wished that there was some way he could help his brother. But they were so utterly different that he and Domitian at times hardly seemed to be speaking the same language. "Perhaps, when I get to Rome, I can think of something . . ." Titus said to himself.

On his way there he stopped to visit L. Annaeus Seneca, his former tutor at the court of Claudius. Titus found the tall, gaunt Spaniard seated on the terrace of his Villa Nomentana, overlooking the Sabine hills. "What are you doing back in Italy?" the Stoic philosopher greeted him, crossly. "I saved your life once from Nero. But I won't promise to do it again. You were in Britain with Suetonius. Why didn't you stay there?"

"Because I want to be a lawyer. How can you practice law in Britain? Since Boudicca burned it, Londinium is in ruins. They may never rebuild it."

"Yes, Nero is thinking of withdrawing the legions and giving up Britain entirely."

As they sipped their wine, Titus told Seneca that he hated the killing necessary in the army but was interested in how Rome's vast empire was governed. That was why he wanted to be a lawyer. The profession of law often led to a political career.

"Will you help me get started?" Titus pleaded.

"If you'll promise not to do anything to annoy the Emperor again. Remember, it was because Britannicus sang too well that he was poisoned. Nero cannot endure being outdone. He is childish in his vanity. And, Titus, the Emperor has always been jealous of you. You excell as an orator, a poet, a singer, and a musician, while he has to strive to be the second-rate artist he is."

"I'll live so quietly in Rome that Nero will never know I am there."

"All right then, I'll do what I can for you, although I haven't the prestige I once had," Seneca replied, looking all of his sixty-five years, old and tired. "Burrus and I tried to make a good ruler out of the Emperor, and for a while, we had a restraining influence on him. But, recently, rebelling against all authority, Nero has rid himself of his mother–a thoroughly bad woman, whom no one regrets–and put Pallas to death. My turn, I fear, may come next. Meanwhile, hoping that he will forget all about me, I've retired to this house in the Sabine hills. I seldom go to Rome."

"You don't need to. A letter will be sufficient."

"Good! Then I'll introduce you to my old friend, Marcus Lepidus. With your fine voice and remarkable memory, I always thought that you should be a lawyer."

So two weeks later, Titus found himself entering the Basilica Julia, built by Julius Caesar on the south side of the Forum, as a clerk in the law firm of Lepidus & Galla. He looked about him in awe at the vast marble hall, crowded with toga-clad men. There were merchants and money-changers there, as well as lawyers, for a Roman basilica was a combination of law court, bank, and town hall.

Titus left the papyrus rolls he had been sent to deliver, and was coming out of the building when he ran into an old friend. "Burrus!" Titus cried, embracing the stocky prefect of the Emperor's Praetorian Guard, who had lost his left arm in battle.

Sex. Afranius Burrus was equally glad to see Titus. As he listened to the young man telling of his experiences in Britain, a thought occurred to him. "Titus, why don't you come to Campania with me?" Burrus suggested. "I'm going there next week to visit my family, and I have a daughter I'd like you to meet."

12

LOVE—ROMAN STYLE

"I CAN'T DO IT, I can't marry Titus Flavius Vespasianus," cried Pompeia Gaia, the older of Burrus' two daughters, age sixteen. "How could our father be so cruel? He knows I'll never wed anyone but Marcellus." And Gaia, thinking of a young neighbor with whom she had played since childhood, burst into tears. "Do you imagine that Titus will try to kiss me?"

Her fourteen-year-old sister, Arrecina Tertulla, was full of sympathy. "I won't give Titus a chance. I'll tag along every minute and never leave you alone with him."

Both girls knew that this would only be postponing the announcement of Gaia's engagement to the son of former Legatus Vespasianus, which Sex. Afranius Burrus, commander of the Imperial bodyguard, greatly desired, as he had written his wife. Marriages in Roman times were arranged by the young peoples' parents.

Determined, if she could, to resist her father's matrimonial plans for her, Gaia was seated with her mother in the atrium (reception hall) of Burrus' villa in Campania that afternoon, when the prefect arrived with his young friend, T. Flavius Vespasianus, from Rome.

As the two men entered the house, Tertulla appeared and, ignoring her mother's frown of disapproval, seated herself demurely beside Gaia. She was carrying out her promise to her sister. Titus looked at the younger girl's exquisite oval face, her almond-shaped brown eyes, and slim figure. "Are you Gaia?" he asked, eagerly.

"No, I'm Tertulla. This is Gaia."

A plain girl with a glum expression turned unhappy eyes in his direction. Obviously disappointed, Titus was barely polite to her, and talked mostly to Tertulla for the next hour.

Things were not going as Prefect Burrus had planned them, and the man who ruled the Imperial cohorts with an iron hand was used to being obeyed. Only one thought consoled him. This unsatisfactory meeting between Gaia and Titus would lead to a closer acquaintance between them that evening at dinner when Roman etiquette prevented her prettier sister from being present. Still considered a child at fourteen, Tertulla would eat in the nursery.

The meal was a dull affair. Gaia, realizing with relief that Titus was not interested in her, hardly spoke. When the last dishes were being brought in, Titus said, "May I ask a favor? It is the custom in Rome for children to meet their parents' guests over the dessert. Please, will you send for Tertulla?"

Red-faced with annoyance, Burrus gave a servant the order. Tertulla must have expected something of the sort, for she arrived wearing her best *stolla,* red ribbons in her dark hair, and a mischievous smile on her face.

Next morning, the prefect was out by a pasture fence, inspecting his cattle, when Titus rushed up to say excitedly, "Tertulla is charming."

"She's only a child," her father reminded him.

"But already she walks with the dignity of a goddess. I love even her name, Tertulla. It was my great-grandmother's name."

All that day the love-sick young man hardly left Tertulla's side. Gaia, to her great joy, he completely ignored. It surprised no one, when several days later, Titus asked Burrus for permission to marry his younger daughter.

"No," her father firmly replied. "Tertulla is too frail to think of marriage. She has a weak heart. That is why my wife remains in the country with our daughters. For Tertulla, doctors tell me, the excitement of Rome could be fatal."

"We'll live there very quietly."

Titus pleaded so hard that Burrus finally gave his consent. But he had wanted his older daughter to marry first, and the words were forced from his lips.

The prefect was pleased to be getting Titus as a son-in-law, however, and a month later Titus and Tertulla were married at the Castra Praetoria, the barracks of the Imperial Guard, in the northeast section of Rome. When the wedding day arrived, relatives and friends filled the house; even Titus' father, Antonia, and Domitian had come from Falacrina for the ceremony.

A Roman marriage began with an ancient rite. When Tertulla came to meet him, wearing a long white tunic and an orange veil covering her head, Titus made a fictitious purchase. He paid an *as* (penny) to her father and received his bride. The priest then sacrificed on the household altar to Ceres, goddess of marriage, to avert ill fortune. Then Titus slipped a plain gold ring on the third finger of Tertulla's left hand, for the Romans believed that a nerve from this finger led directly to the heart.

A nuptial feast followed during which Vespasian, ignoring Antonia's angry looks of reproof, amused the guests with his coarse peasant jokes. He was a bit drunk and celebrating, for at a low point in the former general's life, his boy Titus had risen to a position any young man might envy, by becoming the son-in-law of Sex. Afranius Burrus, commander of the Imperial bodyguard. The Praetorians, having made emperors of both Claudius and Nero, were a great political power in Rome.

When the feast ended it was time for the groom to pretend to take forcefully his bride from her mother's arms (an act symbolizing the Rape of the Sabine Women) and escort her to his new home—a small house Titus had rented on Quirinal Hill, near where he had lived as a child. Like most Roman houses, its rooms were chiefly on the ground floor, so that Tertulla would not tax her weak heart by having to climb any stairs.

Preceded by flute players, the wedding guests set out on foot, Domitian throwing candies to the onlookers who lined the streets. When the procession reached his door, Titus carried Tertulla over the threshold, for it was considered bad luck if a Roman bride stumbled on entering her new home.

They began their married life as young couples usually do, expecting to live happily ever after. Titus enjoyed being a lawyer. A gifted orator with a remarkable memory, he could speak at length in court without notes. Also an expert at shorthand, he liked to compete with the secretaries at Lepidus & Galla to see which of them could write the fastest. Being able to imitate any handwriting, he jokingly said that he would have made a good forger.

He had chosen to enter the profession of law because, as a lawyer, Titus felt he could best render public service. Instead, he found his time largely occupied in acting as aide (and often nurse) to the elderly Marcus Lepidus.

Titus must be at the famous lawyer's home each day by sunrise, to open the door for his *salutatio* or calling hour. Even then, groups of people seeking help were always waiting to crowd into Lepidus' *tablinum* (office) to ask for free aid and advice. Lawyers were forbidden to accept fees. Instead, they expected valuable presents, and Lepidus' rich clients were only too glad to recompense him well. He did not bother with poor people.

Business in the Basilica Julia began at nine o'clock. Shortly before then, Marcus Lepidus set out for the Forum riding in his litter, accompanied by Titus on foot and a retinue of slaves and hangers-on following. All day long Titus, who was quick at remembering faces, must remain at Lepidus' elbow to whisper to the old man the names of those who spoke to him.

Lepidus & Galla handled chiefly wills and divorce cases, but on a day when Lepidus was at his seaside villa and Titus was holding the *salutatio* in his absence, a different type of client timidly entered the house.

"I live in Falacrina near your father's farm, so I've come to you for help," a shabbily dressed peasant said to him. "A rich landlord is trying to rob me of my land."

The poor man's farm consisted of only two *jugerae* (about an acre), but they were fertile, and a certain Q. Vibius Crispus wanted to absorb them into his vast estate. Knowing the situation, Titus was sympathetic. Everywhere small farmers, like his father, were being compelled to sell their land to rich men who lived in Rome and farmed their vast acreage with overseers and slave labor.

"I'll fight this villain Crispus for you," Titus assured the Sabine farmer. "Don't worry, my friend, you won't be robbed of your land."

A week later, Titus came home one evening to find Tertulla seated by their pool in the peristyle. She listened while Titus told her how he had served an injunction against Vibius Crispus, hauled the avaricious millionaire into court, and was preventing him from getting the peasant's farm for a mere pittance. It was Titus' first big case. At last, he was being the type of lawyer he wanted to be, helping the poor fight the rich. He could not understand why Tertulla should turn pale.

"I've heard my father speak of this man Crispus," his young wife said in an anxious voice. "Titus, do be careful! He's a bad, vindictive person, and a drinking companion of Nero."

As Tertulla spoke, cries were heard coming from their porter's lodge and the noise of a struggle. The porter Gaius appeared, running. "Master!" he gasped. "Crispus is here, with an escort of gladiators! I tried to stop them from coming in. They mean to—"

"—give you a lesson for daring to appear in court against me, Vespasianus," shouted a burly man, with a cruel face. Behind him stood four armed bodyguards.

Tertulla rose, trembling, to her feet. His face grim, Titus walked up to Vibius Crispus. "Leave this house at once," he ordered. "Leave this house, or else—"

"Or else what?" sneered the older man.

"I'll have to throw you out."

"You attacked me publicly in court. You made me look ridiculous. Do you imagine that I'm going to leave without—"

"I do, at once," Titus broke in. "What's more, Crispus, I'm not afraid of you and your armed men, and I shall continue to expose your avarice. This land-grab from a helpless Sabine peasant isn't the only crime you've committed."

Confronted by Titus' angry, determined face, the older man lost courage. "All right, I'll go," he muttered, "but, Vespasianus, you'll live to regret what you've done. You have no idea the tears I shall make you shed."

Leaving the house, Vibius Crispus' wicked little eyes lingered upon Tertulla. He had heard how dearly Titus loved his pretty, young wife, and a vicious idea entered Crispus' head. Bent on revenge, he went straight to Nero.

13

THE SEDUCTION OF TERTULLA

SEVERAL DAYS LATER, with Titus busy at the Basilica Julia, Tertulla was feeding her collection of exotic birds. Standing by her aviary, she remarked to big black Clodia, their one slave, a short distance away in the kitchen, "I hear that Nero is a dreadful person."

"Never believe all you hear," said a voice behind her.

A gross young man, paunchy and spindle-legged, had come into the peristyle. He had grown disgustingly stout, his face brutal from dissipation, and his red hair inherited from his father's family, the Ahenobarbi, instead of being cut short like most Romans, hung in ringlets about his thick neck in the hair style affected by low-class charioteers and actors. Recognizing the intruder from statues of him she had seen, Tertulla stammered, "You're . . . the Emperor?"

"I am," Nero replied. "Won't you ask me to sit down?"

"Certainly." Tertulla led the way to some chairs by the pool. When they were seated, the Emperor asked, "Where's that husband of yours?"

"In court."

"He leaves you alone all day? Aren't you lonely?"

"No, Caesar, I have my birds and a cat for company. Besides, I'm not alone. My cook watches over me. Clodia is a fierce, black woman from the Sudan. If anyone came here to harm me, she would leap at his throat."

Nero's eyes, bright with desire, lingered upon pale, fragile Tertulla. "Still, a pretty girl like you must find it dull with only pets to amuse you. I shall have to bring my harp and sing to you. I'm the finest musician in the world. Everyone says so."

Behind them, the gravel of the path crunched under a heavy military boot. Coming toward them was the captain of the Praetorians, the six-foot, muscular bodyguards that accompanied the Emperor wherever he went. The plume-helmeted soldier saluted. "Caesar, Titus Flavius Vespasianus has arrived," he announced.

A moment later, Tertulla's husband appeared in the peristyle. He looked surprised on seeing who his visitor was and said coldly, "Hail, Caesar!"

"Why such formality?" demanded the Emperor. "You used to call me Nero. We grew up as boys together. I thought we were friends."

As if he had not heard a word, Titus replied, "Tertulla and I are honored to receive you in our home."

"Are you? Then I shall come again. Meanwhile, you and your wife are invited to my next banquet."

"Tertulla is not well. We seldom go out socially."

"Oh, some gaiety will do her good! Tertulla looks pale and sad. Titus, are you neglecting your wife? I shall have to try to cheer her up—" Nero stopped abruptly for fear that, by saying too much, he might give away what he had in mind doing. The shy, modest Tertulla was hardly his type of woman. But she was Titus' wife. And hadn't he always wanted what Titus had?

With a disarming smile, the Emperor rose and started toward the atrium, where his bodyguard waited to escort him out to his litter. But before leaving, he turned to Titus. "Why didn't you invite me to your wedding?" he demanded. "Why did I have to hear, from Vibius Crispus, that you were back in Rome and had married Burrus' daughter?"

Titus remained silent.

"I should be angry with you, Vespasianus," Nero went on. "Instead, to show you how forgiving I am, I intend to send you on an important mission. The King of Parthia is coming to Rome next week. Will you go to Puteoli, where he is to land, and greet him for me?"

What could Titus do but say yes?

"Good!" the Emperor exclaimed, getting into his litter. "I trust we're going to be friends again."

With Tertulla's husband sent off to Puteoli, Nero came to Titus' home one night in his absence. Gaius, the porter, was tied up and gagged. But where was Clodia? His escort of hard-faced Praetorians searched the house for the African woman, while the Emperor walked through the peristyle and into the *cubiculum* (bedroom) where Tertulla lay asleep. Sitting down beside her, he put out his hand. His touch roused her. "Titus . . ." his wife murmured, lovingly.

"I'm not Titus."

"Who are you?" the girl whispered, half-awake.

"Nero, who loves you. Give me a kiss."

Tertulla was like a maddened little cat. Frantically she pushed away the stout, repulsive man, reeking of perfume.

His grip hurt her, and she cried hysterically, "Go or I'll scream!" But before she could, he had clamped his short, fat fingers over her mouth. After that, it was like a nightmare as the helpless girl felt the vile creature, seated on her bed, caressing her hair, her cheeks, her neck. His podgy fingers were about to . . . Tertulla screamed.

Hearing the frantic cry for help, big black Clodia, who had been hiding nearby, managed to break past the soldiers stationed outside the door and burst into the room. With no regard as to whom he might be, she seized the intruder by his long red hair and dragged him off Tertulla's bed onto the floor.

Then the savage African woman's courage deserted her, for over Clodia stood one of Nero's soldiers, his dagger raised and pointed at her throat. Reluctantly, she released her hold and stood up.

His guards helped the Emperor to his feet. His fat face purple from humiliation and rage, Nero, rearranging the folds of his rumpled toga, strode from the room.

He had gone; the house grew still. The terrified women strained their ears to listen. Presently, out in the street, they heard the measured step of the Imperial Guard, marching off beside the Emperor's golden litter.

She was no Poppaea. Nero could not induce Tertulla to cheat on her husband. Finding himself up against what was rare in Rome, a virtuous woman, a week later the Emperor sent for a dissolute Sicilian, C. Ofonius Tigellinus, a former horse breeder whom he had made the head of his secret police.

Nero talked; Tigellinus listened.

"We must be careful, Caesar," the Sicilian cautioned. "You

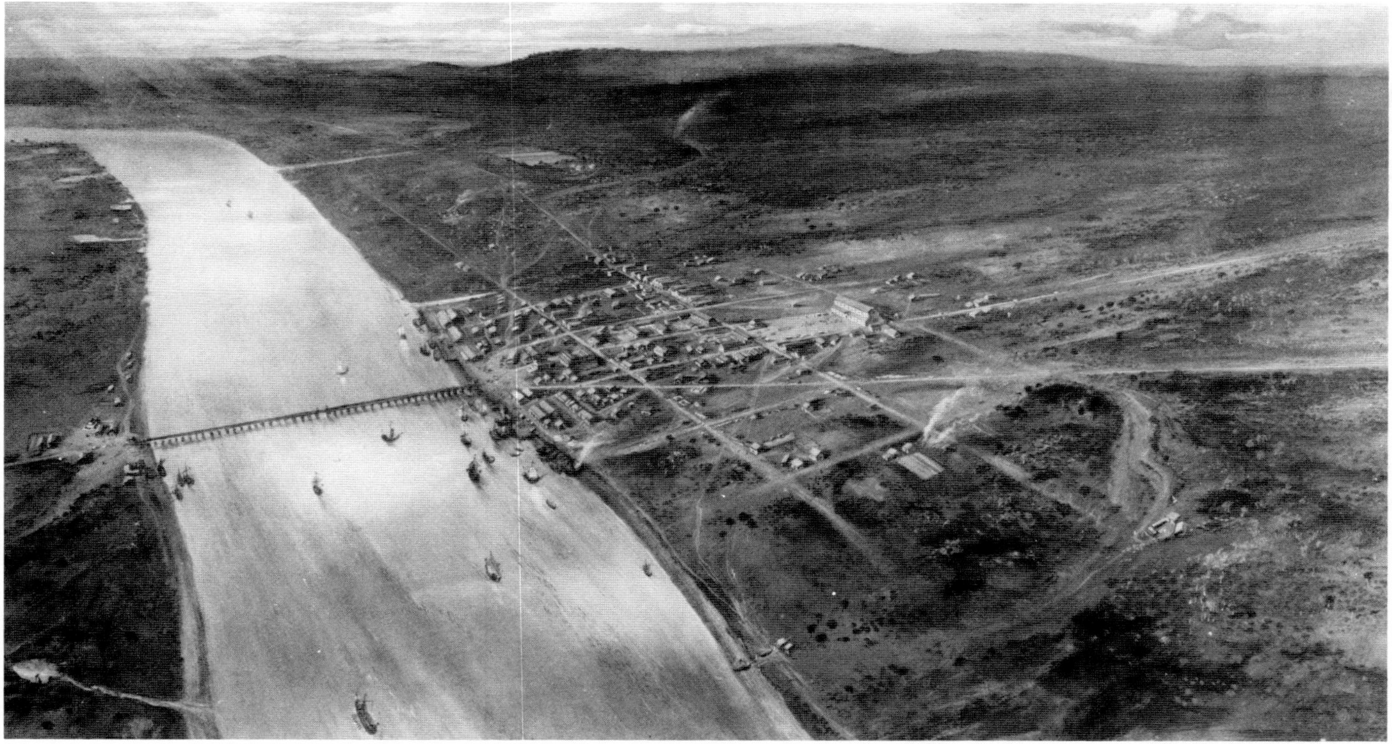

The Museum of London

LONDON IN THE FIRST CENTURY A.D.
by Alan Sorrell

Alinari-Art Reference Bureau

BRITISH TRIBAL CHIEF, FIRST CENTURY A.D.
Lateran Museum, Rome

Alinari-Art Reference Bureau

ROMAN LEGIONARIES
Mostra Augustea, Rome

Radio Times Hulton Picture Library

STATUE OF THE QUEEN OF THE ICENI
Westminister Bridge, London, England

Radio Times Hulton Picture Library

THE ROMAN BATHS AT BATH, ENGLAND, EXIST TO THIS DAY

Alinari-Art Reference Bureau

VESPASIAN
Uffizi Gallery, Florence

Alinari-Art Reference Bureau

TITUS
Villa Albani, Rome

Oscar Savio, Rome

COIN MINTED BY CLAUDIUS TO COMMEMORATE HIS CONQUEST OF BRITAIN

Alinari-Art Reference Bureau

CLAUDIUS
Uffizi Gallery, Florence

Alinari-Art Reference Bureau

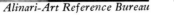

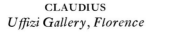

MESSALINA
Uffizi Gallery, Florence

Alinari-Art Reference Bureau

NERO
Uffizi Gallery, Florence

Alinari-Art Reference Bureau

BRITANNICUS
Uffizi Gallery, Florence

Alinari-Art Reference Bureau

AGRIPPINA
National Museum, Naples

Alinari-Art Reference Bureau

BERENICE
National Museum, Naples

Alinari-Art Reference Bureau

TITUS
Uffizi Gallery, Florence

Alinari-Art Reference Bureau

VESPASIAN
National Museum, Naples

Alinari-Art Reference Bureau

SENECA
National Museum, Naples

Collection Viollet

TITUS
The Louvre, Paris

Alinari-Art Reference Bureau

THEATER OF MARCELLUS, ROME

Alinari-Art Reference Bureau

BATHS OF TITUS, ROME

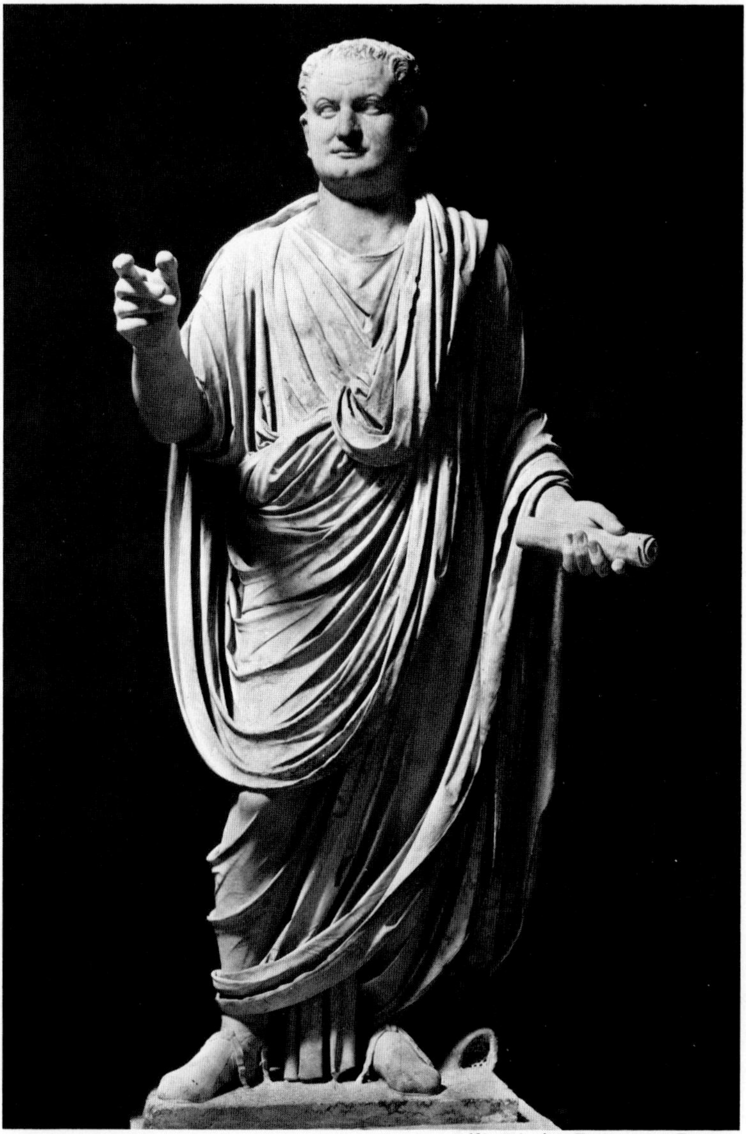

Alinari-Art Reference Bureau

TITUS
Vatican Museum, Rome

cannot kidnap this girl. Remember, she is no tavern wench, but Burrus' daughter."

This reminder made even the ruthless Nero pause. No one, not even the emperor of Rome, dared to risk offending the commander of the Praetorian Guard. It was the Imperial household troop that had elevated Claudius to the purple, after Caligula's murder; they had created Nero emperor; and they could, as easily, dethrone him.

Tigellinus went on. "But there are other ways to separate Vespasianus from his wife."

"Name them," Nero commanded.

"If properly approached, he can be forced to divorce her." The two men exchanged a knowing look. "Leave it to me, Caesar," Tigellinus said. And, a few nights later, he invited Tertulla's husband to dinner.

Titus had returned from Puteoli to learn with horror of Nero's attempted rape of the defenseless Tertulla, which might have succeeded except for Clodia. Bitterly now he regretted his attack upon Q. Vibius Crispus, who in revenge had drawn the Emperor's attention to his pretty wife.

"What can Tigellinus want of me?" Titus thought that evening as he was ushered by a servant into the Sicilian's elegant house near the Forum. His host greeted him in the atrium. "Before we eat, I must step over to the Mamertine and speak to the warden," the police officer said. "Would you like to go with me?"

After a short walk across the Forum, the two men came to the notorious Mamertine Prison below the Capitoline Hill. Doors were unlocked, and there was a sickening smell coming up from below the spiral staircase down which they were descending.

"Come along," Tigellinus kept saying.

They were now in one of the dark passageways, which ran under the Capitoline. Its walls were damp and slimy. Rats scuttled away at their approach.

"An interesting place, the Mamertine," the older man turned to say. "Since you've never seen it, Vespasianus, I'll take you on a tour of inspection."

Tigellinus called the head jailer, who preceded them down a corridor flashing his lantern into one cell after another, so that Titus could see what befell those who saw fit to displease the Emperor. He was sickened by the sights he saw—prisoners who had once been men, now but skeletons in chains, their filthy rags alive with vermin.

Ahead of them, they heard blood-curdling screams, and the warden's lantern shown down into a dark pit where rats swarmed and squeaked in a ferocious chorus as they fought one another over a dying man helpless to defend himself. His hands had been cut off.

"For refusing to sign a divorce agreement. Stupid fellow!" Tigellinus sighed. "Well, come along, Vespasianus, you've probably seen enough and are hungry for dinner."

Hungry! Titus wanted to vomit.

"You'll feel better shortly," his companion remarked as they came out of the prison into the night air of the Forum. "The Mamertine always upsets those who visit it for the first time."

Back in his house, the head of Nero's secret police devoted himself for the next hour to being a genial host. While they were being served food that stuck in Titus' throat after the gruesome sights he had seen, the burly, gray-haired man dining with him chatted about recent sporting events. And

Titus wondered again, why he had been invited here to-night?

He was not left long in doubt. The meal over, Tigellinus turned to a servant. "Get me that scroll of papyrus you'll find on my desk."

He placed it before Titus.

"I don't understand . . ." stammered the younger man, glancing in disbelief at the document. It was an Imperial command that he divorce Tertulla.

"You're here to sign that paper. Now do it!"

The shock of Tigellinus' words went through Titus like a knife. He felt ill and turned his eyes away, unable to look any longer into the cold, brutal face confronting him.

The police officer rapped impatiently on the table with his knuckles. "I said, sign it!"

"Never!"

"Oh, yes, you will . . ." Leaning across the table, Tigellinus lifted one of Titus' hands and pretended to study it. "You've nice hands, Vespasianus. So, once, did that poor creature you saw in the Mamertine. I'm sure you won't make the mistake he did, refuse to sign a request from the Emperor."

Titus felt sick. He wanted to leap to his feet and dash out of the house. But he no longer could. Two burly men had come, swords in hand, to stand on either side of him. He was unarmed and helpless.

"I should have shown you another interesting place, the Mamertine torture chambers," the Sicilian's voice purred on. "What ingenious instruments they have there! The gauntlets, for instance. A man hangs from them for days in agony. All because he has refused to do as the Emperor wishes."

Titus shuddered. The sweat ran down his body.

"And you should see the spikes on the iron collar. Not pleasant when pressed into your neck, Vespasianus. How would you like to be locked into such a collar for months? But of course you won't be, for you're not going to be obstinate and force me to send you to the Mamertine. Just sign that paper before you."

Tigellinus nodded to one of his men, who thrust a pen into Titus' hand. He flung it aside. "No!"

The police officer sprang to his feet. "Sign, you fool! I've stood enough. Sign or you go to the Mamertine."

They were putting the pen back into Titus' trembling hand. They were guiding it over the paper. He had signed.

Immediately, his host became again affable and smiling. "What a wise young man you are, Vespasianus! Anything you want now, in politics or in the army. Didn't the Emperor make Otho the governor of Lusitania for giving him Poppaea?"

What Titus replied he never knew, nor did he remember much of the rest of that ghastly evening, until at midnight he finally escaped from Tigellinus and hurried to the Castra Praetoria to ask the advice of its prefect, Sex. Afranius Burrus. Titus had been forced to sign a divorce agreement, but he still had his wife, and was determined to keep her.

"Run away!" his father-in-law advised him. "Do what Julius Caesar did when Sulla tried to make him divorce Cornelia. He fled with her to Rhodes. Get to Ostia as fast as you can. The Emperor will send my men after you, but I'll pretend that you've gone to Brindisi, and by sending them in the wrong direction, perhaps give you time to escape."

So at two o'clock in the morning, disguised as peasants, Titus and Tertulla mounted fast horses and set out for the coast. The fifteen-mile ride, mostly at a gallop, almost killed poor Tertulla. Titus carried an exhausted girl aboard the first boat in Ostia that was sailing. Where would they go? Anywhere. What did it matter? Just so long as they were together. But when the captain told him his destination, Titus cried, "Oh, no, not there!" He had imagined starting a new life with Tertulla in Greece or Egypt, where the warm climate might make her well, but they did not dare stay in Italy an hour longer.

So Titus set out for his third visit to the cold, damp island of Britain, this time with a sick wife. It was the worst possible place he could have taken her.

A year after Queen Boudicca had burned it to the ground, Londinium, to everyone's surprise, was being rebuilt. But it was still an unwalled, primitive, frontier town, too crude and unhealthy a place for the ailing Tertulla to remain. So Titus took his wife to Aquae Sulis (Bath) on the river Avon. Invalids came there to rid themselves of their rheumatism and other ailments by bathing in the hot medicinal waters that were a blessed relief in Britain's dampness and eternal drizzle. Over the only natural hot springs on the island the Romans had built a marble swimming pool, surrounded by a colonnade. Daily, Titus brought Tertulla to these baths of Minerva to bathe, but nothing did her any good.

One day, after Titus had made his usual offering for Tertulla's recovery at the shrine of Minerva, patroness of the spa, he sat down by chance on the steps of the pool beside a fierce-eyed old man in a worn goatskin cloak, who was washing his feet.

"I hope your Roman goddess answers your prayers, young man," the stranger said, "but if you've brought a loved one to Aquae Sulis to get well, have them drink from my magic cup. Let me show it to you." Reaching into a sack, he brought out a worn silver goblet. "Jesus of Nazareth drank from this cup at the last meal he had with his disciples in the home of Mary, mother of Mark." The old man held the chalice reverently in his hands. "It has miraculous powers. During the thirty years that I was imprisoned by the Romans, I kept myself alive by drinking from it."

Then he introduced himself. He was a Jew, Joseph of Arimathaea, and the crime for which he had been arrested by the Romans was for asking Pontius Pilate to let him place the body of Jesus of Nazareth in his tomb (John 19:38). "I don't suppose you've heard of Him?" Joseph asked.

"Indeed, I have," Titus replied. "My father helped Claudius conquer Britain. Among his troops were soldiers from the Twelfth Legion that had been stationed fourteen years previously in Jerusalem, at the time we had that trouble there over this Jesus of Nazareth, who called himself the King of the Jews. They told us about it."

After that, the old Jew and the young Roman often met at the baths. Joseph of Arimathaea had come to Britain to win converts to the Christian faith. Carrying a precious relic, the cup used at the Last Supper, he was searching all over Britain for a place from which to preach.

"How would you like to be my first convert?" Joseph asked.

Titus smilingly shook his head.

"I fear that I shall make a poor missionary." The old Jew looked troubled. "Am I using the wrong words? I cannot convince even you."

Titus had no desire to desert the Roman gods and goddesses for this new faith, but it was to Joseph of Arimathaea he turned one day, when the doctors warned him that the end was near. Tertulla looked tiny lying in their big bed. He sat down beside her. "Am I going to die?" she whispered.

"No, my darling, you mustn't. How could I live without you?"

Titus kissed his wife's cheek. And the chill of her skin frightened him. In despair, he remembered Joseph's goblet. Hadn't the old Jew said that by drinking from it he had been kept alive in prison for thirty years? Titus sprang to his feet. "Tertulla, I'll go fetch the magic cup. You'll drink from it and get well. You will. I swear it."

Running over to the baths of Minerva, Titus searched frantically for Joseph of Arimathaea. He never found him. Carrying the chalice that became known in the Middle Ages as the Holy Grail, he had gone on to Glastonbury to build there the first Christian church in Britain.

That night, Tertulla passed away, and a week later, Titus heard that his father-in-law, Sex. Afranius Burrus, had died from what seemed to be a sore throat.

But had he? Travelers, arriving in Britain from Rome, told how Nero had sent C. Stertinius Xenophon, once Claudius' doctor and now his, to the bedside of the ailing Burrus. After that, what happened? Had Xenophon, on orders from the Emperor, caused the prefect's death? While pretending to paint Burrus' tonsils with medicine, had he put a feather dipped in poison down his throat? Titus was sure of it. And that Nero, to punish Tertulla's father for helping her to escape from him, had committed another in his long list of crimes by doing away with the uncorruptible old soldier who made him emperor.

Titus remembered all the heartaches Nero had caused him,

beginning in his boyhood with the poisoning of his dog. He had killed Ajax, he had killed Tertulla, two beings whom Titus loved. For hadn't Nero caused the death of Titus' ailing wife by forcing her to flee to cold, damp Britain? Quivering with hatred, Titus made up his mind for the second time to return to Rome. This time, to get his revenge.

14

MARCIA—UNFAITHFULLY YOURS

"HUSH!" murmured T. Flavius Sabinus wearily as he listened to his wife lying on the bed beside him. Would she ever stop talking? Aloud, he said, "It's after midnight. Isn't it time we both got some sleep?"

That only started Paulita off again. "So your nephew came to see you? About what? Isn't it enough that you rescued Titus' father from bankruptcy? What did he want?"

"I told you," came the exhausted reply. "He's back from Britain. His wife died there, and Titus seems different somehow, bitter and revengeful. He muttered about having a private score to settle with the Emperor, and asked me if I could get him something to do at the palace."

"You? You couldn't get Titus made dog catcher!" Paulita's money had helped Sabinus become governor of Moesia, and after ten lucrative years on the Danube, he was now mayor of Rome. She never let him forget it. "What can Titus be up to? A job at the palace? He can't be hoping to break into society, can he? If so, Titus should find himself a rich wife. Someone like Marcia Furnilla, whose money would help him, as I helped you."

"Marcia! With her gladiators and racing drivers, what would she want with a husband?"

"If the girl became pregnant by one of them, a husband might prove convenient."

Sabinus couldn't resist saying, "Surely, my love, you wouldn't want your niece—a descendant of the second king of Rome—to marry into that low-class Flavian family? Country yokels, you call us." There was no reply. Believing that Paulita had gone to sleep, Sabinus drew a breath of relief. He drew it too soon. His wife was only thinking.

"I have it! We'll marry Titus to Marcia," exclaimed a voice beside him in the darkness. "He's poor, but handsome, and with her money—" Paulita said no more, but several nights later Titus was invited to a family party—just his Aunt Paulita, his Uncle Sabinus, and Marcia Furnilla.

Titus gasped on being introduced to the lovely blonde. His blood raced. He could not understand why. Marcia showed no interest in him whatsoever; she was cool, haughty, and very conscious of her own importance, not only as a descendant of Numa, king of Rome in 714 B.C., but left an orphan at an early age, now in her own right an extremely wealthy woman. During the meal, she talked mostly about her racing drivers and horses.

Titus, who cared little about sports, hardly spoke. He just sat looking at Marcia. She was decidedly mannish. She bred stallions in Campania and raced them under her own colors —orange and white—the only woman in Rome to own a racing stable. But later that evening when Titus took her home, Marcia's hard blue eyes grew soft, and her perfume intoxicated him as he lay beside her in the litter.

Greeted by a snarl as they entered her palatial home on the Aventine, Marcia laughed. "That's only Janus, my pet ocelot." She took Titus' hand. "Come along, you fool! Janus is chained in the garden. He won't hurt you."

Nervously, Titus entered the atrium and sat down, close to Marcia. "Darling . . ." he whispered, trying to kiss her.

Her strong hand shot out and gave him a hard slap. "How dare you!" Marcia shrieked, with fictitious indignation. She liked men to treat her roughly. "I hope you get a black eye from my fist. You deserve it."

"You vixen! You put your thumb in my eye," Titus said, between kisses. "Just for that, you're going to marry me."

And she did.

The ceremony took place in Marcia's luxurious home several months later, before the aristocracy of Rome. Vespasian, Antonia, and Domitian came from their Sabine farm for the wedding, as they had when Titus married Tertulla, but this time, awed by so many grand people, the groom's family was lost in the crowd.

When the guests had left and the bridal couple was alone in their *cubiculum* (bedroom), Titus proceeded to do what a few words spoken before a priest at the household altar had given him the right to do—untie the knots of Marcia's marriage girdle. A roar stopped him. "That's only Janus," his wife shrugged. "He sleeps with me. You'll have to get used to him."

"I will not! Either Janus goes or I do."

For the sake of peace, Titus finally gave in, and learned to share his wife's bedroom with a savage ocelot that growled at him whenever he came near her. It was sometime before he found out about Attila. But, by then, he tried to pretend to himself that he no longer cared.

Nero had murdered Burrus, his father-in-law. And it had taken great courage on Titus' part for him to return to Rome. Before he could get his revenge, would the Emperor, who never forgave a humiliation such as having Tertulla snatched from under his nose get Titus first?

That was why Titus had married Marcia Furnilla. Not for love, or because of her wealth and social position, as his Aunt Paulita thought, but to save his neck. Marcia was a close friend of the Empress Poppaea. Using the excuse that Octavia had failed to give him a child, Nero had divorced his wife a year ago and married his mistress. And Titus figured that Tigellinus, who had succeeded Burrus as prefect of the Praetorian Guard, would think twice before harming the husband of Marcia Furnilla.

The Emperor's divorce and remarriage had caused an uproar. The Roman people, who had accepted in silence his poisoning of Britannicus, his murder of Agrippina, and the "liquidation" of Burrus, were indignant at the virtuous Octavia being supplanted by the dissolute Poppaea. Rome was shocked when Nero, urged on by Poppaea, had his former wife imprisoned on the penal island of Pandateria. There, the helpless Octavia was seized by her jailers one day, gagged to stop her screams, and thrown alive into a cauldron of boiling water.

Titus heard of Octavia's ghastly death with horror. Tenderly he remembered Britannicus' gentle sister with whom he had played as a boy. What a monster Nero had become!

More than ever Titus longed to bring about his downfall. But could he?

It was some time before he thought of a way, but he did, and the test of whether he could outwit his old enemy and survive took place on the August night in 63 when Marcia and her husband received their first invitation since their marriage to a banquet at the palace, and Nero and Titus met again after several years.

As was the Roman custom, the Emperor's guests ate reclining on couches placed around three sides of a low table which was served from the fourth side. A single dining couch held three people, and Titus found himself chatting that evening with two men lying beside him. They were both Jews. One of them, a frail man in his mid-thirties, turned out to be King Agrippa II of Judaea, the great-grandson of Herod the Great, while his companion—a bearded fellow some ten years younger—was a Hebrew rabbi named Joseph ben Matthias, who had come from Jerusalem to ask Nero to pardon some Jewish priests whom the Romans had arrested.

As they ate with fingers or spoons, knives and forks being unknown, Egyptian dancers whirled before the Emperor's guests to the sound of zithers and flutes. Then, while they lingered over dessert and wine, he rose to entertain them. A slave brought him his harp, and Nero sang some comic songs set to bawdy tunes which he had composed. As he acted out the lyrics with obscene gestures, his voice cracked. The applause was polite when he finished, but perfunctory.

Now had come the moment that, for Titus, might mean life or death. What would the Emperor say, when he first saw him? "Come!" Titus said, and taking his wife Marcia by the hand, they pushed their way through the crowd up to the royal dais, where the Imperial couple were lying on silken couches, dining from dishes of gold.

"Marcia, darling!" Poppaea cried, on catching sight of her friend. "So you finally married. Is this your husband? Isn't he handsome!" The two women kissed. Titus bowed to the Empress. Then, turning to the frowning Emperor, he said with a straight face, "Nero, those songs were sung magnificently. You've never been in better voice."

This blatant lie may have saved Titus' life. Nero was intensely gullible. Always ready to believe any amount of flattery, his scowl vanished. "Do you really think I sang well? I thought on those high notes—"

"Your voice was a little weak then, but you could improve it by gargling, morning and night, with honey."

"Honey?"

"Yes, honey fermented with wine, if gargled, strengthens the vocal chords. That was what I used to make Britannicus do. I taught him to sing exquisitely. Remember?"

"Very well!"

"With a little training, Nero, you could perform before a larger audience than this, in private among your friends. Just think how the Roman people would enjoy hearing your glorious voice! Have you ever considered appearing in public? Say, in the theater of Marcellus? Before a crowd of several hundred people?"

"Often, but I wouldn't dare. What would the Romans say if their Emperor became a public entertainer?"

"They would love it!"

Nothing pleased Nero more than to be treated as a distinguished artist. And here was the man who could help him to become one! In comparison, what did the loss of Tertulla matter? Rome was full of pretty girls.

"Titus, I'm delighted you're back in Rome," the Emperor said genially on dismissing him. "Come and see me, tomorrow. I want to hear more about how to strengthen my voice."

So the next morning, three men hurried to the palace on the Palatine. Titus came first, accompanied by a Greek masseur. He was followed, a half hour later, by Tigellinus.

On entering the Emperor's private apartments, the commander of the Praetorian Guard stopped in amazement, hardly believing his eyes. Nero was lying on a bed on his back. Beside him stood a masseur and the very man whom Tigellinus had come to tell the Emperor that they must arrest at once.

The Greek, under Titus' instructions, was rubbing his Imperial patient with both hands. Following an upward movement toward the Emperor's throat, the masseur raised his hands after each stroke and shook his fingers vigorously, as though to drop off any impurities.

"Tigellinus, you're interrupting us! What do you want?" Nero asked, crossly. "Wait outside. I'll talk with you after my massage."

Fifteen minutes later the Emperor came sauntering out into his dressing room, where the prefect humbly waited. Nero held a silver bowl from which he gargled, spitting the liquid onto the floor. "It's honey and wine," he explained between retchings. "Gargling, so Titus Flavius Vespasianus tells me, gives greater power to the lungs."

"Titus Flavius Vespasianus!" gasped Tigellinus, livid with frustration and rage. "Caesar, he's just the person I've come to warn you against! Look out for that man. Why do you suppose he has returned from Britain? To avenge his father-in-law's death, of course. We must have him arrested—"

"Don't you dare!" Nero cut Tigellinus short. "Who do you think is going to manage my concert next month in the theater of Marcellus?"

15

THE EMPEROR TURNS PROFESSIONAL

NERO COULD TALK of nothing now but the day when, in the theater of Marcellus, the public would be allowed to hear his "heavenly voice." In preparation, he kept down his weight by taking laxatives; he gave up eating fruit, believed by the Romans to be bad for the vocal chords; and to avoid "wasting his breath," spoke only in whispers. But he kept postponing his debut. Until now, his audiences had all of them been friends and hand-picked. What if his first public concert was a fiasco?

The Roman people would not hesitate to hiss even their emperor off the stage. And Titus, for fear this might happen, hit upon a bright idea. From the many idlers in Rome, he recruited a fan club of young men, whom he arranged to have attend Nero's performance in the theater of Marcellus, seated inconspicuously in the audience.

Unknown to the Emperor, Titus rehearsed his paid applauders. "I'll signal to you when you must start clapping," he told them, "and when Nero strikes a high note, all of you are to cry 'Bravo!' "

At last, the great day came. A huge crowd poured into

the theater of Marcellus, scarcely believing that their emperor would actually sing from its stage. Inside the building, Titus' claque was already in their seats; and in his dressing room, Nero nervously awaited the time when he must walk out onto the stage and perform. This was what the Emperor most loved doing—in fact, actually lived for—yet he was sick with stagefright.

"Caesar, you're to go on after Volus' dogs and before the acrobats," Titus told him. Fearing that the concert might go badly, he had arranged to have other artists appear with Nero on the bill.

The long-awaited moment finally arrived. Volus ran off into the wings with his trained dogs and, carrying his harp, the Emperor, trembling with nervousness, came out onto the stage.

At the conclusion of the act, Titus lifted his hand to signal for the applause, and his hired fan club responded from their seats to the cue with thunderous clapping. "Encore! Encore!" they shouted. The audience, copying the professional handclappers, heartily joined in.

After the almost deafening ovation had died down, Titus hurried back to the Imperial dressing room, to be greeted by a happy man. "I wasn't booed! They loved me!" Nero cried, beside himself with joy.

Inwardly exalting, Titus urged him on to his ruin, for acting, a respectable profession in Greece, was not considered respectable at all in Rome. Actors were slaves or freedmen, almost never freeborn men. "Caesar, since you were such a success here, why don't you sing at the theater in Neapolis?" Titus suggested.

It was a clever speech. Flattered, Nero jumped at the bait,

and heartily agreeing to everything that Titus said, embarked upon the slippery slope to his doom.

To have their emperor appear on a vaudeville bill at the theater of Marcellus, with acrobats and a troup of trained dogs, was bad enough. It lowered the dignity of the throne in the eyes of the Roman people. They were shocked. But after a few weeks, to see the emperor perform on the stage of a public theater in Neapolis (Naples)—acting, singing, fiddling, and what was worse, being paid for doing so, like a common actor—was a sight repugnant even to his warmest supporters.

Nero's appearances on the stage had made him more avid than ever for the shouts of the crowd. He had raced for years with friends on his private racetrack, but now driving fast horses across the Tiber in the remote Vatican gardens, where few people could see him, no longer satisfied him. Knowing what the Romans would think of their emperor if he did, Titus tempted him further, "Caesar, why don't you enter the races at the Circus Maximus? Your many admirers should see how well you drive a chariot."

Before long, his subjects beheld a scandalous sight—their Emperor further demeaning himself by taking part in a public race. The Romans were fond of horse racing, but held chariot drivers in contempt. Rich men never drove their chariots at the Circus Maximus. They had professionals, usually slaves, to do that. Yet there was the Emperor, violating the conventional decencies, by openly competing with the scum of the Roman racing stables.

The crowd gasped as Nero—fat, gross, and naked except for a loin cloth—held in his four stallions waiting for the signal to start. Drunk that day, he was thrown out on the first lap. They picked the Emperor up and helped him back into his chariot, but he failed to complete the course. No matter. He won first prize all the same, and was crowned with a gold laurel wreath.

In every race he entered, Titus saw to it that Nero was declared the winner. He slept with his precious wreaths of victory over his bed and, vain as he was, knowing full well to whom he owed these honors, he asked one day, "My dear friend, you've made me a happy man. What can I do to repay you?"

"Nothing for myself, but will you do something for my father?" Titus replied. "You don't remember it, Caesar, but you cashiered him from the army for snoring during one of your musicals."

Nero was amused. What would the former general like? "To be reinstated," his son replied.

"How about being proconsul?" the Emperor suggested. "Possibly in Egypt? Alexandria is a nice place to live."

The Foreign Office, however, objected. Vespasian was an excellent soldier, his services in Britain were still remembered, but what did he know about Egypt? So Nero sent him to the Senate, to learn how to govern the Empire's richest province, and T. Flavius Vespasianus, now fifty-four, came to Rome, annoyed at having to leave his Sabine farm and complaining that the red shoes of a Senator hurt his feet.

Titus' plot to induce Nero to destroy himself was succeeding beyond his wildest expectations. But at home life with Marcia had become one long quarrel. By now he knew all about Attila, an arrogant Sicilian who was her favorite racing driver. Marcia never missed being at the Circus Maximus when Attila was competing in a race, and she paid him a salary of four hundred thousand *sesterces* a year, a fortune in those days. But Titus was unprepared for the sight that met his eyes, when returning home unexpectedly one afternoon, he entered his wife's bedroom without taking any notice of the efforts of her slaves to stop him.

Marcia freed herself from Attila's arms. "Titus!" she demanded, angrily. "How dare you enter without knocking! Have you no manners?"

His temper was as hot as hers. His hand on his sword hilt, Titus strode up to the handsome Sicilian. "Get out, you miserable slave! Do you want me to kill you?"

"Oh, Titus, don't be so melodramatic! Do you wish the servants to hear us quarreling?" Marcia hurried over to slam shut the door. "What an evil mind you have! Attila and I were only discussing my horses. And it's so hot today that . . . well, we shed some of our clothes. Now beg Attila's pardon for calling him a slave. Months ago, he won his freedom by his many victories in the arena."

Sickened by the farce their marriage had become, Titus retorted, "Marcia, I've stood enough! I want a divorce."

"Oh, you do? Well, you won't get one!" His wife's blue eyes grew steely. "Titus, I don't know why you married me. Certainly not from love or because of my money, which you seem to scorn, but for some strange reason known only to yourself. Well, I now have need of you too. Titus, my love, I'm pregnant. And how do you know the child isn't yours?"

Titus didn't. Only that he didn't dare get a divorce. He needed the protection of being Marcia Furnilla's husband until he had his revenge on Nero. So Titus was still living in his wife's house on the Aventine, although they had separate bedrooms, when she gave birth to a daughter six months later.

It was the Roman custom, as soon as a child was born, to bring the baby and lay it at a man's feet. If the alleged father picked the infant up in his arms, by that act he acknowledged the fact that he was its father; if he failed to, he repudiated his wife's offspring. Lying in bed, Marcia asked anxiously, "Titus, are you going to be difficult?"

No, he couldn't afford to be.

Before several witnesses, Titus took the little girl in his arms. She was his. Perhaps? They named her Julia.

16

ROME BURNS

A Roman baby received a name on its ninth day if a boy, the eighth if a girl; and the sultry night of July 18, 64, Julia's name day, found her mother's house on the Aventine filled with guests. Titus' father, Antonia Caenis, and his brother Domitian were in Egypt—T. Flavius Vespasianus, as Nero's proconsul—but Titus' Uncle Sabinus and his Aunt Paulita were there, as were King Agrippa of Judaea, Joseph ben Matthias, and, to Titus' shame and annoyance, Attila. Holding little Julia in his arms, the handsome Sicilian charioteer strutted about showing off the baby. With her dark hair and olive skin, Marcia's child was the image of him.

When everyone had arrived, a priest offered a sacrifice on the household altar, Julia's *praenomen* was bestowed upon her with due solemnity, and the feasting began.

Two hours later, when the guests had all eaten and drunk well, several of them wandered out onto the terrace. Gazing down into the valley between the Aventine and the Palatine, Joseph ben Matthias exclaimed, "What's that?" A column of black smoke was rising from the Circus Maximus.

"It looks like a fire," Titus said.

His wife came hurrying out onto the terrace. "A fire?"

Marcia asked. "Where is it?"

"Down by the Circus," Titus told her.

"Another fire?" Paulita turned to her husband, the mayor of Rome. "Sabinus, must you go? Can't your firemen put it out?"

"It would be a good thing if all of Rome burned down," was Marcia's opinion. "Nero said, only the other day, that he'd like to see the whole city destroyed, so he could rebuild it properly."

Smoke and flames continued to rise from the valley and, remembering his duties as mayor, T. Flavius Sabinus hurriedly left to call out the city's fire brigades, for the conflagration was spreading. A high wind had fanned it. From the racecourse below, the flames had inched their way up the Palatine Hill and crackling flames were dancing in the cypress trees of the Imperial gardens.

Titus ordered his horse.

"I'm going with you," King Agrippa said. So did his Jewish friend, Joseph ben Matthias, and the three men rode off, down the slopes of the Aventine into the burning city. By that time, the fire had spread to the Forum, and the streets of Rome were blocked with frightened people fleeing from their homes. Riding along the Via Sacra, whose shops were ablaze, Titus caught sight of some men flinging lighted torches into the wooden buildings. One of them ran past him, shouting, "The Day of Judgment has come!"

"They're Christians," Agrippa explained, "followers of that troublemaker named Christus, whom we crucified in Judaea back in the reign of Tiberius. They believe the end of the world is coming, and their Messiah will return to earth, to judge the living and the dead."

Further on, they found Mayor Sabinus directing his city police. They were chasing people out of their homes and setting fire to the buildings, trying to make a firebreak to keep the flames from spreading. A hopeless task. How could they? Riding along the Via Lata, the three horsemen came upon a burning house. Smoke was pouring from its windows. Joseph ben Matthias dismounted and went over to pound with his fist on the door. "Anyone in there?" he shouted.

"Help! Help!" replied a weak voice.

Titus forced open the door. Inside the house, a small, bald-headed man sat slumped in a chair. Agrippa inquired, "Are you all right?" And the man gasped, "Yes, only . . . overcome . . . by the smoke . . ."

Titus and his friends put out the fire. While they did so, the little man, looking intently at Agrippa, asked, "Aren't you the King of Judaea?"

Agrippa nodded.

"You don't remember me," went on Paul of Tarsus, "but it's thanks to you that I'm alive and safe here in Rome."

Seeing Agrippa again brought back to Paul that day in Caesarea, when he had been taken from prison to plead for justice before the King of Judaea and his sister Berenice (Acts 25:23). Being a follower of Jesus of Nazareth, how he had feared them! What would these Herods do to him? They were a family of murderers. Hadn't their great-grandfather, Herod the Great, killed all of the children of Bethlehem in the hope of doing away with the infant Jesus (Matt. 2:16)? Their great-uncle, Antipas, beheaded John the Baptist and sent Jesus to his death? And their father, Agrippa, killed James, the first of the Apostles to die for Christ? So Paul of Tarsus had stood that day before Agrippa II and his sister Berenice, expecting the worst. But, to his surprise, they werc kind to him.

Now in Rome, six years later, Paul reminded the King of Judaea of their first meeting. "I told you then that I had been kept in prison by the Romans for two years to save me from being lynched by the priests in Jerusalem, who accused me of having profaned their Temple. And since I could not get a fair trial in Judaea, I begged you to let me go to Rome and appeal to the Emperor, as I had the right to do, being a Roman citizen. And you agreed that I could go under military escort. Don't you remember?"

"No," replied Agrippa. "Frankly, I don't."

The fire burned for eight days. When it was stamped out finally, two-thirds of Rome lay in ashes and four hundred thousand people were homeless. Mayor Sabinus put his nephew Titus in charge of getting the refugees food and shelter. Tents were erected on the Campus Martius, and Titus sent urgent appeals to Campania for wheat, oil, and clothing, which he distributed to quiet the people, who were accusing the Emperor of deliberately setting the city on fire so that he could build a new Rome.

The belief gained credulity when Nero began doing just that. Rome's narrow streets were widened; huge blocks of tenements torn down; and since his palace on the Palatine had been damaged, he started to build himself a new one. A mile of sumptuous buildings beside an artificial lake between the Forum and Esquiline Hill, his Domus Aurea, when finished, was the most grandiose palace ever erected by a Roman emperor. Its name, Golden House, was due to the gold-plated tiles on its roof, and so much of the precious metal was used inside and out, on cornices and the capitals of columns, that the huge building sparkled in the sunshine.

Shocked by Nero's selfish extravagance when so many of his subjects were still homeless, living in makeshift shelters on the Campus Martius, the Romans were more convinced than ever that it was the Emperor himself who had started the Great Fire, in the most thickly inhabited section of Rome, to acquire enough space for his new palace.

Such talk was dangerous, but Nero shrugged it off. "Oh, I'll placate them!" he said. So day after day, the gladiatorial combats, the chariot races, and the fights between wild beasts went on, as well as the free distribution of corn. Still, the Romans grumbled.

"They're bored," Tigellinus told him. "There's nothing so monotonous, Caesar, as continuously seeing condemned prisoners being fed to the lions. We must give the public something new and amusing to watch."

The Christians, he thought, might do as suitable victims. They were a small sect, mostly slaves, and since they refused to worship the Emperor, disliked in Rome. Why not fasten the blame on these unpopular and defenseless people? During the Great Fire, many Christians had been seen helping the flames to spread, for they believed the wicked city of Rome must be destroyed to prepare for Jesus' Second Coming.

"We'll accuse the Christians of arson," Tigellinus went on, "and silence this talk that it was you, Caesar, who was the incendiary."

So the persecution of Jesus' followers, as scapegoats, began. Nero lent his Vatican gardens for the spectacles. And the Roman people, satiated with attending brutal gladiatorial combats and beast fights, were given a "new and amusing" entertainment. Dressed in wild animal's skins, groups of trembling people were driven by whips into the arena, and packs of savage hunting dogs were let loose on them. The audience howled with laughter at the comical sight of the half-starved hounds chasing the fleeing Christians, hampered by their long animal skins across the sand, knocking the helpless people down, and tearing them to pieces. While a water organ played loudly to drown out their screams, the hysterical mob in the grandstands shouted, "Death to those who set fire to Rome!"

The Romans were not all of them heartless brutes, however. There were decent people, like Titus, who deplored all this cruelty.

Going about Rome distributing food baskets to the people made homeless by the Great Fire, Titus often stopped in at Paul of Tarsus' small house on the Via Lata to check on him. With the Christians being persecuted, he feared for his safety. Freed by Nero after two years in Rome, Paul lived alone. Luke, the Greek physician who had come to Italy with him, had returned to Judaea to gather information for a life of Jesus of Nazareth he wanted to write; and Mark, who had accompanied Paul on his missionary journeys, was now the secretary of Simon Peter, the head of the Christian sect in Rome.

Little by little, Titus learned about Paul: how, once a strict Pharisee from Tarsus in Cilicia, he had persecuted the Christians; then one day on the road to Damascus, a vision of Christ spoke to him; and since then, a changed man, Paul was devoting himself to telling about Jesus, not only to the Jews but to the Gentiles, as he called the non-Jews, and writing letters to the Christian churches he had founded in Asia Minor.

One night, Titus found a cart before Paul's door, and the Apostle about to leave his house. "I'm going to one of our services," he explained. "Nero is making things so difficult for us that we no longer dare to meet, except furtively. Simon Peter, our leader in Rome, is to speak to us tonight. Won't you come?"

Titus agreed to go.

"I'm glad that you're to hear Peter speak," Paul said as they drove out along the Appian Way. "He is a former Galilean fisherman. Peter and Andrew, his brother, were Jesus' first disciples. Peter can remember his actual words, while I only saw Our Lord once in a vision. That is why Peter can tell about Him so much better than I can."

On the Via Appia, outside the city walls, the Romans buried their dead, but the Christians, too poor to build tombs above ground, had cut underground galleries, called catacombs, in which to bury theirs. Afraid of Nero, they met in them in secret.

Stopping his cart, Paul took Titus down into one of these subterranean chambers, where a small group of people was assembled, holding lighted candles. Beyond them, a tall, gray-bearded man stood before an altar, whom Titus knew to be Simon Peter.

"This is Mark, Peter's secretary." Paul introduced a young man who came forward to greet them. "It was in the house of Mark's mother in Jerusalem that Christ ate that last Passover supper with his disciples. Mark was too young then to remember Our Saviour very well. But Peter is helping him to write down the story of Jesus of Nazareth for the first time, by telling him all that he can remember about the Master."

The younger Apostle smiled at Paul, but Titus could feel the antagonism toward himself—a Roman and a pagan—as he led them to their seats. Then he forgot all about Mark, for the service had started and Peter began to speak. Seated beside Paul in the semidarkness, Titus listened in astonishment to what the former Galilean fisherman was saying, for he was preaching about the equality of man, a doctrine the cast-ridden Romans considered seditious.

"A slave and his master are brothers, equal in the eyes of God," Peter assured his little congregation. And he promised them a life after death, in which the Romans did not believe.

When his sermon was over, women brought out bread and wine, and Peter said, "This is my body, take and eat . . ." The bread was passed around. Then, lifting a goblet, he told the kneeling people, "This is my blood, shed for you . . ." When his turn came, Titus drank from the same cup as the others. Blood? How absurd! The Roman knew cheap wine when he tasted it. But the Christians drank from the goblet reverently, and the service over, kissed each other good-by.

There was no farewell kiss from Mark. His scowling expression seemed to say: Why has Paul brought this pagan here? Will he turn out to be an informer? Paul felt differently. He trusted Titus. On the way back to Rome, Paul said to him, "I'm glad that you've eaten of His flesh and drunk of His blood. Now you are saved."

It was midnight when Titus reached home. Marcia met him at the door. "Where have you been?" his wife demanded. "In some disreputable brothel? You look guilty."

Without replying, Titus hurried past her into his bedroom. The Christian rites during which bread and wine were consecrated and taken by the congregation, symbolizing the body and blood of Christ, shocked the Romans. They regarded the Eucharist as a cannibalistic feast. And although

Titus knew that he had eaten bread, not human flesh, nor drunk blood from the goblet Peter handed him, the thought of having attended such an orgy was so revolting to the Roman that he felt sick.

Next morning, Titus hurried to the baths to cleanse himself, both physically and spiritually. There something happened to him that put all thoughts, except of Nero, out of his mind.

17

CONSPIRATORS IN CRIME

The odd thing about a Roman house was its absence of bathrooms. A Roman did not take his bath at home but went daily to the *thermae* (public baths), where he met his friends, gossiped and arranged business deals, all the while going through the pleasant ritual of bathing. After stirring up his circulation by playing games, the bather progressed through the increasing heat of various hot rooms, until he sweated all over; he finished off his bath with a cold swim in the pool, enjoyed a massage, dressed, and went home to dine.

The morning after his visit to the Christian catacombs, Titus was lying on a slab of marble in the *unctorium* (massage room), being annointed by a Greek slave with sweet-scented olive oil, when he overheard conversation nearby. "Why, Consul," chided a Greek youth giving a rubdown to a plump man trying to lose ten pounds, "what about these new rolls of fat? Been attending too many banquets?"

"Relax, float off . . ." purred Titus' masseur, and turning on his face, he heard no more. But later in the gymnasium, meeting the stout man again, Titus recognized him as Gaius Calpurnius Piso.

"Vespasianus, I'd like to discuss something with you," the

consul said. What was it? Piso woudn't say, but he was so persuasive that Titus agreed to be at his home the following afternoon. Already there when he arrived were Senators Atticus Scevinus, Faenius Rufus, and Marcus Lateranus.

"Let's go where we cannot be overheard," cautioned Piso, and he took his guests out to his garden. When they were seated, their host lost no time in bringing the conversation around to Nero.

"First, our Emperor disgusted everyone by becoming an actor. Now he has lost the respect of all decent people by his cruelty to the Christians. They're a dangerous sect, preaching the equality of man, and so likely to incite our slaves to rebellion. They should be repressed but not torn to pieces in the arena by dogs, nailed to the cross, or turned into living torches to light Nero's parties. Who enjoys such revolting sights, except the Emperor? We must rid ourselves of this mad man. But, gentlemen, what then? Nero has no son. Who will succeed him? That's why I've invited you here. We must be prepared to replace him with someone."

Scevinus spoke up, "Someone like Seneca."

"He would be ideal," agreed Titus, "I, too, would like to see the last of Nero. But what chance have we, a few individuals, to bring such a thing about?"

"An excellent one," Piso declared. "Vespasianus, you will be amazed at the number of men who have shown themselves eager to join us. But we need a leader, such as Seneca. He is old but greatly respected."

"You," Scevinus said, looking at Titus, "are a close friend of his. Can you get him to join us?"

"I'll see if I can."

Knowing that Piso wanted a prompt answer, Titus rode

out the next day to Seneca's Villa Nomentana, four miles from Rome. He found his former tutor at the court of Claudius looking ill and half-starved, for since Burrus' death, afraid that Nero would poison him next, Seneca ate nothing but nuts and fruit he picked himself.

"You're mad," the Stoic philosopher exclaimed when he heard the reason for Titus' visit. "Nero still has the loyalty of the Praetorian Guard. What makes you think that you, a handful of his enemies, can force him to abdicate?"

"We're not a few but many." Titus handed Seneca a list of names that Piso had given him. He read it, then tossed the paper aside. "Very interesting. But, pray, leave me out of this. I'm sixty-nine, too old, too tired . . ."

"We're committed. We cannot draw back now," Titus told him, "and Piso, Scevinus, and the others would like to think that if we succeed in restoring the Republic, you will be willing to head it."

"No, I'll never return to the Palatine," Seneca kept insisting, but in a flattered voice that indicated—well, why not? So the next day when Titus repeated this conversation to his fellow-plotters in Rome, Piso exclaimed, "Don't worry! When the time comes, the old man will be with us."

Now that the conspirators felt they could count upon Seneca, they began to discuss how best to eliminate Nero. There was a diversity of opinions. Some of them wanted to kidnap the Emperor and send him into exile, but the majority of those consulted thought that he should be assassinated.

Titus was shocked by such talk.

"We all of us want to be rid of Nero, but let's stop short of murder," he pleaded with the others. "Why is it necessary? The Emperor has so disgusted the Roman people by appearing on the stage—and I'm proud to say I encouraged him in this way to ruin himself—that he may soon be forced to abdicate. Isn't it enough for us to continue to stir up this resentment?"

No one listened to Titus.

Instead, the conspirators went on to plot the best way to commit the murder. Before long, they had it all decided—the time, the place, and the method. Nero was to be stabbed to death at the Circus Maximus during the games in honor of the goddess Ceres. Quintanus and Scevinus volunteered to bring their daggers.

Titus refused to join in their plans.

Nobody had done more than he had, since his return from Britain, to weaken the throne. By catering to Nero's vanity, Titus had encouraged the Emperor to make such a spectacle of himself on the stage that the Romans had by now had enough of him. Nero was destroying himself. So why resort to bloodshed?

Returning home that day, Titus made up his mind to disassociate himself from the Pisonian Conspiracy, which was getting out of hand.

He came upon Marcia seated in the atrium reading a copy of the *Acta Diurna* (*Daily Doings*), a newspaper founded by Julius Caesar that was posted daily in the Forum. She looked up to say, "One hears of nothing but horrors these days! More shops in the Forum have been robbed . . . there's been another hold-up on the Via Flamina . . . and we're warned about swimming in the Tiber—the garbage, thrown from the barges, is polluting the river. Oh, here's some good news! Those Christian rabble-rousers, Peter and Paul, have been arrested."

* * *

Fleeing from Nero's persecutions, Simon Peter had hurried to leave Rome, but a short distance out on the Appian Way a vision of Jesus appeared to him. Peter asked, "*Quo vadis, Domine?*" And Christ seemed to answer, "*Eo Roman interum crucifiggi.*" ("I am going to Rome to be crucified a second time.") Peter was ashamed. He returned to Rome and gave himself up.

Now, several months later, Simon Peter sat in his cell at the Mamertine Prison, his feet in water. Two guards knelt before him. Dipping his hand into the water, Peter baptized them. "In the name of the Father, the Son, and the Holy Ghost–" What was that? Footsteps! The kneeling soldiers jumped up, guiltily. Listening intently, the prisoner silently prayed. Peter was sentenced to die, but when and how he had not been told. Was this the executioner come at last to do his work, down in this dark, isolated cell?

Titus appeared. "Go," he ordered the guards. "The warden has given me permission to be alone with the prisoner."

The soldiers saluted and went.

Today, Simon Peter, for the first time, sat in a corner of his cell chained to the wall, and Titus' heart ached at this new humiliation. He said to him, "I've just come from seeing Paul. His cell is freezing cold. He tells me that he has written to Timothy to send him a coat, but I'll try to get him one in Rome. And Paul sent me to ask you, Peter, what can I do for you?"

"I've a wife and children in Judaea. Will you write and tell my family that I love them?"

"Willingly."

Titus was leaving, when Simon Peter called him back. "Surely, you realize the risks you've been taking, visiting a condemned man in his cell?" he asked. "Don't come here again, Titus, for your own safety. But to show my gratitude before we part, let me baptize you in the only true faith, as I did the soldiers. Look, it's a miracle. See, what came an hour ago—" He indicated the water covering the floor of his cell. "I prayed, a spring bubbled out of the stone floor, and I christened my guards with it. I'll do the same for you, but you must come closer, for yesterday they came and chained me to the wall and now I cannot move."

"No!" Titus backed away instead, for having dipped his hand in the water, Peter was making strange gestures, touching first his right shoulder, his left shoulder, then his chest. "A miracle? Don't be absurd! That's only water oozing from a broken pipe. I'll get it fixed."

Titus hurried up the stairs.

"There's a bad leak down there," he told the warden. "Have it repaired or move the prisoner, Simon Peter, to a dry cell."

The prison official promised to attend to the matter, and Titus returned home from the Mamertine that day, glad that he had been able over the last month to alleviate somewhat the sufferings of those two condemned Christians, Peter and Paul, whom he had grown to like and respect. His heart lighter from having done a good deed, the Roman entered his house, and was startled to find a man standing in the peristyle. "Vespasianus, I've been waiting for you," Tigellinus said.

Titus did his best to keep his voice steady. "What do you want?"

"A little chat. Can we talk here?"

"Certainly." Titus drew up two chairs. The commander of

Nero's Praetorian Guard sat down, smiling his usual nasty smile, and Titus knew that something abominable was coming. "My dear fellow, aren't you keeping dangerous company these days?" he asked. "Visiting those dangerous Christian radicals, Peter and Paul, and plotting with Piso?"

"So you know all about me? Tigellinus, you're well informed."

"I have to be. As head of the Imperial secret police, it's my duty to protect the Emperor's security. Titus, I suspected you from the moment you returned from Britain. I tried to warn Nero, but he wouldn't listen. So I let you go free, but under close vigilance. My intelligence service has kept me informed. I have agents in the wine shops and brothels. Even the public lavatories are unsafe to talk in. Do you suppose I wouldn't learn of your meetings with Piso and his friends? Surely, remembering our visit together to the Mamertine some years ago, you know of the ingenious ways I have of making such people as Scevinus talk? Vespasianus, didn't you know better than to trust that imbecile?"

Little by little Titus learned to his horror (for Tigellinus liked to stick in the knife and twist it slowly around, to make sure it hurt) that it was Atticus Scevinus who had given their secret away. Drunk one night, the Senator boasted to a servant, "Milichus, sharpen my dagger! For I'm to restore the Republic with it." Suspecting what his master was about to do, Milichus informed on him, hoping to get a reward for saving the Emperor's life. Instead, Scevinus and Milichus were both arrested. Threatened with torture, Scevinus broke down at the sight of the hot irons, confessed the plot, and named his accomplices.

"They will all of them die in the torture chamber," Tigellinus remarked, coldly. "All but Seneca, whom the Emperor has graciously allowed to take his own life."

"That good man . . . is dead?"

Titus hid his face in his hands. He remembered what Seneca had said to him. "Having killed his mother, his wife, his stepbrother, and Burrus, who is there left for Nero to murder but his old tutor?" For years, the philosopher had looked upon each day as his last.

"Yes," Tigellinus replied, "and it took Seneca a long time to die. Not even the hemlock that Socrates drank—and it's still the best poison—had any effect. So we had him locked in a vapor bath, where he suffocated."

The burly, hard-faced Sicilian was enjoying himself. He sat back, watching Titus' grief. Memories of that infamous prison, the Mamertine, still nauseated Titus. He remembered the sights that had sickened him, and the horrors in the torture chamber he was spared then but would surely see now—the hot irons, the gauntlets, the iron collar. His nails biting into the palms of his hands, Titus asked, "You've arrested the others. Now you've come after me?"

"You?" Taking a malicious pleasure in keeping him in suspense, Tigellinus took his time answering. At last, he said, "Naturally, I had agents planted among Piso's conspirators. They reported to me that you, Vespasianus—and you, alone—pleaded with those would-be assassins not to murder the Emperor. So Nero has decided to spare you. You are to be deported. Tomorrow, you'll be taken to Ostia, under heavy guard, and put on a ship bound for Egypt."

Not to be branded with the hot irons? Torn limb from limb by the gauntlet? Or left to starve in the iron collar?

The relief was so great that Titus could scarcely murmur, "Thank you . . ."

"You're to stay in Alexandria with your father. Understand?" Tigellinus went on. "Don't ever dare to show your face in Rome again."

Titus was still numb. He could feel nothing, but after Tigellinus had gone, he staggered to a basin and vomited.

18

NEARING FORTY AND TENSE ABOUT IT

How could Judaea, that tiny country where Jesus was born, dare to defy Rome? But the brave little nation did. Riots broke out in Jerusalem in A.D. 66 and the Emperor, no longer able to ignore the unrest, sent troops to restore Roman authority. Being nearby, the obvious person to command them was the fifty-seven-year-old governor of Egypt, T. Flavius Vespasianus, a veteran of the Conquest of Britain, who started for Judaea with two legions, the Fifth Macedonia and the Tenth Fretensis.

"I can't get along with the Flavians, nor can I do without them," Nero said, so in spite of his doubts as to Titus' loyalty since the Piso Conspiracy, he appointed Vespasian's son a general at twenty-eight and second-in-command of the expedition to Judaea.

Titus had been living in Egypt since his banishment from Rome for taking part in the plot against Nero's life, and the year of 65 was a bad one for him. Refusing to share her husband's exile, Marcia had divorced him, only to be killed four months later in a chariot race. Nor had he been reunited with Julia; Marcia's daughter, after her mother's death, remained in Rome with her Aunt Paulita.

Well, that was all past history now, and hoping to repair his shattered life, Titus joined his father with the Fifteenth Legion from Egypt at Ptolemais (Acte) on the Phoenician coast.

Their strategy was to reduce Judaea piecemeal, leaving the capture of Jerusalem until the last. So on May 21, 67, the Romans first marched on the fortress of Jotapata, ten miles north of Nazareth. This stronghold was held by Joseph ben Matthias, the Jewish rabbi whom Titus had met in Rome three years ago, now governor of Galilee. His forces held out for an incredible forty-seven days before the Romans' battering rams crumbled Jotapata's walls, and Vespasian attacked, with his son Titus leading the assault.

When the fort fell and the Galileans had to surrender, Joseph ben Matthias did not commit suicide as the other last-ditch holdouts did. Instead, losing his nerve at the last moment, he went over to the enemy, and on being brought before Vespasian in chains, tried to escape the cross or the slave ship by predicting that Nero would not rule much longer, that Vespasian would shortly become Emperor, to be followed by Titus.

Could anything be more absurd? Emperor! The son and grandson of a humble tax collector? No one had ever ruled the Empire but a member of the aristocratic Julio-Claudian family. So the modest Vespasian dismissed Joseph's words as ridiculous flattery. However, having admired the Galilean's bravery at Jotapata, he decided to spare his life. Joseph would be held a prisoner, but kindly treated.

After the fall of Jotapata, six thousand Jewish prisoners of

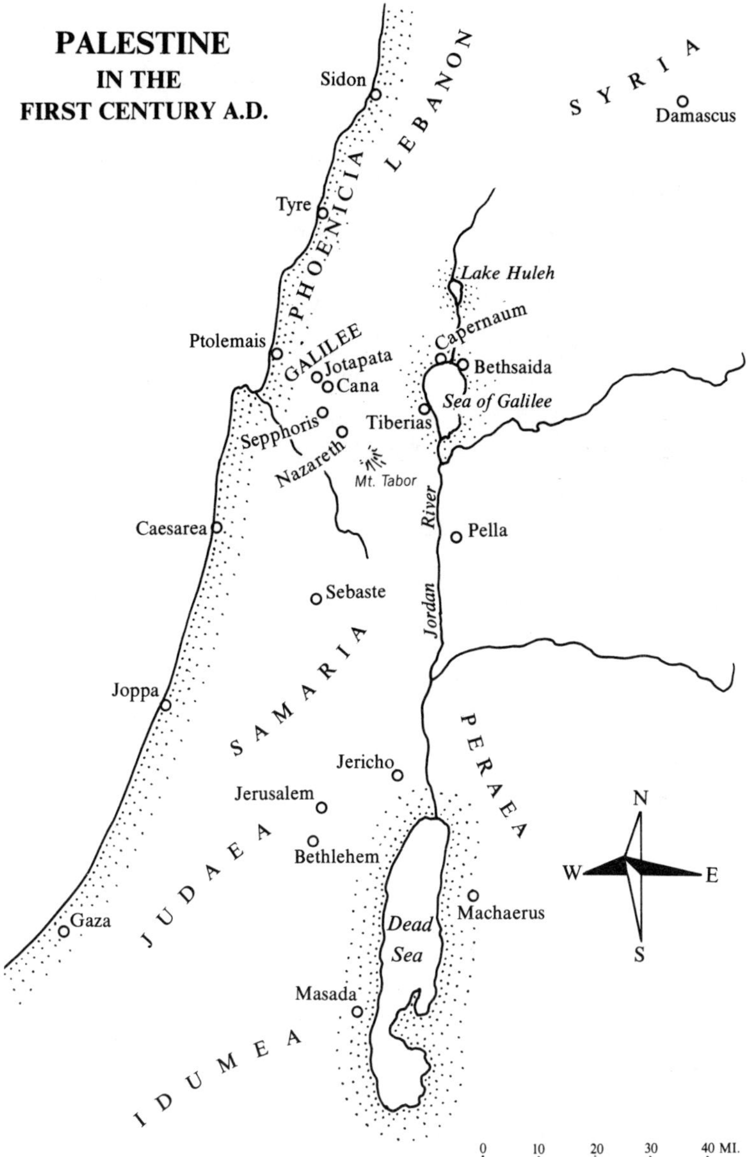
PALESTINE
IN THE
FIRST CENTURY A.D.
Sidon
LEBANON
SYRIA
Damascus
PHOENICIA
Tyre
Lake Huleh
Capernaum
Ptolemais
GALILEE
Jotapata
Bethsaida
Cana
Sea of Galilee
Tiberias
Sepphoris
Nazareth
Mt. Tabor
River
Caesarea
Pella
Sebaste
Jordan
SAMARIA
Joppa
PERAEA
Jericho
Jerusalem
N
JUDAEA
Bethlehem
W
E
Machaerus
Gaza
Dead Sea
S
Masada
IDUMEA
0
10
20
30
40 MI.
0
20
40
60 KM.

war were sent to Greece to dig the Corinth Canal; the Army of the East went to camp at Sepphoris; and Vespasian and Titus accepted the invitation of one of Rome's most loyal client kings, Agrippa II of Judaea, to visit him at Tiberias. He was living in his father's old palace in Galilee, the Herod family being so hated by their Jewish subjects for always siding with the Romans that Agrippa no longer found it pleasant to remain in Jerusalem.

On the day the Romans arrived in Tiberias, a crowd of hostile Galileans lined the streets to see the legionaries who had destroyed their key fortress of Jotapata and captured Joseph ben Matthias, their ablest general.

Titus, astride his white horse Castor, led the escort of cavalry that preceded Vespasian's chariot. Seeing ahead of him the square on which faced Agrippa's palace, he reined in the impatient Castor to await the long file of horsemen, four abreast, coming up the hill behind him.

From a balcony of the palace, Agrippa's elder sister, Queen Berenice of Cilicia (southern Turkey) leaned forward, eager to see the man about whom she had heard so much. Taking a bunch of flowers, Berenice tossed them at him, then watched in horror as the nosegay struck Titus square in the face. He looked up angrily at the balcony. But on beholding the culprit, eyes wide with fright, the Roman general, smiling his forgiveness, blew her a kiss.

She was lovely. When would he see her again? That evening, Titus stood eagerly awaiting Berenice's arrival in the hall of Agrippa's palace overlooking the Sea of Galilee, where the King of Judaea and his court had assembled to do honor to T. Flavius Vespasianus and his son. They were all there, except one. And then she came.

The wine was flowing freely, the room ringing with voices, when suddenly everyone stopped talking. All eyes turned toward the door. A tall, beautiful lady was arriving. She walked in, proud and erect. Exquisitely dressed and decked with jewels, Berenice looked like the queen she was, her red hair wound about her head in braids interwoven with pearls.

Leaving Vespasian's side, Agrippa went to greet the elder of his two sisters, to bring her over to be presented to his Roman guests.

Titus had heard considerable about this fascinating woman. Berenice had already had three husbands, two of them kings. And how many other men? In her girlhood Agrippa I had given her in marriage to a rich Egyptian–Mark, son of Alexander of Alabard, the head of the Jewish colony in Alexandria; when he died, Berenice's father had chosen for her next husband his own brother Herod, King of Chalcis, and she had two children by him before he was killed in 48. Twice widowed at twenty, Berenice had then become the wife of Polemo II, King of Cilicia, whose capital was Tarsus in Asia Minor.

People could tell Titus plenty about the Queen of Cilicia, for she was often in Judaea living with her unmarried brother Agrippa–incestuously, according to whispered gossip–but about Berenice's husband, they knew little. Polemo never came to Judaea with his wife. They were said to be unhappily married.

Now the King of Cilicia was absent, as usual, and Berenice was presiding over Agrippa's court as if she were his queen. After the banquet Titus pushed his way through the crowd surrounding her. "Aren't we ever to be allowed to talk to one another?" he asked. Not a brilliant opening, but all the Roman could think of at the moment. Taking the stately

Jewess by the arm, he steered her off into a corner, away from the others.

"I wanted to see if my eyes were deceiving me," Titus said, when they were seated. "They didn't . . . you're gorgeous."

Berenice was indeed. A regal woman, charming, intelligent, and–so he would discover–firm in her convictions. From a distance she had looked to be young, serenely beautiful, and elegant. On closer view, she was still serenely beautiful and elegant, but not young. Nearing forty, he would imagine.

Before Titus' arrival, Agrippa had warned his sister, "He's a widower, recovering from an unhappy marriage, and off all women at present. He thinks of nothing now, but putting down the Jewish revolt. So don't fall in love with him, Berenice. You'd only be wasting your time."

Meeting the handsome Roman, then, was something of a challenge. Being actually thirty-nine, eleven years his senior, the thrice-married beauty was pleased when she saw that she attracted him.

"I heard about you in Rome from a countryman of yours, Paul of Tarsus," Titus said. "He told me of having been arrested in Jerusalem by the Temple priests and how he came to ask Agrippa to let him go to Rome and plead his case before Nero, and that you persuaded your brother to grant his wish."

"Yes, and I wonder why I did. Paul had defiled our Temple by taking Gentiles into it. By Jewish law, his act was punishable by death."

"Your religion means a great deal to you?"

"Yes, the Herods are orthodox Jews. My father thought the Christians heretics, and killed everyone of them he could

CHIEF MEMBERS OF THE HEROD FAMILY:

Herod the Great had ten wives and fifteen children. The names of this vast family given here are only those who appear in this book. Berenice and her brother Agrippa are mentioned in the Bible by St. Luke. Berenice's first cousin, Salome, as a young woman danced before her stepfather Antipas, Tetrarch of Galilee in the days of Christ, and was rewarded with the head of John the Baptist.

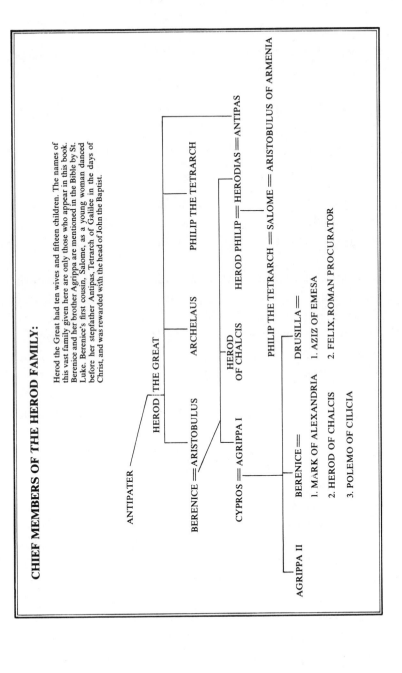

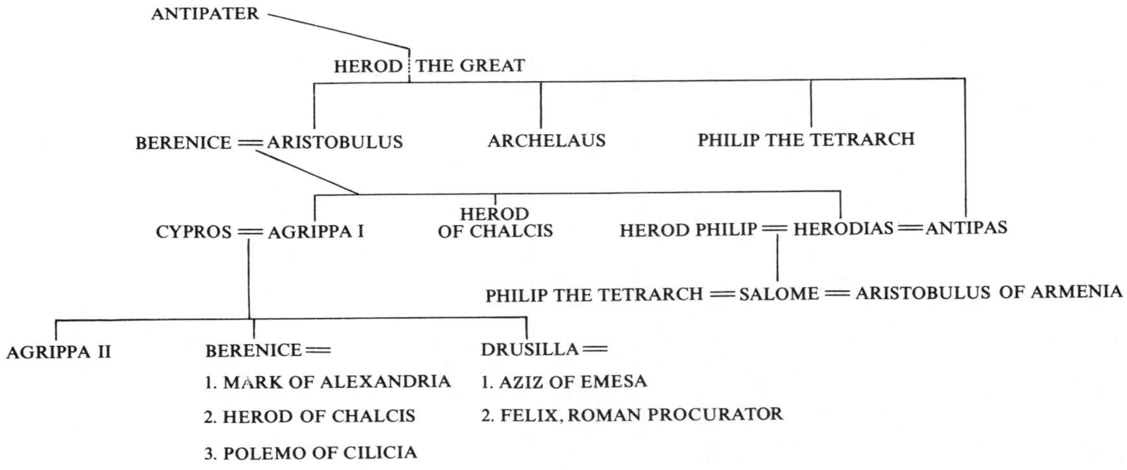

lay his hands on. I don't know why I helped Paul to escape to Rome. Perhaps because he came from Tarsus, and I was his queen."

Soon, however, they had forgotten all about Paul. "I'm glad those flowers I threw at you this afternoon didn't hurt you," Berenice said. And Titus replied, teasingly, "You're pretty rough, aren't you? In future, I'll take to my heels whenever I see you."

Then, far from taking to his heels, all evening Titus never left the side of this beautiful, intelligent, and understanding woman who had come into his life when he needed her most.

Their love affair became known all over Judaea in a month, and it stirred up all the resentment the Jews had long felt for their reigning family. Wasn't it because the Herods had been puppet kings, fawning on the Romans, that Judaea remained a weak client nation? All over Palestine, Herod the Great, Berenice's great-grandfather, had built circus arenas—an affront to the Jews, who hated the bloody combats that delighted the Romans—and a new temple in Jerusalem, very different from Solomon's. It was Greek in architecture and on its main gate Herod placed a golden eagle (the emblem of Rome) in defiance of the Torah injunction that no image of a human being or an animal should adorn the Temple.

Herod's grandson, Agrippa I, had helped to make Claudius the next Caesar when Caligula was murdered, and his son was brought up in Rome. Under Nero, he returned to Judaea as Agrippa II, but he was king in name only, subservient to Rome, and disliked by his Jewish subjects.

They became especially incensed when Agrippa's younger sister Drusilla, seduced by a Roman procurator, Antonius Felix, left her Syrian husband, King Aziz of Emesa, to live in adultery with the uncircumcised Felix who refused to adopt Judaism. And the similar shocking behavior of Drusilla's older sister, Berenice, set tongues to wagging again.

In Jewish eyes, by consorting with a Gentile, Berenice had also become unclean. Moreover, she was a Jew, Titus was a Roman, and with their countries at war, a love such as theirs was wrong from the beginning.

Hearing of it, Polemo of Cilicia wrote angry letters ordering his wife back to Tarsus. What had come over her, a devout Jewess? Her first two husbands had been circumcised Jews. And hadn't Berenice demanded that he, Polemo, be circumcised before she would marry him? She was to return home, immediately.

Her reply was unequivocal: No.

Instead, the Queen of Cilicia remained in Judaea, visiting Titus in camp when she could. During that spring of 67, the Roman legions were on the march again. As they drew the noose tighter about Jerusalem, place after place in Galilee, where thirty-nine years ago Jesus had walked preaching from village to village, fell into Roman hands—Mount Tabor, scene of the Transfiguration; Sepphoris, birthplace of Jesus' mother; Magdala, home of Mary Magdalene; and Bethsaida, the native town of the Apostles Peter, John, and Philip.

Berenice watched the Romans vanquish Galilee, sick at heart, for eventually they would be attacking her beloved City of David. By October, the rebellion had been crushed throughout most of Judaea. Only remaining to be conquered was Jerusalem.

"You must capture our Holy City, I know," the Jewish-born, deeply religious Berenice pleaded with her Roman lover, "but promise me you won't harm the Temple."

And Titus promised.

Then, in June of 68, came staggering news that abruptly cancelled all of Vespasian's plans. Nero was dead. And the Roman Army of the East could not proceed against Jerusalem without orders from the new emperor.

Titus heard of Nero's death with joy. He had his revenge. And hadn't it all turned out as he had hoped it would? For it was not Nero's crimes, but the disgrace of the Emperor's theatrical tours, when he made a spectacle of himself on the stage, that had disgusted the Roman people beyond endurance and finally the army. The first to revolt were the legions under Servius Galba in Spain. They advanced upon Rome, and Nero, deserted by everyone, even his Praetorian Guard sworn to protect him, at thirty-one committed suicide.

A.D. 68-69 is known as the Year of the Four Emperors. None of them lasted long. After seven months, the Praetorians found the elderly Galba too stingy, and he was murdered at the instigation of a younger general–Poppaea's former husband, M. Salvius Otho, governor of Lusitania (Portugal).

When they made Claudius emperor, it had never occurred to the Praetorian Guard that the emperor could be anyone but a descendant of Rome's first Caesar, the great Julius. But the Julio-Claudian line ended with Nero. The army was now in power. In the future, the emperors would all be military men.

So Otho, in his turn, was overthrown by Aulus Vitellius, commander of the legions in Germany. And Otho killed himself after a reign of only three months.

It was now apparent that any man could make himself emperor if he had a strong enough army. Vitellius' elevation infuriated Vespasian's devoted legions, and they demanded that he make a bid for the throne. In July, 69, T. Flavius Vespasianus was proclaimed emperor by his troops in Judaea, and the Army of the East set out for Italy to confirm his title. Joined by seven legions from the Danube, the Flavian forces swept down upon Rome.

Within the city, Vespasian's brother, Mayor Sabinus, tried to rally the Romans to the Flavian cause. Vitellius crushed the uprising with bloody butchery, and Sabinus fled to hide in the Temple of Jupiter with his eighteen-year-old nephew, Domitian. During the fighting Jupiter's golden temple on the Capitol went up in flames, Domitian escaped, but Sabinus was caught by Vitellius' soldiers and killed.

Bitter street fighting followed between the rival armies. As the Flavians fought their way into Rome, Vitellius fled to his palace on the Palatine and barricaded its doors. Domitian, with some soldiers, broke in. There was a cruel streak in Vespasian's younger son. He enjoyed inflicting pain on others. So now Domitian took a savage delight in avenging his Uncle Sabinus' death by personally cutting off the Emperor's head and helping to throw his mutilated corpse into the Tiber.

After only a six-months' reign, Vitellius was dead; and on December 21, 69, the Senate declared the sixty-year-old commander of the Army of the East to be the ninth Emperor of Rome. Vespasian sailed for Italy at once, leaving to his son the difficult task of capturing Jerusalem.

Berenice returned to Cicilia; and at the head of four legions, Titus started inland from Caesarea, glad now to be able to empty his mind of everything but how to finish off the Jews.

19

GO DOWN FIGHTING

"When ye shall see Jerusalem compassed with armies, then know that the desolation thereof is nigh. Then let them which are in Judaea flee . . ." Christ, foreseeing the catastrophe that was to take place, thus spoke on the day before His death (Luke 21:20-21). Obeying His command for them to escape to safety, Jesus' disciples hurried that May 10, 70, to leave the doomed city for the town of Pella, south of the Sea of Galilee.

The little band of Christians had no sooner disappeared over the hills of Judaea than Titus Flavius Vespasianus appeared before Jerusalem with a Roman army consisting of four legions—the Fifth, Tenth, Twelfth, and Fifteenth—to lay seige to the town. He pitched his camp on a hill called Scopus, part of the Mount of Olives, and looking down on the walled city, saw the same Jerusalem that Jesus had seen forty-one years before. Herod's Temple was finished. Otherwise, little there had changed.

Built upon three hills, Jerusalem was strongly fortified by a series of walls. The one to the south enclosed the southwestern quarter of the city on Mount Zion. The second ran from Herod's palace on the west to the Temple hill on the east. Beyond this lay the new suburb of Bezetha that had sprung up north of the town. This too was encircled by a third wall begun by Agrippa I (Berenice's father), twelve years after the death of Christ, and not yet finished. This then, on the north, was Jerusalem's weakest point. Elsewhere, on its south, east, and west sides, the city stood at the head of a precipice and those who wished to capture it must do so uphill.

Although he needed to take Jerusalem in order to crush the revolt, Titus hoped that it would not be necessary for him to harm the Jews' Holy City. Their resistance, he thought, would be brief, for within Jerusalem its defenders, the Zealots, as the ardent nationalist party was called, had split into two squabbling factions that were destroying each other —the extremists (led by a Galilean, John of Gischala) hating the moderates (under Simon bar Giora, an Idumean) as much as they did the Romans.

So Titus did not storm Jerusalem immediately. Before attacking Agrippa's wall on the north, he sent Joseph ben Matthias to plead with his countrymen, John and Simon, to surrender. Titus could not have chosen a worse emissary. The Jews hated the governor of Galilee for having defected to the Romans. They considered Joseph to be a traitor and a coward, who should have died at Jotapata rather than be taken prisoner, and his pleas to them to surrender met with derisive laughter.

Titus had no other choice then than to give his second-in-command, General Tiberius Alexander, the order to attack. The Romans' huge battering rams were rolled up to Agrippa's wall and the siege of Jerusalem began.

By late June, the Roman legionaries had penetrated two of

the city's walls and fought their way from house to house to the base of the Temple, the center of rebel resistance, and Titus called off his assault. Rather than continue this senseless killing, he paraded his four legions before the Temple wall, hoping that a display of Roman strength would so intimidate the Jews as to induce them to give up without further bloodshed. It achieved nothing. Confident their God watched over them, and that the Lord would save them from the Romans as he had once done from the Egyptians, the followers of Simon bar Giora and John of Gischala had no thought of yielding.

So Titus tried persuasion again. He sent Joseph ben Matthias to make a second plea to the insurgents.

When Simon and John refused to surrender or accept any terms offered them, the commander of the Army of the East saw that there was only one way left to force the Jews to surrender—encircle Jerusalem with a wall and starve the city out. It would take time to bring the Zealots to their knees, but Titus could only gain by waiting.

Each legion was assigned a section to build and the high, earthen rampart, five miles long, was finished in three days. There was no way now to get supplies into the besieged city and any Jew who tried to sneak outside the walls and forage for food was caught by the Romans and crucified in sight of the town. Finally, within twelve miles of Jerusalem so many trees had been cut down to make crosses, on which hung the rotting corpses of dead Jews, that the city was surrounded by a forest of crosses and wood was scarce.

As the weeks passed, and the food supply dwindled, the famished Jews were driven to eating leather shoes, old hay, decayed meat, and such things as even animals would not

JERUSALEM
A.D. 70

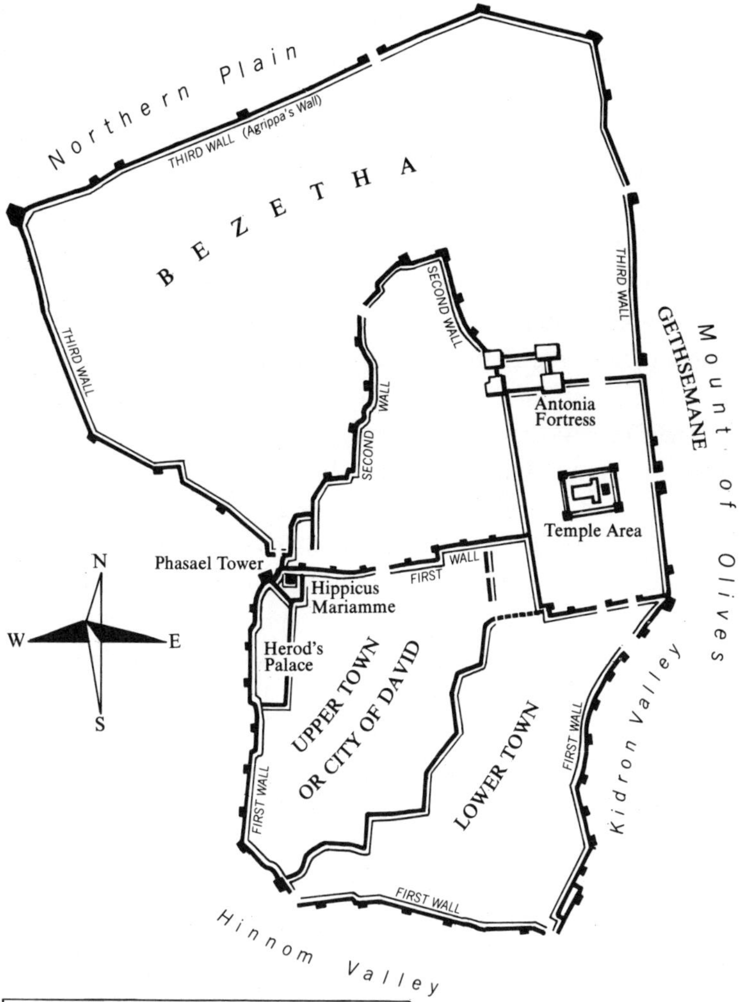

The Jerusalem that Jesus knew was divided by walls into separate defense sections. In A.D. 70 the Roman general Titus attacked the city from the north, near the left angle of the Third Wall.

touch. People searched the sewers for cow dung. Which was best? To stay within the city walls and die of hunger? Or try to escape from Jerusalem and be hung on a cross? Feeble from gnawing hunger pains, the emaciated Jews scratched among the refuse and fought off packs of starving dogs for a few morsels to eat.

Only then did Titus move his legions in.

By July 24 the siege had so weakened the Jews that they put up little resistance, and with a minimum of effort and small loss of life, the Romans captured the city's strongest fortification, the Antonia Tower, which Herod had built on the northwest corner of the Temple area and named after his Roman protector, Mark Antony. Once Pontius Pilate's judgment hall from which Jesus was led out to his crucifixion, the Antonia had served until four years ago as a barracks for the Roman legions by which Jerusalem was kept in subjection.

Now the grim fortress overlooking the Temple was torn down, and Titus gave his troops a demonstration in personal bravery, as in hand-to-hand combat with the retreating Jews, he led the Roman forces across the Temple enclosure. The Zealots were fighting now to save their beloved Temple. The thought of a Gentile defiling the House of God by setting his unclean feet in it could not be borne. So when the legionaries reached the entrance, they came face to face with both factions—the men under Simon bar Giora and John of Gischala united at last in a desperate effort to keep the infidels out.

Battering rams were powerless against the huge stones with which Herod had built his Temple. In order to force an entry, Titus had his legionaries form a solid wall of locked shields above their heads to protect themselves from the Jews' rain of arrows and burning oil; and like a tortoise under its shell, they advanced on the western Temple wall and set fire to its gates. Flames melted the great silver doors. But the Romans were hardly within the Court of the Gentiles from which Jesus had driven the money-changers (Luke 19:45) before Titus ordered the fires his soldiers had started to be put out. Had he not promised Berenice to spare her great-grandfather's magnificent Temple?

Capturing it unharmed from an army of religious fanatics, however, would not be easy. Erected on the site of Solomon's Temple on Mount Moriah, Herod's Temple consisted of a series of courts raised in terrace-fashion on ascending levels, which, as the worshiper climbed to the Sanctuary, became holier and holier. The first area within the walls was known as the Court of the Gentiles, because non-Jews were forbidden, under penalty of death, to go farther. In the middle of this vast square, with colonnades on all sides, lay the inner Temple built on a higher elevation. Steps led up to the Women's Court, to which they were restricted; and to the Court of Israel, accessible only to male Jews, which surrounded the Sanctuary.

Erected on the site of the threshing floor purchased of Araunah the Jebusite by King David, the Sanctuary was divided into two rooms. The outer one, the Holy Place, contained three things: an altar on which incense was burned, a seven-branched candlestick, and a table for shewbread. Only the priests were allowed this far, and only the High Priest could go farther, beyond a purple curtain into the Holy of Holies, and then but once a year, on the Day of Atonement.

Before the Exile, the Holy of Holies contained the Ark of the Covenant that Nebuchadnezzar had carried off to

Babylon. It was lost during the Captivity. The small, dark room where God lived was empty now. Yet so sacred was it that when Pompey captured Jerusalem in 63 B.C., he had not dared to pollute the Holy of Holies by setting foot in it. Nor, out of respect for the Jewish religion, had the Roman general touched anything in the Holy Place—the golden candelabra beside the altar or the shewbread (unleavened bread) baked into twelve oblong, flat cakes, representing the twelve tribes of Israel, and placed fresh each Sabbath on twelve golden trays before the Lord on a table of gold.

"Our Temple is God's home on earth," Berenice had warned her Roman lover. "Violate the House of Our Lord and the Jews will hate you forever."

Titus remembered this. And on the thirtieth of August as the Romans fought their way into the Temple, driving back the Zealots with frightful slaughter, their commander, seeing smoke and flames rising on all sides, ran among his exultant soldiers shouting, "Water! Water! Put out those fires!" No one paid any attention to him. Mad with greed at the sight of so much gold, silver, and precious stones, the legionaries were indulging in a wild orgy of looting. Believing there to be greater riches beyond, they rushed up the terraces of the Temple to reach the Sanctuary and grab the fabulous treasure they had heard was there.

Imagine their disappointment then, on arriving at the Holy of Holies, to find but a small, bare room. Furious at seeing no gold and jewels in it—merely a stone marking the spot where the Ark had stood—a legionary, cursing angrily, threw a lighted torch into the Sanctuary, and his comrades cheered as they saw its wooden walls catch on fire.

No longer able to restrain their men, Titus and his staff

HEROD'S TEMPLE

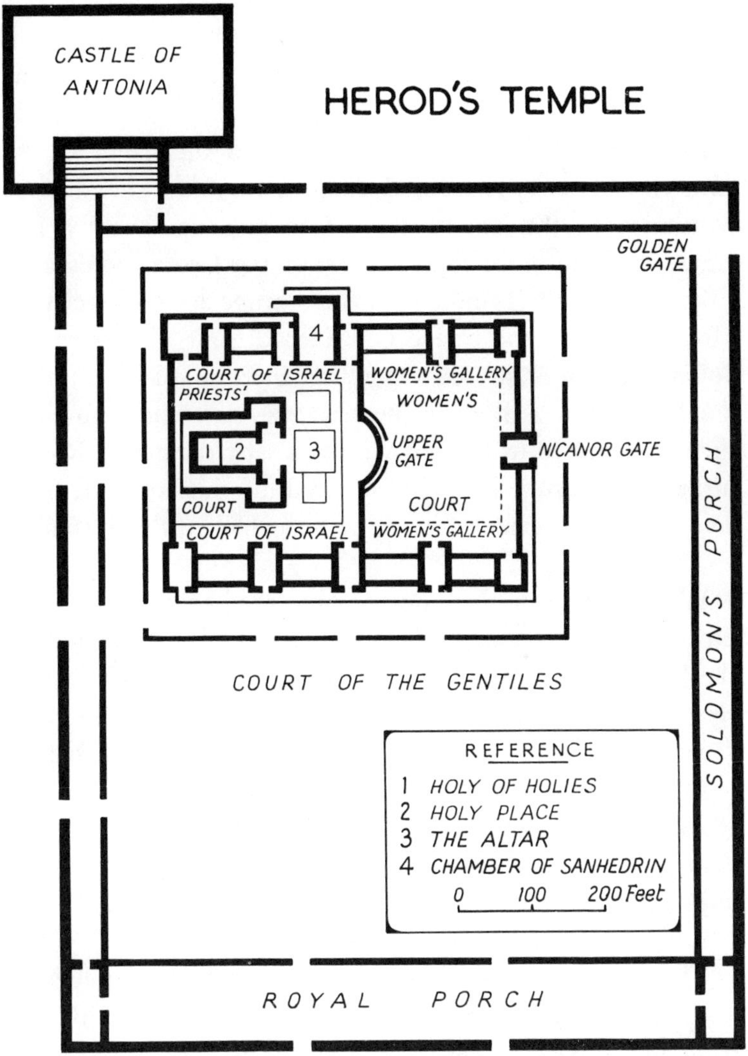
CASTLE OF ANTONIA
GOLDEN GATE
4
COURT OF ISRAEL
WOMEN'S GALLERY
PRIESTS'
WOMEN'S
1
2
3
UPPER GATE
NICANOR GATE
COURT
COURT
COURT OF ISRAEL
WOMEN'S GALLERY
SOLOMON'S PORCH
COURT OF THE GENTILES
REFERENCE
1 HOLY OF HOLIES
2 HOLY PLACE
3 THE ALTAR
4 CHAMBER OF SANHEDRIN
0 100 200 Feet
ROYAL PORCH

officers stood by helplessly watching their soldiers setting fire to other parts of the Temple. Herod's magnificent building, largely built of cedars of Lebanon, became a roaring inferno.

Even then, with most of Jerusalem in the hands of the enemy, and their violated Temple a smoking ruin heaped with corpses, the Zealots refused to give up. With a few survivors, John of Gischala and Simon bar Giora had escaped from the burning Temple and taken refuge across the city on Mount Zion, in the palace that Herod built on the site of Solomon's. Titus offered the rebels there a pardon, if they would surrender. But the beaten Jews attempted to drive such a preposterous bargain with him that the gentle Roman turned indignantly away and ordered his chief of staff, General Tiberius Alexander, to burn Jerusalem to the ground.

This was done.

When the fires died down, and the legionaires rushed through the streets of the burning city in search of plunder, the Romans on breaking into the houses drew back in horror, for they found in them only decaying bodies. So many Jews had killed themselves and their families that a sickening stench hung over the town. It swarmed with flies. Even worse than the smell and the flies was the silence in the empty streets. After five months of siege, Jerusalem was a city of the dead.

Resistance, however, was at an end.

The Zealot leaders, Simon and John, who had hidden in a sewer, were dragged out and kept alive for Titus' Roman triumph; the sacrilegious eagle, emblem of Rome, was placed on the heap of ashes that had been the Temple; and the walls of Jerusalem were torn down. Only one tower of Herod's palace was left standing, to provide a barracks for the Tenth Legion remaining to police the conquered city.

Early in October, with Rome in full control of Judaea, Titus Flavius Vespasianus marched away with his troops, long lines of Jewish prisoners in chains, and miles of oxcarts piled high with booty, bound for the ships at Caesarea that would take the conquerors back to Rome.

The victorious Roman army stopped on the crest of the Mount of Olives, as it had done five months ago. But, this time, Titus looked down upon a once-glorious city that was no more. The Jerusalem that Christ knew was a charred ruin. Even the hillsides, within a radius of twelve miles of the town, were bare. Olive and fig trees a thousand years old, as well as magnificent stands of cedar, had been cut down to make ramps for the Romans' battering rams, for crosses, scaling ladders, and to provide wood for campfires, leaving a forbidding scene of desolation in the midst of which the dead city smoked in its slow burning.

Titus had captured Jerusalem, as his father sent him to do; but because the Jews fought with such fanatical bravery, he had been forced to kill over a million of them and turn miles of beautiful Judaea into a desert. And he wept.

20

JUDAEA RAPED TO MAKE A ROMAN HOLIDAY

On April 8, 71, the Romans were celebrating their victory over the Jews, and the Forum's Via Sacra was lined with excited people, assembled to watch the carts filled with booty and the captives in chains file by. Among the spectators was Mark, the youngest of Christ's disciples, who had fled from Rome shortly after Peter and Paul were led out of the Mamertine Prison to die on the same day, Paul to be beheaded on the road to Ostia, and Peter crucified in Nero's Vatican Circus. Hating all Romans, Mark had escaped to Egypt. Now, seven years later, he was back in Rome to fetch some rolls of parchment concerning Jesus which he had left behind in his hurried flight. And he had come to watch the parade today.

"This triumph may be different from all previous ones," said a woman, standing beside Mark in the crowd. And she told him why.

It seemed that, after the fall of Jerusalem, the Army of the East had wanted to make their thirty-one-year-old commander emperor, instead of his aged father. Titus had indignantly turned down any such proposal. And he wrote Vespasian that, on his return to Rome, they must hold a joint triumph. But would they? No one could tell until they saw the *triumphator's* chariot. Would it contain one man? Or two?

The Emperor had gone out that morning to meet his son, returning from Judaea, on the Appian Way. "Everyone is wondering how Titus greeted him," the woman went on. "Titus' capture of Jerusalem so far outshone Vespasian's campaign in Galilee that people are wondering whether he will allow his father to share today's honors with him. Well, we'll soon know, for here they come!"

From outside the walls where it had assembled, the procession was winding its way into the city. First, down the Via Sacra came the band, playing the marching tunes of the legions. Then, by the grandstands, trundled floats with huge paintings on them, showing scenes from the Judaean war—Romans slaughtering Jews, battering rams knocking down the walls of Jotapata, and the legionaires setting Jerusalem on fire. The crowd shouted and cheered. Only the Queen of Cilicia, seated beside her brother Agrippa, watched the parade pass by, her beautiful face impassive.

That morning Agrippa had asked, "Are you going to Titus' triumph?" And Berenice exclaimed, "No! Nothing would induce me—" It would have been a satisfaction to have stayed away, and let these Romans know how she despised them. Then why had she come? It was to get a glimpse of Titus. She had not seen him in nearly a year, not since before his march on Jerusalem.

So here the Jewish-born Queen of Cilicia was, seated in the Forum, and hating herself for coming. Sick at heart and humiliated, she looked at all the gold, silver, and jewels heaped upon the passing carts that her former lover had brought back from the captured cities of Judaea.

Following the plunder came the prisoners of war. More than a million Jews had died trying to save Jerusalem, but over ninety thousand of them had been brought to Rome to be sold as slaves.

Among them, two wretched prisoners stumbling along in chains brought the bystanders, hysterical with hate, to their feet. Shouting insults at the helpless men, the Romans pelted them with stones and rotten vegetables, for these miserable creatures were the once-proud leaders of the Jewish rebels –Simon bar Giora and John of Gischala. Roped together and flogged every step of the way, Simon and John were being dragged naked through the Forum; and when the parade ended at the foot of Capitoline Hill, they would be led back to the Mamertine and strangled.

Berenice gazed down from the grandstand at the Zealots, her face turned to stone. What if John and Simon should look up? She would die of shame if they saw her seated among their enemies. How could Agrippa watch his people, the Jews, being humiliated with such indifference? And Joseph ben Matthias? Berenice glanced with contempt at her countryman Joseph, seated nearby, who had returned to Rome with Titus.

The parade, to her, seemed endless. Another band passed, then the white bulls destined for the sacrifice, followed by chariots in which rode Tiberius Alexander and other high-ranking officers. After that the army filed by, two cohorts from each legion, behind their eagle standards; then, as a reminder to the provinces of the might of Rome and the folly of revolt, came an impressive display of the catapults, the ballistas, and the battering rams that had crushed rebellious Judaea.

The march-by of the troops lasted for a long time. Then the shouting crowd grew quiet with awe, for down the Via Sacra were coming the sacred objects from the Temple, snatched by the conquering Romans from God's burning house. Carried on the shoulders of laurel-crowned soldiers, who staggered under the weight of so much pure gold, came the table for the unleavened bread set out for the Lord, the huge seven-branched candlestick, the trumpets that had announced the morning and evening sacrifices, and the vessels the Jews had used in their sacred ritual. The bearers lifted these trophies high so that everyone could see them.

The triumph was not over yet. Behind these spoils marched the lictors with their fasces, escorting a chariot drawn by four white horses. They were driven by the commander of the Army of the East, wearing the long red cape of a general falling over his left shoulder—and Titus was not alone. Standing beside him in the vehicle was his father, the Emperor, a fat old man with a laurel wreath on his bald head. Behind them, Titus' younger brother, Domitian, rode on horseback.

When the crowd saw the chariot coming, containing not one man, but two, they went wild. The woman turned excitedly to Mark, "Never has Rome seen a two-fold triumph! Nor one for a father and son!"

"We might have had civil war," people were saying. "Titus, a hero to the army, could have seized the throne from his aging father, but he remained loyal." Within an hour, what had happened out on the Appian Way that morning would be known all over Rome—how Vespasian and his son had met and embraced, and Titus insisted that Rome honor them together.

The Romans admired him for his generous act, and cheering themselves hoarse, pelted their favorite general with flowers. Titus hardly noticed the ovation. Riding through the Forum, his eyes were searching the crowd for a certain face. He saw Joseph, he saw Agrippa, but not Berenice. He had heard that she was in Rome. Where was she?

Titus reacted with anger. He had longed for this day ever since, in Caesarea, his father had hurried back to Rome and left him to capture Jerusalem. Not because of the honors that would come to him, but because on his return to Italy with victorious troops, all the fighting and killing that Titus had always hated would be over. But now his triumph was ruined. Without Berenice present to see the parade, what sense was there to this long ride in pomp through the Forum?

Unable to endure any more, she had fled. And Mark returned that day to the Jewish quarter across the Tiber, wondering whether he was doing the right thing—recording the life and ministry of Jesus of Nazareth in Greek in order to convert the pagan Romans, rather than in his native Aramaic, a language only the Jews would be likely to read. After the cruelty he had seen today, were these Romans worth saving?

But hadn't Jesus preached to all types of men, especially to sinners? So after much soul-searching, Mark decided to continue writing his Gospel (the second of the four in the New Testament, but the first one to be written) in Greek, a language understood throughout the ancient world. For the story of Jesus must be told, he felt, not only to the Jews, but to everyone in the Roman Empire and beyond.

21

THIS TIME FOR KEEPS

AFTER VESPASIAN was acclaimed emperor in Judaea, the nineteen-year-old Domitian, a handsome ne'er-do-well, became prominent for a short time as the only member of the Imperial family on the spot. Domitian's importance vanished when his father returned to Rome, but the brief taste of power turned the young man's head. The day following Titus' triumph, Domitian stormed angrily into his brother's room to demand to know why he was not given a more prominent place in the procession.

"Because you didn't go to Judaea. Did you expect to ride in the *triumphator's* chariot?" Titus laid an affectionate hand on his brother's shoulder. "Domitian, let's not quarrel so much. Today, at the games, you shall be important and give out the prizes."

It took the Romans several days of festivities to celebrate properly the return of their victorious troops from Judaea. So although Titus was angry at Berenice, and thought a great deal about her, he could not get away to ride out to see her and demand to know why she had not attended his triumph.

Besides, Titus had an urgent family matter to attend to. He must go and try to become acquainted with Marcia's daughter. Since her mother's death, Julia had been living with her great-aunt, Paulita, the widow of Rome's Mayor Sabinus. Titus had not seen the girl for six years, not since his exile to Egypt.

So, one afternoon, Julia met him in the atrium of Paulita Sabinus' huge, gloomy old mansion on the Aventine. It shocked Titus when he saw her. Julia was not at all what he had imagined she would be. She was now seven. Not an attractive child. Big dark eyes; long, straight, black hair; a shallow, olive complexion; bad teeth, and too heavy. When they were seated in the peristyle, Titus asked about Julia's great-aunt, bedridden for two years from a stroke. "About the same . . ." she sighed. "Auntie lies there, not knowing anyone."

He tried to make conversation. "What do you need, my dear? Clothes? Money? Pets? I'll give you anything you want."

"You're back in Rome now, Father," Julia cried out. "You'll take me to live with you? I'm so unhappy here—" Her voice broke.

How could he? On becoming emperor, Vespasian had refused to move into Nero's ornate Golden House. With Antonia Caenis and his two sons, the Emperor was occupying a small villa formerly owned by Sallust, the historian. There was no room in it for little Julia. Titus tried to tell her so.

She didn't say anything. She just sat there, tears of disappointment in her dark Sicilian eyes. On the night of July 18, 64, Julia's Name Day, when the Great Fire of Rome had broken out, Titus remembered how the chariot driver Attila had strutted about showing off this girl, a baby then, in his arms. At seven, Julia resembled Marcia's Sicilian lover even more strongly. Titus winced at the thought. And, suddenly, he wanted to get away. "My dear, I'll come to see you often," he promised, getting to his feet.

Julia followed him out to the front door. And Titus forced himself to kiss her. The child clung to him, looking forlorn and lost. "Good-bye, Father . . ." she said. Disengaging himself from Julia's clinging arms, Titus turned abruptly away and hurried out to his litter.

He wished she wouldn't keep calling him "Father."

As if he didn't have problems enough with Julia and Domitian, a week later, when Titus was finally free to ride out the cypress-lined Via Appia and see Berenice, he began to wonder if he might not have a difficult hour ahead. What would she say to him? He had destroyed Jerusalem, her Holy City; he had broken his promise and burned the Temple. Could he justify what his army had done in Judaea?

Several miles from Rome he came to the Herod villa. An African servant opened the door. Titus gave his name and the man ushered him into the atrium and went to inform the Queen of Cilicia of his arrival. Titus waited. He sat there, the commander-in-chief of the mightiest army in the world, the heir to the throne of the Caesars, his heart racing like a bashful schoolboy's.

When Berenice had returned to Cilicia, Titus had expected to get on with the Jewish War and, in time, forget her. After his unhappy marriage with Marcia, he had made up his mind never to become seriously involved with any one woman again. But forget Berenice? Titus wasn't at all sure that he could, for she had brought a sweetness back into his life which, with the loss of Tertulla, Titus thought had gone forever. He realized that now. And he waited.

Meanwhile, seated at a dressing table, the Queen of Cilicia had been anxiously inspecting in a mirror her first gray hairs when her African servant came to announce Legatus T. Flavius Vespasianus. So Titus had come? Did she want to see him? Berenice remembered how in Judaea she had given herself to this Roman with her whole heart, utterly, as only a woman approaching forty does, who, at that critical age, fears that she is having her last affair.

Had she played her cards wrong? If she had acted harder to get, Berenice wondered, could she have saved the Temple? The Roman had broken his word. He had violated the Temple and burned it to ashes. Titus was a second Nebuchadnezzar. Worse, if possible, than the Babylonian king who destroyed Solomon's Temple and carried off the Jews into captivity.

"I shall see Legatus Vespasianus, but only briefly," the Queen had informed the African. "In ten minutes, come and show him out."

Now, as she walked through the peristyle, Berenice saw her Roman lover seated ahead of her in the atrium, his hands (so it seemed to her) stained with Jewish blood. She remembered how, because of him, the courts of the Temple had been engulfed in smoke and flames. And Berenice prayed to the God of Abraham to tell her what to do. The wise thing, of course, was to go back to her room. Instead, she came into the atrium and sat down.

They looked at each other. There was so much to say that Titus hardly knew where to begin. "When we parted in Judaea, I thought you were going back to Tarsus," he said.

"I went, but I couldn't remain there," Berenice replied. "Polemo has divorced me and taken another wife. So I came to Rome, with Agrippa."

"Then why weren't you at my triumph?"

"I was. I stood seeing all of that disgusting spectacle that I could! I'm Jewish, Titus. Why didn't you have me led through the Forum in chains like the other prisoners? It would have been easier to endure than having to sit there and watch . . ."

Since they had last met, the destruction of Jerusalem had come between them, but Titus still felt a great longing for this slender, golden-brown Jewess. So why not say, at once, what must be said?

"Berenice, forgive me! I regret as much as you do that, during the battle for Jerusalem, the temple of this god of yours was burned down. My dear, it was impossible to save it. We had to flush out the Zealots, who had taken refuge there. But I did all that I could, I assure you, to save your great-grandfather's magnificent building. Unfortunately, something went wrong. Before we knew it, the whole place was on fire." Refusing to take all the blame for the Temple's destruction, Titus told her how he had rushed through the smoke, shouting at his legionaries to put out their kindled fires and that he had the soldier executed who flung the first lighted torch into the Sanctuary. "Berenice, I did all I could to save your Temple. Believe me!"

She listened, her lovely, dark eyes stern and disbelieving. "So you're a general who cannot control his men?" she asked, scornfully.

Titus flushed. "Berenice, please understand! Your Temple was no longer holy ground. The Jews had turned the house of their god into a fort. And when has Rome left a rebel fortress standing? A Roman soldier does what he's told to do, my dear, even when he doesn't like his orders."

"But, Titus, you promised me to make the capture of

Jerusalem a merciful one. Was it necessary to build a besieging wall around the city? Then to wait, week after week, while the poor Jews within your wall slowly starved to death? Do you call that being merciful?"

"You heard, too, I suppose, that when we burned Jerusalem, I threw babies into the flames?" he cried angrily. "Berenice, be reasonable! No people in history ever put up such a furious resistance as the Jews. Twice I sent Joseph ben Matthias to plead with Simon and John to surrender. If they had, the Zealots would have spared themselves months of suffering."

It was Berenice's turn to lose her temper. "Because my brave people preferred death to slavery, you massacred them! You stood by, Titus, and let your soldiers break into the Sanctuary and steal objects so sacred to the Jews that even Pompey dared not touch them. It's a wonder the Lord didn't strike you dead!"

"Well, he didn't. No fire fell upon me from heaven. Berenice, let me ask you something . . . If there is any truth in the existence of this god of yours, whom you say is all-powerful, why wasn't he able to protect his Temple?"

She looked past him and said coldly, "The Lord sometimes takes a long time to strike."

Titus saw that, by mocking her religion, he had cut this woman he loved to the heart. If only Berenice would shout at him, denounce him. She sat there, no longer saying a word, and her silence was a deeper reproach. Finally, she said quietly, "I warned you, Titus, that if you violated our Temple, the Jews would hate you forever."

"And will you?"

Humbly, he waited for her reply. And Berenice did not

know whether she wanted to say yes or no. Was she to be a traitor to the Jews like Joseph ben Matthias? Like her sister Drusilla, who left a Jew to live with a Roman? Or her brother Agrippa and all the kings of Judaea who betrayed their country to side with Rome? This time, if she went back to Titus, she would no longer have the excuse that it was to save the Temple. God's House on Earth lay in ruins. And it was this man who had destroyed it. Yet, she loved him.

Looking into Titus' broad peasant face, Berenice replied softly, "Hate you? I've tried to, my dear, but I can't."

The ten minutes were up. The African came to show the Roman out, but on glancing into the atrium, he softly closed the door and went away.

22

A PEASANT ON THE THRONE

VESPASIAN DID NOT CARE about honors for himself. He had but one ambition—to found a Flavian dynasty and have his sons succeed him. A stocky man with a round, bald head on a thick neck, after three years on the throne, he remained what he had always been at heart, an Etruscan peasant. But luckily, at this time, the former mule breeder was just what the Empire needed.

He had inherited from Nero a bankrupt nation and, being an honest, thrifty man, Vespasian set about enforcing a rigid economy on the nation and raised taxes. Especially annoying to the Romans was a tax put on the produce of the city's public lavatories (the dry cleaners of Rome having found that ammonia in urine made it a good cleaner). When Titus protested that a tax on urinals was undignified, his father waved a coin under his nose and asked, "Does it smell?" Meaning money is money, no matter from where it comes.

Ill one day, and thinking he was dying, the Emperor asked how much his funeral would cost. On being told ten million *sesterces,* the frugal old man exclaimed, "Give me a hundred thousand, and throw my body into the Tiber!"

Vespasian was not the least bit ashamed of having come from a middle-class family of little distinction—the first Roman emperor not to be of aristocratic lineage—and disliking Rome, he lived most of the time at his farm in the Sabine hill town of Falacrina where Antonia Caenis, his devoted, hard-working housekeeper, kept everything as it was in his boyhood.

The old miser allowed himself only one luxury; Vespasian liked to build, and ignoring the cost, set about beautifying Rome. He restored the Temple of Jupiter, damaged during the Vitellius-Flavian struggle, and erected in the Forum a white marble building to exhibit the trophies that Titus had brought back from Jerusalem. It was named the Temple of Peace, because, for the first time in the memory of living Romans, the Empire was not at war. This was largely due to Titus' conquest of Judaea. And the popular heir to the throne shoveled away the first pile of dirt from a site where the Via Sacra enters the Forum, and laid the cornerstone for an arch to commemorate his victory over the Jews.

As a result of the Great Fire during Nero's reign, a large part of Rome still lay in ruins. Titus helped his father rebuild it. A lake in the park of Nero's Golden House was drained, and construction began there on a huge arena. Destined to become the most famous monument of ancient Rome, the Flavian Amphitheater later acquired another name—the Colosseum. This was not due to its size, but to an immense statue or *colossus* of Nero which was moved from before his palace to decorate the new Flavian Circus.

Aiding him in these projects, Titus became almost co-emperor with his father. But Vespasian's relations with his second son were less amicable. Effeminacy shocked the rough old soldier, and disgusted by Domitian's use of an expensive, strongly-scented hair oil, Vespasian snapped at the young dandy who always reeked of perfume, "I'd rather you smelt of garlic."

Domitian was not the sort of person the Emperor wanted near him. Refusing to give the young man even a small government job, his father sternly told him to get back to his studies. Domitian submitted, but with bitterness, for he loved power.

Titus, having returned from Jerusalem a hero, only added to Domitian's jealousy and resentment. Feeling himself outclassed, he retaliated, like many a second son, by hating his outstanding older brother. Was it his fault, Domitian thought, that he had been reared in poverty on a Sabine farm, while Titus was educated by Seneca at the court of Claudius? A mixture of malice, envy, and frustration, he set out to build himself up by pulling his brother down. Nobody is perfect; even Titus had a flaw. Domitian knew that it was enough to ruin him, if it became known, for since the Jewish War there was bitter anti-Semitic feeling in Rome.

Seeing a chance to do his brother irreparable harm, Domitian rode to Falacrina one day to inform the Emperor that Titus had secretly resumed with his Jewish mistress.

Vespasian listened to what his younger son had to say, then, greatly upset, sent for Titus. He came to the farm a few days later, and they were no sooner seated at the supper table before Antonia asked, "Is it true what Domitianus tells us? That you are still seeing the Herods?"

His mug of beer stopped halfway to Titus' mouth. "Yes. Why not?"

"Because the Herod family is bitterly hated by both Romans and Jews–that's why!" Vespasian glared at his eldest son over the rim of Grandmother Tertulla's old silver mug from which he always drank. "Titus, your affair with the Queen of Cicilia didn't help us in Judaea," he sternly informed him. "However, I put up with it, although what you could see in a middle-aged woman, eleven years your senior, was quite beyond me. But must you continue to see her in Rome?"

Titus flushed. "Yes," he replied, curtly.

The Emperor's temples throbbed with rage, but he controlled himself enough to say, "Well, I wouldn't, if I were you." And he went on to explain why. "Titus, this woman is a Jewess. We've just conquered her people. And the Romans still feel very bitterly toward the rebels. Remember, it was not only the Jews who died in the late war, but thousands of our legionaries. There is hardly a family in Rome who has not lost a father or a son."

"What has that to do with my private life? Surely, a man has the right to select his own friends–"

Titus tried to say more, but his father wouldn't let him. "By Hercules, not the heir to the throne!" the old man interrupted with an angry shout. Then after taking a long swallow of beer, he continued more calmly, "The Flavians, Titus, are a young dynasty. I'm the first emperor, you will be the second, and then Domitianus. At least, that is my dream. But it can only come true if we continue to please the Romans. Thrust this arrogant Jewess on them and who knows? I sit upon an extremely shaky throne, my son. The aristocracy scorns us. They consider the Flavian family to be upstarts. And we are."

Titus had listened in silence. Much of what his father said

was true. He remembered how the Senators had marched in his triumph—the majority of them reluctantly, filled with contempt for the plebian Emperor and his son whom they were forced to honor.

"Give this woman up, Titus," Vespasian pleaded. "Nero, a descendant of the great Germanicus, could live with a notorious harlot like Poppaea and the Romans excused it. But you can't. Your love for this Jewess will be the ruin of us. Surely, you've heard what people are saying about her morals, that Berenice's affection for her brother was . . . well, far from sisterly?"

Titus' voice cut back like a whip. "How filthy-minded the Romans are! Do you believe such lies? Here's the truth. Now listen! Agrippa is an epileptic. He has been since childhood. After their mother Cypros died, it was up to Berenice, being the elder sister, to be in Judaea with her afflicted brother as much as she could and look after him. He's a sweet man. Naturally, she's very fond of him. That's all there is to it."

Father and son regarded each other coldly, with hard eyes, over the rims of their beer mugs. Two stubborn Sabine peasants, Antonia thought, watching the clash of wills across the table. How alike they looked! Titus was only a more polished edition of Vespasian. Which of them would give in first?

"Don't upset your father, dear," she pleaded. "Titus, you've always been a dutiful son. Not like Domitianus. Forget this woman, and find yourself a lovely girl, nearer your age."

Vespasian nodded. "Antonia is right. Rome is full of suitable young girls." And he went on, sternly, "Titus, you're the heir to the throne and thirty-three now. It's time you married, but you never will, not as long as this Jewess remains in Rome. So Berenice must go away. Back to Judaea, or wherever she likes, but she is to leave Italy immediately. You can tell her that from me."

"I'll do nothing of the sort," Titus replied, through clenched teeth. "Berenice remains in Rome. And I intend to marry her."

Stunned, Vespasian and Antonia sat, gazing at him with shocked and disbelieving eyes. His father finally recovered himself enough to say, sharply, "Marry her? That's impossible! It is forbidden by law for a Roman to marry a foreigner."

"You're the Emperor, aren't you?" Titus reminded Vespasian, curtly. "You can repeal that law."

"Not even Julius Caesar dared to do that, in order to marry Cleopatra."

Titus noticed how, all at once, his father looked very old and sick. "I can wait," he announced with icy calm. "When I become emperor, I shall repeal that law and make Berenice my wife. Who will there be then to stop me?"

"The Roman people," Vespasian said.

23

WOMAN WITHOUT A COUNTRY

After two years of being a model prisoner, the Jewish-born Joseph ben Matthias was set free by the Romans, and on returning to Italy with Titus, Latinized his name to Flavius Josephus. Like a freed slave, he adopted the family *nomen* of his benefactor, for the Emperor had made Josephus a Roman citizen and given him a tract of land in Judaea. That is, if the former governor of Galilee, knowing how the Jews despised him, had courage enough to go back and claim it.

In return, Vespasian wanted Flavius Josephus to write a history of the late war. He knew he could trust him to depict the Romans favorably. No one could be more loyal to a former enemy. So, seated one day at his desk, Josephus unrolled a sheet of papyrus, dipped a sharpened reed into black ink made from soot, and began his book.

"It is probable," he wrote, "that other writers will attempt to describe the war of the Jews against the Romans, writers who were not eyewitnesses of the events, and who will have to rely on foolish or contradictory rumors. I, Joseph the son of Matthias, an eyewitness of these happenings, have therefore resolved to write the history of this war as it actually happened—"

Several months later, long rolls of parchment were piled up on Josephus' desk. He read over what he had written, whistling softly, as he did when pleased with himself. Then the first part of *The Jewish War* was rolled up again, and he sent his history to Agrippa and Berenice to read.

The proud author waited a week. No reply came from the Herods. So, protected by the armed escort without which he no longer dared to travel, Flavius Josephus rode out one day to King Agrippa's heavily guarded villa on the Appian Way. Josephus knew the reasons for these precautions.

The fall of Jerusalem had crushed the Jews, but only temporarily. Since the Lord seemed to have deserted their cause for a while, the Zealots had merely gone underground and, escaping from prison camps and slave ships, infiltrated Rome. The town was full of would-be assassins. Among them was a sect of terrorists known as Dagger Men from their practice of going about with knives concealed up their sleeves, who had vowed to kill all Jewish collaborators with Rome—especially Berenice, Agrippa, and Josephus, three people whom the Jews blamed for their defeat.

That day, as the author of *The Jewish War* waited, Agrippa came into the room carrying his rolls of parchment. Placing them on a table, he greeted Josephus warmly. "Congratulations! I enjoyed your book," he said.

The Galilean listened to Agrippa's praise with indifference. A frail-looking man, tall, and stoop-shouldered, the King of Judaea was a collector of rare manuscripts. Studious, but dull. What did Josephus care what Agrippa thought? It was Berenice's approval he wanted. When she finally appeared, he jumped up eagerly and took a step toward her. Berenice drew back, as from a leper, and said scornfully, "Remain where you are, Flavius Josephus. Don't you dare come a step nearer!"

His smile faded. "I have offended you? You've read my book?"

"Yes, all I could endure of it."

"You didn't like it?"

"Did you expect me to? After *The Jewish War* comes out, there won't be a Jew in the world who won't loath the name of Flavius Josephus—" Berenice sat down, keeping her distance. Josephus noticed that she no longer called him Joseph ben Matthias, but by the Roman name he had adopted.

He tried to defend himself. "I only told the truth," he said.

"The truth!" Berenice's eyes flashed. "How dare you accuse the Jews of rebelling! The Romans oppressed them for a hundred years. Can you blame the Jews for at last striking back? Your book is written entirely to please the Romans. Flavius Josephus, you make me sick with shame!"

Agrippa, a shy man who hated scenes, hurriedly left the room, leaving Josephus to listen humbly while Berenice went on berating him. He had longed for her praise. Sick with disappointment, the author of *The Jewish War* stood Berenice's angry harangue as long as he could, then finally had the courage to interrupt it. He wasn't a traitor, Josephus told her, merely a realist. Aware that the Jews were hopelessly outnumbered, he had wisely chosen the winning side. As for going over to the enemy, hadn't she and Agrippa also fled to the Roman camp for protection?

"It is said in Rome that you're Titus' mistress. If you hate the Romans so, how do you excuse that?"

"I don't excuse it." Tears welled into Berenice's beautiful, dark eyes. "Don't you think that I don't hate myself for loving Titus, every hour of the day."

"Then why not break with him and go back to Judaea?"

She sprang to her feet. "You know very well why, Flavius Josephus, for the same reason that you don't . . . the Zealots would kill us!" For a moment they stood facing each other, two exiled Jews whom the Dagger Men had vowed to exterminate as traitors, and Josephus saw the fear on Berenice's face at the thought.

Then the look of scorn returned. Picking up the rolls of parchment, Agrippa's sister practically threw them at him. "Go, and take your filthy book," she cried in a furious voice. "And never ask me to read any of your writings again."

After Josephus had gone, Berenice went to wash her hands, but she still felt unclean, for she had handled what this man had touched.

By the time he was thirty, Flavius Josephus already had had three wives—the first, in his youth in Jerusalem; the second, he deserted in Caesarea to go to Galilee and fight the Romans; and the third, he abandoned in Alexandria to return to Rome with Titus. Recently, Josephus had fallen in love with a luscious Jewess from Crete. The fact that he already had a wife and son in Egypt was a small matter to him. Josephus could forget a woman as easily as he could change sides.

Agrippa had also adjusted well to exile. His life in Judaea as King of the Jews had not been a pleasant one, and he was glad to be back in Rome. Only Agrippa's sister found it hard to start a new life.

How long could this situation with Titus go on, Berenice

wondered, sick at heart. She knew she was sinning against God by loving an uncircumcised Roman, yet she wanted to go on sinning. She and Titus had reached the point of no return. There was no going back. They talked of marriage, but both of them knew that it was mostly talk. Could it be otherwise? The impasse was still there—the law forbidding a Roman to marry a foreigner, which Vespasian, disliking Berenice, refused to repeal.

"It won't be long," Titus assured her. "My darling, as soon as I become emperor, we will be married. You'll be the empress then and Rome will have to accept you. Didn't Nero finally force the Romans to tolerate Poppaea?"

Meanwhile, they did not dare to be seen often together in public, for Domitian was letting people know that the heir to the throne was in love with a Jewess and hoped to marry her, and the Romans were reacting with indignation. When the Herod litter passed through the streets, it was frequently stoned, and Berenice's bodyguard had to push back the angry crowds milling about her. Their anti-Semitism, since the fall of Jerusalem, was largely due to the presence in Rome of thousands of Jewish prisoners of war, and this unpaid labor, engaged in building Titus' Victory Arch and the Flavian Amphitheater, was making work scarce for the average Roman.

Nero's Lake, only a few hundred yards from the Forum, had been drained by Roman engineers, and on the still-marshy ground there was rising a huge oval structure that, when finished, would be three stories high. The immense arena was being constructed of travertine blocks, a limestone quarried in Tivoli, and it was backbreaking work. The Jewish prisoners must unload the heavy stones from the ox-carts that brought them from Tivoli, and hoist them into place, high on walls of the amphitheater erected by now up to the first floor. The long lines of ragged Jews, chained together, were kept hard at work with whips. Even the old and sick did not dare to relax and sit down for a minute.

Many of the Roman overseers were cruel. If a prisoner fell over faint from exhaustion, the officer in charge would bend over him, a lighted torch in his hand, and touch the Jew's flesh to find out. Was the man dead? Or only shamming? Simulating death, to get a moment's rest? If the wretch cried out in pain, the foreman gave the prone figure a vicious kick with his hobnailed boot. "Get up, you!"

Thus the Colosseum was being built, and hearing daily of these atrocities, a hatred of the Romans and a great longing for her own people came over Berenice at times. "It's horrible! We must atone to the Jews for what's being done to them," she told Agrippa. "Let's build them a synagogue, here in Rome. One as fine as the Temple they lost in Jerusalem."

So on Passover, a day when Berenice felt very close to her own race, she had herself carried in a litter over to a district on the right bank of the Tiber, near the Porta Porteo, where the Jews lived. None of them had forgotten Nero. Afraid that similar persecutions would begin again, most of the Jews of Rome had hidden their grief over the fall of Jerusalem, but in all their hearts the bitterness was there. As soon as Berenice crossed the Tiber, she felt herself in enemy territory; the Herod litter was recognized, and Berenice saw loathing in the faces she passed.

Near where the Apostle Peter had once lived, her litter bearers stopped before the home of Aron, the High Priest. He received the sister of the king who had deserted his people in their time of need, his eyes hostile.

Berenice gazed at the old man's stony face, and all

the courage oozed out of her. "Forgive us," she pleaded. "Agrippa and I regret the loss of the Temple as much as you do . . . we will build you another . . . a synagogue, here in Rome, to make up for it . . . We'll do anything, only forgive us!"

"We do not want your synagogue."

His words cut through Berenice like a knife. She was stunned. The High Priest had turned away. Summoning a young man from the next room, he ordered him to show the lady to the door. Head high, but biting her lips to keep from crying, Berenice walked out to where her litter was waiting.

As she was carried away, back in his house, Aron the High Priest, was saying, "Well, now you've seen her!"

The young man was trembling with anger and frustration. He had suffered greatly during the siege of Jerusalem; his sister had been raped by the Romans; his parents had died of starvation; and he, himself, had been captured and brutally tortured. After the city fell, managing to escape, he had joined the Dagger Men. No one was more dedicated to the Jewish cause.

The youth tried the edge of his knife with his thumb. It was very sharp. Angrily, he demanded of Aron, "Why didn't you call me sooner? Why did you let her get away?"

"It is Passover," the High Priest reminded him. "It is not right to kill on a holy day. Not even a traitor. But there will be other days."

24

THUMBS DOWN ON BERENICE

It would be hard to have to tell Berenice that she must leave Rome. The separation would be painful for him, too, but after what had happened, Titus was convinced that she must go. Berenice had found her little lap dog poisoned. "It's to show you that someone can get into your bedroom," he explained, and doubled her guards. Since then, Berenice wore a steel cuirass. She slept with a knife under her pillow.

Agrippa and Josephus had also had several narrow escapes. One of the Dagger Men, posing as a barber, nearly succeeded in cutting Agrippa's throat. In the Forum one day, Josephus' litter had been overturned. There was the flash of knives, and the Jewish turncoat barely escaped with his life. The men's safety didn't concern Titus so much. They could look after themselves. But nothing must happen to Berenice.

"If an assassin is out to kill you, all the bodyguards in the world cannot stop him," Titus told her. "To be safe, you must get out of Rome."

"You mean, leave you?"

She had refused to go.

But now, badly frightened since the death of her little

dog, Berenice was willing to listen to him. She believed the Dagger Men intended to poison her too and, like Seneca, would eat nothing but oranges and nuts that could be peeled, for food that hands had touched might be contaminated. Nor would she drink any wine. Every day, parched with thirst, Berenice had herself carried to the Tiber. When she got there she jumped out of her litter and, falling upon her knees, drank from the river as though she could never get enough. The water from the Tiber might be polluted, but, at least, it was free of poison.

Berenice grew pale, thin, and too nervous to endure much more. So, taking her in his arms one night, Titus kissed and caressed her, and when she was soft and yielding with love, he told her why she must go away.

In Rome it was impossible to protect her. The city was filled with strangers. Any one of them could push past her bodyguard and plunge a dagger into her breast. In a smaller town, where every criminal was known, he could have her better protected. It would not be a separation, really. If she went to some place, say a hundred miles or so from Rome, he could visit her often. No, he wasn't getting tired of her. Berenice mustn't say such a ridiculous thing. It was because he loved her so much, that for her own peace of mind, as well as his, she must leave Rome.

"For how long?" Berenice demanded.

Vespasian's attacks of gout had greatly aged Titus' father. He spent all of his time with Antonia at the farm and rarely came to Rome anymore. "Perhaps a year. Maybe two," Titus replied. As soon as he became emperor, he promised to marry her. Everything would be different then. It would be longer since the Judaean revolt, and the Romans would feel less bitter toward the Jews.

Berenice wiped away her tears. She believed him. Titus wasn't getting tired of her. He was only suggesting this separation because he loved her so much. "I could go to Pompeii and stay with Drusilla," she said.

Pompeii? Why not? Berenice's younger sister, Drusilla, who had left Felix Antonius, the former Roman governor of Judaea, was living there with her boy, Antonius Agrippa. It was just the spot, only a three-days' journey by carriage from Rome, and Titus would feel safer about Berenice in Pompeii, for little crime was committed in that quiet market town on the Bay of Neapolis. In fact, visitors thought Pompeii to be a dull place. Nothing, they complained, ever happened there.

"You'll come and see me?" Berenice asked.

"Every month."

Titus pleaded. He stroked and kissed her. And Berenice finally agreed to go. But that night, lying in bed, unable to sleep, she thought about something she usually tried hard to forget—the eleven years difference between their ages. Titus, a robust thirty-four, had as much life before him as there was behind. But how many years of loving and being loved lay ahead for her, a woman nearing fifty? Ten more years or fifteen? Berenice didn't want to leave him and waste a moment of this. Not a single second.

They finally did part, however, for what they thought would be a year or two. It was actually six. Vespasian, who came from tough Etruscan peasant stock, took a long time to die.

When Titus destoyed Jerusalem, nine hundred Jews had managed to escape into the Judaean wilderness to carry on the struggle against the Romans. Now, for an incredible three years, they had been living in the ruins of a fortress that

Herod the Great built at Masada on a thousand-foot mountain overlooking the Dead Sea, near the site of the ancient cities of Sodom and Gomorrah.

In the spring of 73 when Berenice joined her sister Drusilla in Pompeii, the Tenth Legion that Titus had left to police Jerusalem set out to wipe out this last stubborn nest of rebels. Its sheer rock face made Masada almost inaccessible. But the Romans managed to reach the summit. However, when they broke into Herod's crumbling old fortress ready for a fight, instead of the struggle the Romans expected, they found only smoking ruins and silence. The entire Jewish garrison, after a heroic last stand, had committed suicide. Rome had triumphed again.

With the fall of Masada, the Jewish revolt came to an end. One by one, the Dagger Men were rounded up and executed, and the Zealot guerillas, who thought of themselves as patriots, but whom the Romans considered terrorists, became but revered names in Jewish history.

Freed by the collapse of Jewish resistance from fear of any further attacks on her life, but unable to return to Rome so long as Vespasian lived, Berenice, bored in the quiet commercial city of Pompeii, bought a villa at Herculaneum, a more cultured town a few miles away. Agrippa went to live with her. And Josephus moved to Cyprus, to continue his writing, away from the distractions of Rome.

Titus continued to be his patron. Always interested in the arts, the heir to the throne was encouraging Pliny (Gaius Plinius Secundus), who had been one of his staff officers in Syria, to begin an encyclopedia of all sorts of scientific things. And he was befriending a struggling, young writer named Tacitus.

Frequently, Titus visited his father at the farm, and sitting out under the trees, the two former soldiers talked about Britain, where both of them had fought. The Roman invasion that stalled under Nero had been renewed by Vespasian, and by now the south of Britain was thoroughly Romanized. The Ordovices of Wales, however, were still causing trouble. And Vespasian sent that able Gaul, Cn. Julius Agricola, with whom Titus had served under Suetonius in Britain, to complete the conquest of the rest of the island.

As the spring of 79 approached, Agricola and his legion commanders had subdued Wales and were making plans for a march north into Caledonia (Scotland). But the old Emperor was never to hear of their arrival at the Tay the following year. For several months he had been feeling ill, but Vespasian continued a bad habit of drinking quantities of cold water when hot and thirsty, which his doctors thought unwise, for it caused him chronic intestinal trouble. They could do nothing, though, with the stubborn, seventy-year-old Etruscan.

On June 24, weak from dysentery, Vespasian was lying exhausted and his sons, Titus and Domitian, were sent for. They hurried to the family homestead at Falacrina, to be at the bedside of their ailing father. His housekeeper for twenty years—the frugal, hard-working Antonia Caenis, who had helped the old miser scrimp and save and amass a fortune—had died four years ago. He was very much alone.

Vespasian was by no means a prude. He had always loved to crack jokes and tell stories, some of them very indecent, and the genial old man could be witty even on his deathbed. He knew he was dying, and alluding to the Roman custom of deifying their dead emperors, he exclaimed with a flash of his old spirit, "Make way for me on Olympus, Jupiter! I feel myself becoming a god!"

He did not want to die. At least, not in bed. So at the last moment, Vespasian exerted all of his remaining strength in an effort to get to his feet. He stood beside his bed for a time, legs apart, fists on his hips, a strong man with a tired face, but a determined jaw. Then with the words, "An emperor ought to die standing," Vespasian, after a reign of ten years, fell forward dead into the arms of his eldest son.

Titus laid him gently back on the bed, and Domitian, looking across their father's body at his brother, felt wildly elated. Only one life now stood between him and the throne.

25

THE LONG GOOD-BY

NEVER BEFORE in Roman history had a son succeeded his father on the throne. Vespasian, by closely associating his firstborn with him in the government, had realized his ambition to establish a Flavian dynasty. Without opposition, Titus Flavius Vespasianus became the tenth emperor of Rome and the best-liked ruler of the Empire since Augustus. This was largely due to his benevolent nature. The man who had been forced to destroy Jerusalem in a bloody war was actually a gentle person, who hated all fighting and killing. Titus considered a day wasted when he had not done someone a kindness, and shed tears if he had to sign a death warrant. "I wish I could not write," he would say.

At the age of forty, with a strong face and the body of a sturdy Sabine peasant, Rome's new Caesar looked like the healthy, good man he was. Titus had a remarkable memory, wrote verses and speeches in both Latin and Greek, took down notes in shorthand, and still composed songs he sang to his harp.

The provinces had taken the hint from Titus' crushing of the Jewish revolt, and during his reign, the Empire remained at peace except for the campaign in Britain where Agricola was continuing his advance into Caledonia (Scotland). The legions knew little about this sparsely inhabited land into which they were marching, and the Emperor eagerly followed Agricola's route into the unknown. Was there water north of Caledonia, he wondered. If so, did that make Britain an island? And was it true that another large island lay to the west of Britain, out in the Atlantic?

There was a keen interest in geography at this time, due to the *Natural History* that Pliny had written and dedicated to his friend, Titus. Other authors were busy. Tacitus was writing a book about his father-in-law, Agricola, who was extending Roman rule in Britain, and Josephus was working in Cyprus on his autobiography.

The reign of Titus, who came by his love of learning from his old tutor Seneca, came to be known as the Silver Age in Roman literature. Not quite in a class with Augustus' Golden Age, when Virgil, Horace, and Ovid were living, but a time when Martial and Juvenal enjoyed poking fun at the vices of the day.

Nero's Golden House was being torn down to make way for a public bath, and Titus was continuing to build the Flavian Amphitheater that his father had started. He was working hard at being emperor and doing a good job, the Romans thought. The only fault they could find in him was that he had a Jewish mistress and planned to marry her. For Titus' first act, on becoming emperor, had been to send for Berenice. He wrote her:

"Come to me. Come. Come quickly."

The Romans had not resented Vespasian's long association with Antonia Caenis. That humble freedwoman kept in the background, and Vespasian had never considered marrying

THE ROMAN EMPIRE
AT THE TIME OF TITUS
(A.D. 39-81)

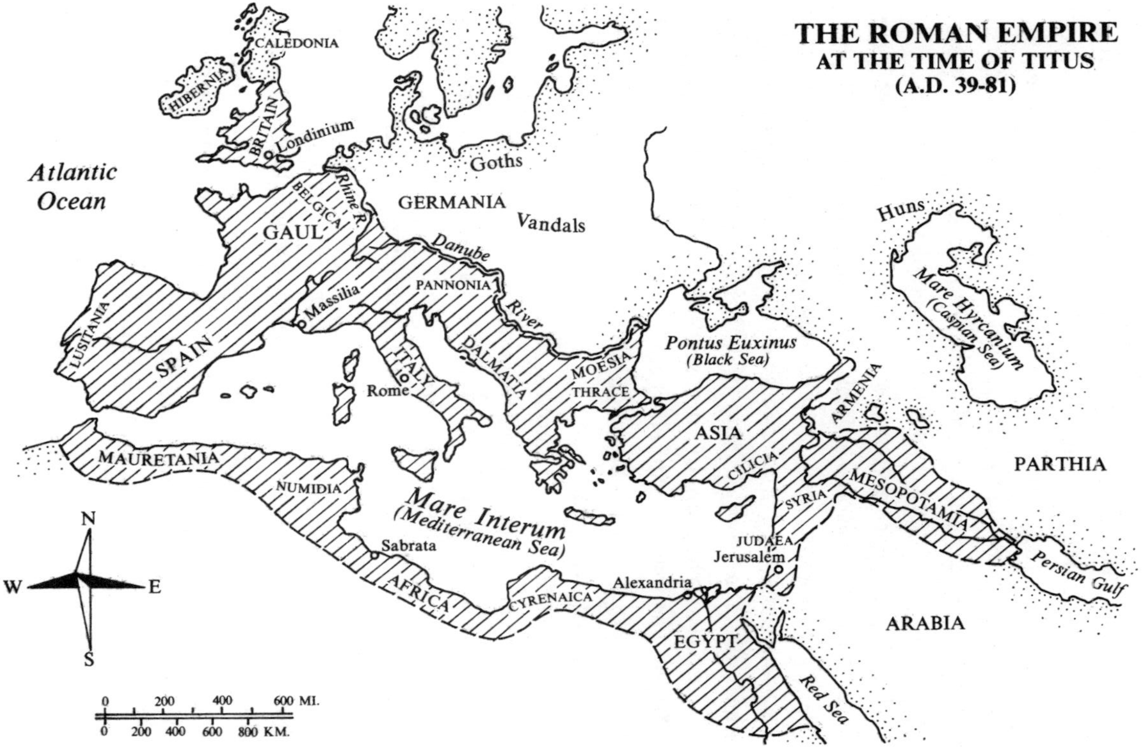

her. Besides, Antonia was a Roman citizen. Agrippina, a murderess, could become empress, since she had Claudian blood; but Berenice, although formerly a queen, was a foreigner and a Jew. That was too much for the Romans. In their eyes, she was another Cleopatra, and hadn't public opinion kept even Julius Caesar from marrying the Queen of Egypt?

The harassment of "that foreign tart" started before Berenice was back in Rome a week. At first, it was but whispered gossip, then anonymous articles began to appear in the *Acta Diurna*, reminding its readers of all the old scandals—Berenice's divorce from Polemo of Cilicia; the mysterious death of her two children by her second husband, the King of Chalcis (had she murdered them?); and the rumor that, before meeting Titus, Berenice was living incestuously with her brother, Agrippa.

The attacks on her morals were everywhere, mostly as graffiti, insults scrawled on the sides of shops and houses. No one—least of all Berenice and Titus—had to be told that these slanderous wall-writings were inspired by Domitian, for no one could match the Emperor's brother in the art of vituperation.

Every morning Berenice sent her servants to whitewash the walls of Rome and hide the lies about her. Unfortunately, some of the filth escaped them. Titus, riding to inspect his Victory Arch one day, reined in his horse to read in horror an inscription that demanded in enormous letters: JEWISH WHORE GO HOME! It was signed: THE SENATE AND PEOPLE OF ROME.

In a rage, the Emperor directed the removal of the insulting graffito. Then he stormed back to the Palatine, and from his palace, summoned the Senate to appear before him and explain. They came, solemnly filing into the room to sit down.

Brogi-Art Reference Bureau

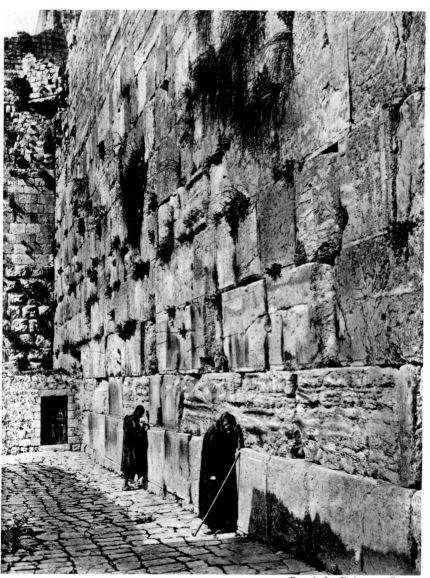

THE WAILING WALL, JERUSALEM

Collection Viollet

TRIUMPH OF TITUS AND VESPASIAN
by Giulio Romano, The Louvre, Paris

Brogi-Art Reference Bureau

HEROD'S PALACE, JERUSALEM

Alinari-Art Reference Bureau

VESPASIAN'S TEMPLE OF PEACE (LEFT, FOREGROUND)
The Forum, Rome

THE COLOSSEUM IN THE TIME OF TITUS

Alinari-Art Reference Bureau

RUINS OF THE COLOSSEUM, ROME

Alinari-Art Reference Bureau

THE ARCH OF TITUS AND THE COLOSSEUM

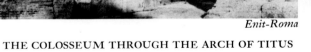

Enit-Roma

THE COLOSSEUM THROUGH THE ARCH OF TITUS

Anderson-Giraudon

ARCH OF TITUS, ROME

Alinari-Art Reference Bureau

THE ARCH OF TITUS

Alinari-Art Reference Bureau

THE SACK OF JERUSALEM
(Interior of the Arch of Titus)

Alinari-Art Reference Bureau

TITUS' TRIUMPHAL RIDE THROUGH ROME
(Interior of the Arch of Titus)

Alinari-Art Reference Bureau

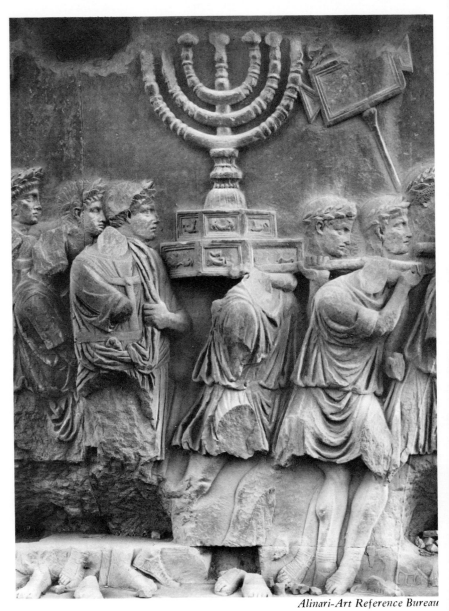

GOLDEN CANDELABRA FROM JERUSALEM

Anderson-Giraudon

THE SEVEN-BRANCHED CANDLESTICK (CLOSE-UP)

Alinari-Art Reference Bureau

TITUS
Vatican Museum, Rome

Alinari-Art Reference Bureau

TITUS' DAUGHTER JULIA
National Museum, Naples

Alinari-Art Reference Bureau

BERENICE
National Museum, Naples

Alinari-Art Reference Bureau

DOMITIA
Uffizi Gallery, Florence

Alinari-Art Reference Bureau

DOMITIAN
Capitoline Museum, Rome

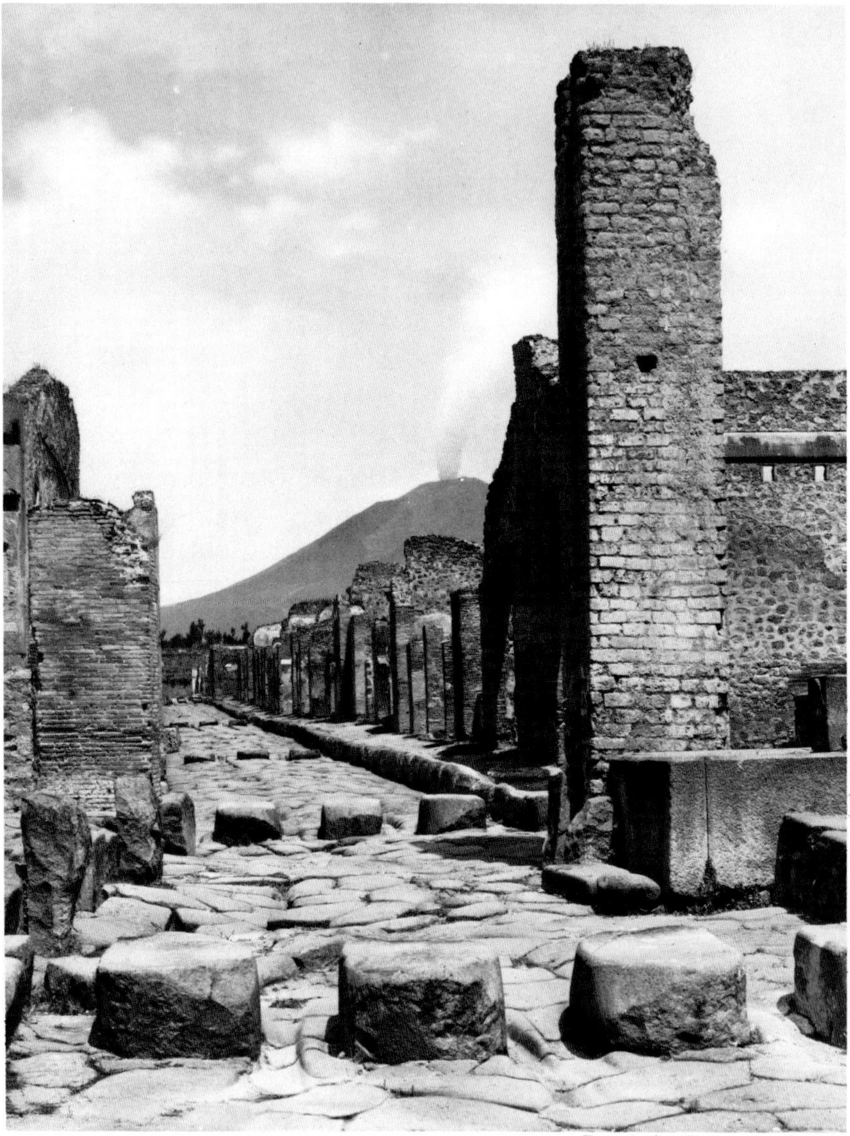

Brogi-Art Reference Bureau

RUINS OF POMPEII

No sooner had the toga-clad Senators taken their seats than Titus, steely-eyed and shaking with anger, launched forth into a fevered speech. He demanded that the attacks against the former Queen of Cilicia cease. Immediately. He reminded the Senators that Berenice had once ruled in Tarsus as queen; that she came from the noblest Jewish stock, being a granddaughter of Aristobulus, Herod the Great's second son by the first Mariamme. Berenice was far better born that he: a direct descendant of Isaac's son Esau, the elder brother of Jacob, and through her grandmother Mariamme, of several early kings of Israel.

"I shall be proud to marry this noble lady and make her my empress," the Emperor informed his Senate. There was an embarrassed silence. Titus had only to look at the rows of stony faces seated before him to know what thoughts were in the Senators' minds.

Finally, the representative from Gaul rose to say, "Caesar, we indeed all hope that you will marry and give Rome an empress. But let me warn you! Nothing will induce the Romans to accept, as your consort, a woman of Jewish blood. Have you forgotten that there is a law forbidding a Roman to marry a foreigner?"

No, Titus had not forgotten. Hadn't his father reminded him of it, long ago? "I shall repeal that law," Titus curtly replied to the Senators. "Go now and draw up such a bill. Bring it to me tomorrow."

The Senate retired to deliberate. Then, unable to face the Emperor with their decision, they sent him a letter instead. It was signed by the Senator from Sicily, Gaius Paulus Brunus, a hanger-on of Domitian.

When he unrolled the papyrus sheet and read it, Titus flushed with anger, for the purpose of the letter could be discerned only too clearly behind the polite phrasing. The Senate refused to pass the bill the Emperor requested, and if he wished to retain the cooperation of the Senate and the love of his people, Berenice of Cilicia must leave Rome. Immediately. Otherwise, the document hinted, Titus might lose his throne. And who would replace him? Domitian.

He must choose then? His throne? Or the woman he loved? Titus exploded with rage. He had been emperor for only two months. Could he give up all that he planned to do? The finishing of the Flavian amphitheater? Agricola's conquest of Caledonia? And his triumphal arch?

It fell to a trusted servant to bring him, a few days later, an even more strongly worded ultimatum from the Senate. It stated that the continued presence of Berenice of Cilicia in Rome was a threat to the tranquility of the Empire. If the Emperor forced this notorious woman over fifty on the Romans as their Empress, they might revolt. So she should leave Rome, at once. And he must promise never to see her again.

Titus bowed his head in grief. He remembered how he had said to his father, "When I become emperor, I shall repeal the law forbidding a Roman to marry a foreigner and make Berenice my wife. Who will there be then to prevent me?"

"The Roman people," Vespasian had replied.

They made their farewells on a mid-July night in 79, within the intimacy of the Herod villa. Next day, accompanied by a long train of oxcarts containing her possessions and an escort of servants on horseback, Berenice departed south along the Appian Way to Brindisi. Where was she going after that? She did not know. Nor did it matter? Titus had chosen the throne and given the Senate his solemn promise that he and his Jewish mistress would never meet again.

26

FOR TWO NIGHTS ONLY

WHAT PLEASURE was there now in life for Titus? After Berenice left Rome, he tried to exhaust himself with work, so that the lonely nights without her would not seem so long. He remained at his desk all day, driving his harassed secretaries crazy, until after a month the strain exacted its toll.

"You need a rest," the Emperor's doctor told him. "Why don't you go to Capri? It's the vacation spot of the Caesars."

Titus agreed. Anything to get out of Rome with its memories of Berenice. Hard work could not make him forget her, so why not try a change of scene?

A few days later, wishing to be alone, the Emperor went off to Capri with only one servant for a holiday on the island off Neapolis (Naples), several miles out into the Mediterranean, where the Emperor Tiberius once had a villa.

Titus fell in love with his vacation spot at first sight—a modest inn perched on a cliff that dropped steeply to the blue Mediterranean, with a breathtaking view of Mount Vesuvius rising serenely into the sky across the Bay of Neapolis. Here, where no one but the proprietor knew who he was, the lonely Emperor thought how he would live in the sea from dawn to dusk and perhaps forget.

The owner of the inn, Felix Cuspius, came out to greet

him. He bowed low. "Caesar, what an honor!" Then, proudly carrying the Emperor's baggage, the stout, genial proprietor showed his distinguished guest up some stairs to a room.

It was a large one. Titus walked over and stood gazing out of a window at the placid cone of Vesuvius in the distance. Directly below him was a terrace, laid out with orange trees in tubs, tables, and dining couches. The room was spotless; the view, superb. The innkeeper was pleased when the Emperor expressed his delight. Going over, he tried the door to an adjoining room. It was locked.

"I am sorry, Caesar, that I cannot give you this one," Felix said, "but some ladies from Herculaneum have engaged it."

Dinner would be at seven-thirty, the innkeeper went on to say, and his wife was in the kitchen now preparing the main dish—lobsters caught that morning in the Mediterranean. He was sorry there were so few guests at his inn. The season in Capri, this year, had not been a good one. "We're almost empty. Just you, the ladies from Herculaneum, and a few others . . ." The proprietor sighed regretfully, went out, and shut the door.

His servant brought the Emperor a basin of hot water. He bathed, changed from a tunic and boots into a toga and sandals, and went downstairs and out onto the terrace that he had seen from his window. There, a table and a reclining couch had been reserved for him. To his right he saw two women at a nearby table. The younger of them turned and stared up with startled, disbelieving eyes.

Titus recovered himself first. "I'm alone," he said. "May I join you?"

"Of course," Berenice replied. The Emperor reclined beside them, and she introduced her sour-faced, elderly companion.

"Emulla, a neighbor in Herculaneum. This is Paulus Justin, a friend of my brother Agrippa," she explained to her. "What a surprise! I haven't seen Paulus for years."

Emulla and Titus nodded to each other and agreed that it was nice for old friends to meet again. Especially, like this, by chance. The wine the Emperor ordered was brought. He poured out three glasses. Looking into each other's eyes, Berenice and Titus drank deeply. Emulla barely took a sip.

After a while the Emperor told the ladies why he had come to Capri. "For a rest and some sun." They had been there several days, Berenice said, and found the island delightful. "Paulus, don't fail to walk along the cliffs," she chattered nervously on, trying to make conversation. He promised he would.

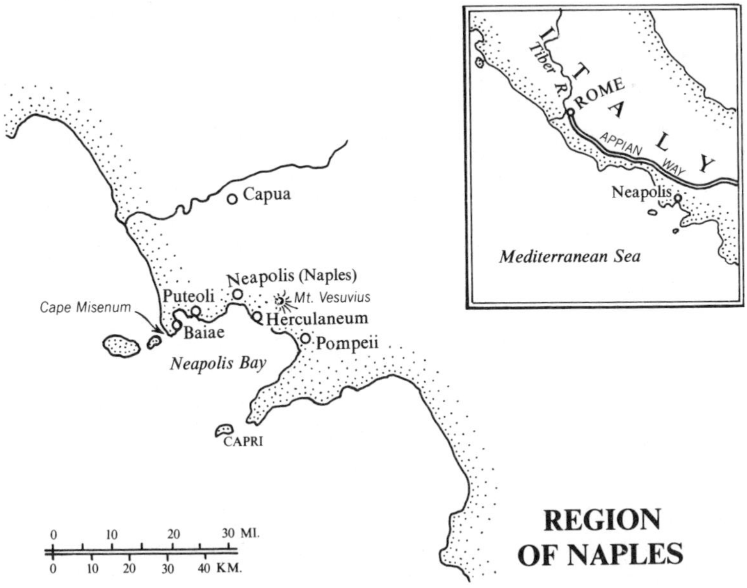

The lobster came and went. The second bottle of wine was emptied as they ladled thick cream over their strawberries. Then Berenice rose. "What a peaceful scene!" She indicated Vesuvius across the bay. "They say it's a volcano, but since the mountain hasn't erupted in thousands of years, it's not worth losing any sleep over, is it? . . . Well, I must get to bed. Emulla and I are leaving for Herculaneum in the morning. Good-by, Paulus, it's been nice seeing you again. Remember me to your wife and children."

Before she left the terrace, Berenice's hand lightly touched Titus' shoulder. Then the two women were gone. A short while later, a light came on in the room next to his. Titus waited until it had gone out. Then he followed her, pausing only to thank Felix's wife for the lobster.

"Two very quiet ladies," the innkeeper informed him. "I'm sure they won't bother you."

"One of them, I believe, is next to me. Where is the other?"

"Down the hall."

It was nine-thirty when Titus tried her door. He found it unlocked and, stepping into Berenice's room, softly closed the door behind him. The moonlight shone through the half-closed shutters upon the woman he loved, lying on the bed, as he knew she would be, waiting for him.

Titus woke in his own room at dawn. For a long time, he lay remembering the sweet scent of jasmine, a perfume that Berenice always used. Then he got out of bed and, wearing only sandals and a tunic, went out into the hall, past her door, and down the stairs to the beach.

For a half hour the Emperor swam in the blue Mediterranean, then coming out of the sea invigorated and happy, he walked back to the inn. He shaved, dressed, and had finished breakfast before Berenice came down to join him. To his surprise, she looked tired and toyed with her food. All of a sudden she stiffened, and he saw that she was looking past him with terror in her face.

Turning his head, Titus saw a man with an ugly scar on his cheek reclining by a table on the far side of the terrace. "What is it, my darling?" he asked.

Berenice's eyes never moved from the distant figure. "It's the same man," she whispered. "He's been following me. Ever since I went to Herculaneum."

The man with the scar seemed to realize that he was being watched. Looking up, he gazed at Titus and Berenice indifferently for a few moments. Then he went on with his meal and soon was gone.

"The fellow looked harmless enough," Titus said. "Darling, are you sure he is the same man?"

Berenice tried to drink, but her hand trembled. "Absolutely. And now he's seen us together. What if he tells?"

"Oh, I wouldn't worry about it!" Titus shrugged. To calm her, he pretended indifference, but when they had finished eating, somewhat upset himself, he went to have a talk with the innkeeper. The man was a stranger to him, Felix said, who arrived late last night. His name was Cassius Longinus, and he had told him that he was a jewelry salesman from Messina.

"Anyway, the fellow has left and gone on," Titus returned to Berenice to report. "So let's forget about him."

"Yes, nothing must spoil this morning," Berenice replied, for she had agreed to postpone her departure until afternoon.

The morning was theirs! Leaving Emulla on the terrace of the inn, Titus and Berenice went off with a picnic basket to explore the island. At noon, seated among the ruins of Tiberius' old palace, they ate their lunch and then made love. But, afterwards, she cried bitterly in Titus' arms. This time, when they parted, it would be forever. They could not hope to meet like this, by chance, again.

"Berenice, my darling," Titus whispered, holding her close. "It's been sweet, this stolen meeting, but so short. I can't bear to have it end. Not today, anyhow. Do we dare risk it? One more night?"

"My dearest . . ." She kissed his broad face, holding it lovingly between her hands. "I long to stay with you. But what if that man tells? Titus, you promised. Remember? You gave the Senate your solemn word that you would never see me again. They'll never believe that we didn't plan all this."

Titus soothed her, stroking her hair and kissing her. Finally, he made her smile. "Please, sweetheart, another night, even if all of Rome hears about it! Are two nights worse than one?"

"No, I suppose not, but what if that man tells?"

"Well, if he does, what can we do about it? The harm is done. But the fellow was probably only a jewelry salesman from Messina, as the innkeeper says. So let's forget about him."

"Yes, of course, we must," Berenice agreed.

They drank until the wine bottle was empty. Then the lovers walked, hand in hand, back to the inn. They found Emulla waiting for them on the terrace. "We're staying another night," Berenice announced to her, as casually as she could. "I must go and tell the proprietor." Titus saw the woman stiffen. She's on to us! he thought.

"Darling, are you sure your friend is to be trusted?" Titus asked, when Emulla had been dismissed indoors on some transparent excuse.

"I think so—" Berenice replied, after a moment's hesitation. "Emulla moved into a villa next to mine, shortly after I went to Herculaneum. I don't know anything about her actually, except that she's been nice to me."

The woman had expressed a desire to see Capri. So that afternoon, to keep up appearances, they took Emulla to visit the Blue Grotto, and at dusk the three of them dined again on the terrace, as they had on the previous evening.

Berenice ate little. Shortly, pushing away her untouched dessert, she rose. "Come soon," she whispered to Titus behind Emulla's back, and disappeared up the stairs.

That night, for two heavenly hours they made slow, sweet love. Then, after Titus had slept for a while in her arms, Berenice whispered, "You must go now." He slipped out of bed and knelt to kiss her eyes and mouth good night. "We'll meet in the morning," he promised.

"Yes." She lighted the oil lamp beside her bed. "But, before you go, dear one, let me look at you." She scanned his beloved face, as though trying to imprint on her memory every detail. Finally, after kissing him long and passionately on the lips, she extinguished the light.

"Good night, my dearest love," Berenice sighed.

As he bent for a last kiss, Titus tasted the tears on her cheek. Then, in the dark, he felt his way to the door. "Don't worry, my darling," he turned to say. "There will be no parting for us tomorrow or ever again. I'll work out some way."

Titus closed the door between their rooms and went to

bed. His mind was made up. He would marry Berenice, even if it cost him his throne. But the next morning, when he came down to breakfast and looked for them, the ladies from Herculaneum were gone.

"They asked to be called early," the innkeeper informed him, "and left here soon after sunrise."

Titus understood. Berenice, no more than he, could endure a final good-by. A week later, in Rome, a courier brought him a letter from her. He unrolled the parchment to read:

Beloved:

The so-called salesman from Messina was an informer and Emulla a spy, so I have discovered. Both of them in the pay of your detestable brother, Domitianus. All of Rome will soon know that we met in Capri. He will see to that. So good-by, my sweet love. Good-by, my darling. I love you with all my heart. But we must never meet again. It would be the ruin of you.

Send Agrippa to Egypt, as ambassador, for my sake. He loves Alexandria. That is all I shall ever ask of you. As for me, I am going to Pompeii to live with Drusilla and her boy, for I am afraid to remain in Herculaneum alone. There is bitter anti-Semitism here. Even more so than in Rome.

I love you, I have my memories, and in Pompeii I shall try to make a new life for myself. Titus, I am telling you this time where I am going—to Pompeii—so that, under no circumstances, must you ever come there. So good-by, forever this time, my dearest love.

Berenice

It was not long, thanks to Domitian's evil tongue, before a couple of hundred people in Rome knew that the Emperor had broken his promise to the Senate. He had gone off to Capri and there, by arrangement, met his Jewish mistress.

Hearing the talk about him on all sides, an angry Titus summoned the Senators to the Palatine again, and when the lawmakers had gathered before him, he cried out in anguish and despair, "It's a lie! Far from planning to meet the former Queen of Cilicia in Capri, we both found ourselves there together, purely by chance."

Titus saw that no one believed him.

The representative from Sicily, a man in Domitian's pay, spoke up. "No one on earth is going to believe that!" His voice grew wrathful. "Caesar, your love for this woman has become the scandal of Rome. Because of it, the Empire is in a turmoil. We warned you, several weeks ago, that if you continued to see this notorious Jewess whom the Roman people refuse to have as their Empress, you might lose your throne. Well, it now looks as though you would, unless you send her into exile, out of Italy, where there will never be any likelihood of you two meeting again—purely, by chance—"

"What do you mean?" Titus demanded.

"Exactly what I say. The Senate is waiting, Caesar, to hear your decision. And it is no longer a request, but a command. Make your choice. Do you intend to give this woman up and remain on the throne? Or be replaced by your brother?"

What would being emperor mean to him, without Berenice at his side? An angry retort was on Titus' lips—"I will abdicate." But, after a brief two months on the throne, he could not bring himself to utter those words. Instead, he told the Senators, "I must have time to think. Come back next week and I will give you my answer then." And the toga-clad men filed solemnly out of the room.

But they never came back. For the next day was August 24, 79, when Vesuvius erupted and buried the towns of Pompeii and Herculaneum under a rain of lava and ashes.

27

DEATH OF A ROMAN TOWN

THE ANIMALS of Pompeii were the first to recognize the signs of oncoming danger. Horses and dogs seemed to be unusually nervous, as if they knew, long before people did, what was going to happen. Six-year-old Antonius Agrippa (called by everyone, Tony) had never seen his spaniel act so strangely. Hector was running about, barking incessantly.

Coming to the door of her house, Drusilla watched her son's dog dashing around in circles. Then she glanced up at the sky. "Berenice, come look at the birds!" Drusilla called to her sister. "They're flying, scared, in all directions. Do you think a storm is coming?"

No one realized what the animals were trying to tell them—that, in a few hours, the prosperous seaport of Pompeii would be wiped off the map. For that twenty-fourth of August, seventy-nine years after the birth of Christ, was a day there like any other. Nearby Vesuvius seemed as always. It was known by scientists to be a volcano, but since the peaceful mountain had never erupted in the memory of man, the towns of Pompeii and Herculaneum were located at its base, and vineyards covered its slopes, for volcanic soil produces bumper crops.

It was noon. Taverns rang with the demands of hungry people, and house slaves were busy over the stoves, when a violent cracking sound came from Vesuvius. Yet not until a rain of red-hot pebbles and ashes poured down on their heads did the Pompeiians guess the truth. The sleeping volcano had exploded. Gushing from its crater, cascades of burning lava came rolling down the mountainside carrying away homes, scorching vineyards and, on reaching the sea, churning up giant waves of boiling water.

People ran screaming from their houses into the street, and fled to the open country, for fear of being trapped in the red-hot lava or buried in the fallouts of ash. But flight offered no escape. The streams of boiling mud moved as fast as a galloping horse. In a few hours, every town within a radius of fifteen miles of Vesuvius disappeared under a thick layer of lava and burning cinders, on which for three days more the deluge of liquid rock, hot ashes, and poisonous gases belched forth by the volcano continued to fall. Cooling, it formed into a solid crust, twenty feet deep.

Surprised by the first shower of ashes, the thought of most Pompeiians had been to get away as fast as possible. They dragged their horses, mules, and donkeys out of the stables, mounted them, and beat the frightened animals into a gallop. Everything that could be ridden was put to use. That is why only corpses of dogs were found in the ruins of Pompeii—those unfortunate pets, whom no one had thought to untie when their owners fled.

Hector was not going to let his young master, Tony, forget him. His frantic barking drowned out the cries of the people in the street. Berenice jerked open the front door. "Drusilla!" she called to her sister. "Hurry! Fetch Tony. We must get away. Immediately."

They rushed from the house to find themselves amid the wildest confusion, for the street outside was blocked by a river of frightened, hysterical people, as everyone in Pompeii tried to escape at once through the east gate of the walled town, because it was the one farthest from Vesuvius. Afraid of being trampled upon by this frenzied mob in which everyone thought only of their own safety, Drusilla, in tears, wanted to turn back.

"Back? Where?" Berenice demanded. Behind them, the town of Pompeii was being reduced to a mass of collapsed buildings, crushed under the heavy fallouts of ash. So what choice had they but to be swept along by these terrified people, many of whom had stripped off most of their clothing so as to be able to run faster? A woman was trying to flee, weighed down with an infant moving inside her. Another had a baby clasped to her breast, and two small children running beside her. Tony was not the only one with a pet. An old man had a goat he was struggling to drag along.

Panting and exhausted, Berenice, Drusilla, and her boy managed to squeeze through the one-arched gateway, only to be faced with new horrors. They were now clear of the walled town but from Vesuvius behind them there drifted a huge, mushrooming, black, cauliflower cloud which hung over them, and fiery ashes continued to rain down on their heads.

"Shake them off! They'll scald you to death!" a man shouted at Berenice. Drusilla, her hair and clothing encrusted with the burning black ash, sank in despair to her knees. "I can't go on . . ." she sobbed.

"You must, dear." Berenice lifted her fainting sister to her feet. "You must!"

A few people had dropped to their knees, exhausted like

Drusilla, but most of the crowd trudged on, their faces blank and despairing. They thought that the whole world was being destroyed by the gods and not just Pompeii. So there was no escape. They fled without any special destination in mind, except to put as many miles as possible between themselves and Vesuvius.

"There's a stream ahead," someone said.

Filled with hope, the fleeing crowd quickened their dragging steps, hurrying to reach a river in which they might be able to wash off this thick coating of hot ashes that clung to them like glue. Could they live to get there? Tony's little legs had given out. Berenice was carrying the tired boy, who was sobbing bitterly because he had lost his dog.

"Have courage, Drusilla!" Berenice urged on her exhausted sister. "The river isn't far now. Think how good that cold water is going to feel."

Just then, a tongue of flame shot out of the cone of Vesuvius; and, by its light, Berenice saw a sight that stunned her. Instead of a cooling stream ahead, a high wall of boiling mud was racing down the mountainside directly at them, setting houses on fire before rolling on over their remains. Firmly trapped in this cement-like hell were already a dozen unfortunate people, who had been in its path when the river of steaming lava caught up with them. Unable to escape, the poor creatures were imprisoned in it now, up to their necks. As they were swept along, all they could do was to cry out pitifully for help.

Even as she watched, Berenice knew there was nothing she could do, nothing anybody could do. She was still lying beside the lava flow, unconscious, when a rescue party found her. But, by then, Drusilla and little Tony had long ago sunk into the hot mud and disappeared.

28

HELL ON NEAPOLIS BAY

THE DREADFUL NEWS was flashed to Rome by signal towers. And Rome responded with sympathy for the victims of Vesuvius and charity for the survivors. The morning after the eruption, the Emperor Titus, his face showing the strain of a sleepless night, started out for Campania with the first rescue team to go to the assistance of stricken Pompeii and Herculaneum.

Changing mounts as each horse was exhausted, the men covered the 150-mile journey in eighteen hours and, on reaching the Bay of Neapolis, stopped, stunned, before the desolation they saw ahead. Although the sky was again a clear blue, Vesuvius was still smoking and its slopes, covered with vineyards a week ago, were now bare earth. Along the flanks of the mountain, not a village, not a farm remained. Everything was buried under a deep layer of volcanic mud, hardening, but scarcely cool.

Reaching the little that was left of Pompeii, they found only silence and death. Nearly all of the city had been destroyed. Titus and the men with him searched the ruins, but it seemed hardly possible to them that anyone, or anything, could have outlived one of the greatest volcanic eruptions in history. Virtually every building was gone, and the streets were blocked by streams of lava that in places had piled up as high as the tops of doors and windows. In a few hours, Vesuvius had made Pompeii look like nearby Herculaneum, a dead town, filled with dead people.

But, incredibly, there were a few survivors.

Fearing that the volcano might rumble into life again, those who escaped were reluctant at first to return. Then, clad in whatever odd bits of clothing they had fled in, a few people began coming back to search for the dead and missing, or to dig hopelessly through mountains of rubbish, trying to locate where their homes had been.

Not having eaten for days, these forlorn refugees were ravenously hungry; and the food the Emperor had hurriedly collected in Rome and paid for with his own funds, was all there was. The little found among the ruins was unfit to eat. Pompeii's water was no longer safe to drink. And the danger of an outbreak of plague was serious. Flies and rats swarmed over the human dead and the animal carcasses lying about in the ruins.

But, with the Emperor in charge, things began to improve. He had organized the relief work in Rome after the Great Fire back in the time of Nero, so now Titus set out to do what he could for Pompeii and Herculaneum. A hospital tent was erected; and rescue teams began shoveling out the houses and hauling their foul contents away from the town, while others collected the living into a refugee camp where food, medicines, and clothing were distributed to them.

Next came the grim task of burning the dead on a funeral pyre outside the town. Corpses piled up faster than they could be destroyed—the bodies of those, who, trying to save their jewels, gold coins, and silver plate had dallied too long in their homes and paid for their avarice with their lives, and the remains of those too old or infirm to flee. Sickened by the stench of decaying bodies, Titus, hollow-eyed from lack of sleep, toiled day and night, directing the rescue work.

And, everywhere, he searched for Berenice.

A week later, gangs of men and boys, who had worked for days without adequate food or rest, were still trying to free people trapped alive in the ruins. Many of them died as they were being gently lifted out.

In many cases, those who lived suffered a worse fate than the dead. Carried to the hospital tent, these wretched creatures called out incessantly for water to relieve their thirst. Yet few of them could drink. The flaming sulphuric fumes they inhaled had burned their throats so horribly that they could no longer swallow. Water choked them; they must be turned over and made to spit it out, and still they cried pitifully for more.

Others rolled on their cots in agony, begging to be killed. Anything, to end their sufferings. One woman was different. She was determined to live, and in spite of her ghastly burns, sang softly to herself to keep up her courage.

It was Berenice.

Lying there helpless, she thought of the miracle that had happened to her: she was alive. How had she escaped? All Berenice could remember was of being directly in the path of a torrent of hot, fluid rock pouring down the slopes of Vesuvius to the sea, that had swept Drusilla and Tony away from her. Losing sight of them, and nearly demented, she had run along beside the lava flow calling frantically to her sister and nephew, until she fell exhausted into a ditch.

Berenice did not know it, but falling into that irrigation

trench had saved her life. The cascade of molten rock and debris that carried off the others, missed by inches the ditch in which she lay and rolled on. Although badly scorched from lying, face down, in a pool of steaming mud for hours, Berenice survived. They found her. Men had come along, placed her on a stretcher, and brought her here.

For days now, Berenice had been lying in this tent full of suffering people, their bodies raw with burns. Like the others, she incessantly craved for but one thing. Water. Nobody heeded her pleas. The inadequate nursing staff was far too busy to attend to everybody.

A man came walking through the hospital tent, stopping beside one bed after another. Weakly, Berenice called out to him the plea of everyone. "Water! Give me water!" The sound of her voice, faint as it was, brought the man over to her bed. Pity in his eyes, he stood looking down at the woman lying there, her face hideously disfigured, burned almost beyond recognition.

Trying to alleviate the sufferings of the injured and dying, this man had only three hours sleep in the last forty-eight and, exhausted with fatigue, he thought at first his tired eyes were deceiving him. "Who are you?" he cried. The woman looked up, her face terrible to see.

"Titus," Berenice whispered, "don't you know me?"

29

THE SCORNED DON'T CRY

79 A.D. was an unlucky year. The eruption of Vesuvius in August was followed that September by an epidemic of plague in Rome, believed to have been caused by the clouds of deadly asphyxiating gases that rose from Vesuvius. Titus was in Capri at the time, nursing Berenice back to health, but he hurried to Rome to care for the sick and dying, as he had done at Pompeii.

A month later, the Emperor was called back to Rome by a third disaster. A great fire was sweeping through that crowded city. Titus was in despair. Was his reign to be nothing but a series of catastrophies?

Far from it. The reign of the tenth Emperor of Rome would become famous for several building projects. Work on Titus' Victory Arch in the Forum had stopped due to labor troubles, but his public baths being erected on the site of Nero's Golden House were nearing completion, the last stones being hoisted into place on the Flavian Amphitheater, the great arena begun by his father. And Titus returned to his Capri villa, late one night, well pleased.

He was seated at his desk there the next morning, when an aide appeared, "Will you speak," he asked, "with the former Queen of Cilicia?"

Titus stood up to receive her.

She came in, a tall gaunt figure, and stood facing him in silence until the aide closed the door behind her. Could this pale, broken woman be the once-lovely Berenice? Although her ghastly burns had healed, her face was permanently scarred, her beauty gone forever.

He drew up a chair for Berenice and they both sat down. "Darling, how are things in Rome?" she asked.

"Going well." Sitting back, Titus began to tell her about the entertainments he had in mind to give after his Flavian Circus, the largest in the Empire, seating fifty thousand people, was dedicated. "I intend to offer the Romans something new to watch–athletic events, foot races, and discus throwing as at the Greek games. And this will please you, Berenice–very little cruel animal baiting or gladiatorial fights."

Knowing how the Jews had refused to attend the bloody shows in the arenas that Herod the Great built in Judaea to please his Roman friends, Titus promised Herod's great-granddaughter that, if he could prevent it, nothing of a brutal nature should take place in his new arena. It would be the one circus in the Empire never to be spattered by blood.

"I've thought of a novelty for opening night, sure to delight the audience. The spectators are to be showered with little wooden balls containing coupons that can be exchanged for the articles marked on them, such as clothing, horses, or cattle. And on that gala evening, my dearest, you shall sit beside me in the Imperial box–"

"No, Titus, that's what I came to tell you," she interrupted him. "I won't be at the opening of your circus. I'm better now, almost well, and I've decided to go away."

"Away? What do you mean?"

"I've done you harm enough, my dear. I want to go out of your life. This time, forever. No, don't argue with me, Titus. I thought it all out during the long weeks I've been ill. My darling, we were never meant for each other. Our love was wrong from the beginning. Too much stands between us—the gods and goddesses you believe in, and the One God I worship."

"Berenice, don't talk such nonsense."

"It isn't nonsense. Let me explain. Once I wanted to be your wife and empress, but since I almost died at Pompeii, that no longer seems to matter very much. When Vesuvius rained hot cinders down upon my head, something happened to me. The Jews sprinkle ashes on their heads to purify themselves on Atonement Day. Well, the cinders from Vesuvius falling on me cleansed me of my sin of having loved you, Titus, not one of God's Chosen People. Vesuvius has made me pure once more. It is as though I were reborn. And, my dear, I want to remain that way. Pure. I can never live with you again."

Titus understood. They had been passionate lovers, but since Pompeii, they seldom even kissed. "So you want to leave me?" he asked.

"Yes, my dearest. All I went through during the eruption of Vesuvius ruined my health. I no longer have sufficient strength to fight the enmity of the Roman people. Darling, we're beaten. Isn't that so?"

Titus could not deny it.

"And I hope you realize who is responsible for it." Berenice's tired eyes lit with anger. "Who has worked on the anti-Semitic prejudices of the Romans so that you've never dared marry me? Well, I'll tell you, it's your detestable brother. If I were to attend the opening of your circus in Rome, Domitianus would see to it that the audience pelted me with rotten eggs!"

"My dear, you're imagining things."

"I'm not. I've told you, often enough, that your brother should be exiled to Germany or Britain, where he cannot harm you."

"I could never do that."

"No, of course, you couldn't. Not until you find Domitianus plotting to kill you to get the throne. Don't say then that I didn't warn you—" Berenice's scarred face became almost beautiful again, her eyes were so filled with love and tenderness. "Titus, you're such a dear, gullible fool! You never believe ill of anyone. What is going to happen when I'm no longer here to look after you? Because I won't be soon. I'm sailing tomorrow."

"For Alexandria? To stay with Agrippa?"

"No, back to Judaea."

"Berenice, where will you be in Judaea? I must know."

"If I tell you, you'll promise never to come there?"

Sadly, Titus nodded his head.

"All right then, I'm going to Machaerus to be with Salome." And since he didn't understand, she explained, "It's because of what happened there fifty years ago. Do you want to hear about it?"

Titus did. So Berenice told him how her first cousin, Salome, nineteen at the time, had danced one night in the fortress of Machaerus, east of the Dead Sea, before her stepfather, the Herod who sent Jesus to his death. Salome had pleased Herod Antipas, so as a reward the tetrarch of Galilee had given the girl-dancer what her mother, Herodias (the sister of Berenice's father), had told her to ask for—the head of a prisoner he had, John the Baptist. This desert hermit had denounced Antipas for his second marriage (illicit by the laws of Moses) with his sister-in-law, Herodias, for whom he had left his wife. So now Herodias, by having the Baptist beheaded, had her revenge.

"But her young daughter, Salome, never recovered from the horror of that night, of seeing the executioner go with his sword down into the dungeons of Machaerus and return with the Baptist's head," Berenice said. "Afterwards, always highly emotional, Salome married twice—first, her elderly Uncle Philip, and then his grandson Aristobulus, the son of my second husband, King Herod of Chalcis. Today, with my stepson, she rules Armenia. Fifty years have passed since the night the Baptizer was murdered, but, Titus, I've had such incoherent letters from her recently that I'm frightened."

"Tell me about them, dear, if it will help."

"Well, Salome writes me that the sight of John the Baptist's head, as they brought it to her on a silver platter, still warm and dripping blood, is ever before her eyes. In dreams at night, the vision forms, dissolves, then forms again. The Baptizer died once, Salome says, but she dies over and over every night. Titus, I too have nightmares. I hear the cries of those innocent children in Bethlehem that my great-grandfather Herod slaughtered. Salome is returning to Judaea. She wants me to join her at Machaerus. Perhaps, where the Baptist was murdered, together we can exorcise our dreams."

"So your mind is made up? To leave me?"

Coming nearer, she put her arms around him. "Please, Titus, let me go and help Salome. Let me do one good deed in my life. I've done so much evil."

Angry suspicions came to him. Had Berenice grown tired of him? Was she returning to Judaea with another man? He asked her roughly, "This story about your going to help some crazy woman come to her senses, is it simply an excuse to leave me?"

Berenice smiled. "You're very smart, my dear. I didn't think that you would suspect. Yes, it's an excuse, in a way." Looking deep into his eyes, she went on. "Listen, Titus, and I'll tell you why I am really going. If I remain in Italy, you'll never marry again, and you must—and have a son. Do you want to see Domitianus become emperor?"

He ignored her last remark. "So it's good-by then, forever?"

"Not necessarily. When we both die, we may meet again up in that heaven the Jews and Christians believe in, but not the Romans. I would like to think so, my dear, and that you and I will go to the same place, even though we worship different gods. How stupid of the Romans to think that death ends everything! Titus, don't you want to live again in a better world? I do. I've had such a miserable time in this one."

Berenice and Titus both rose. He held out his arms and they clung together and kissed with tear-wet faces. Then they stood, silent. There was only one word left to say, *vale* (good-by). But neither of them could bring themselves to pronounce it.

"*Vale*," Berenice whispered, at last. "My beloved, I can't believe this life on earth is all there is for us. There must be another world where it won't matter that you're a Roman and I'm a Jew, and we can be happy together forever. So when I get there, darling, I'll be looking for you."

30

BIG AND BLOODY

DOMITIAN WANTED to be the greatest. If unable to compete with Titus, he couldn't be the greatest, so he would be its antithesis, the worst. He never had any trouble in achieving that ambition. The dissolute life of the Emperor's brother was the scandal of Rome. Especially notorious was his liking for unpleasant practical jokes. Domitian's pets included deadly Egyptian snakes, lions, and leopards. When his rowdy companions had gotten themselves sufficiently drunk at his wild parties, Domitian would lock the doors, douse the lights, and let his vicious animals into the room in the dark. He roared with laughter when his guests were hurt in the ensuing panic.

This sadistic younger brother of the Emperor was no unsightly monster but a tall, handsome fellow with only one blemish—thin hair. Domitian was extremely sensitive about his baldness, for it made him look older than he was, twenty-nine, and he became furiously angry if anyone teased him about it.

By refusing to allow his younger son to have a share in ruling the Empire, Vespasian had turned him into a playboy. Titus was trying to rectify that. Some army discipline would do his brother good, he thought, and remembering the advice Berenice had given him, he offered Domitian the command of the Roman Army on the Danube.

"What are you trying to do?" he cried. "Get rid of me?"

Such insubordination shocked General Tiberius Alexander, Titus' chief of staff. "Why doesn't Domitianus want to leave Rome?" he demanded. "Is it because he prefers to remain here, Caesar, and plot against you? You should send him to the Danube by force, and if he refuses, kill him."

"Can you imagine I would do that to my own brother? I would rather die than kill others," replied the man who had destroyed Jerusalem. Titus still remembered with remorse what he had been forced to do in Judaea.

So, instead of exiling Domitian, Titus tried his best to win his affection. He even suggested to his brother that he marry Marcia's daughter. Julia was sixteen now. Not attractive. Dark-skinned, fat, and cowlike. Domitian was not interested. A hard-faced beauty named Domitia Longina had caught his eye. The fact that she was already married to Aelius Lamia, a wine merchant, did not deter him. Domitian seduced her, had Lamia murdered in the street, and wed his handsome widow. Julia should have thought herself well rid of such a man.

Other Roman Emperors had built for their own amusement, but the Flavians–Vespasian and Titus–built for the public good. Desperately lonely since Berenice's return to Judaea, Titus was trying to fill his empty days by occupying himself in finishing his arena, his baths, and his arch in the Forum.

The first of his projects to be completed in the spring of 80 were the Baths of Titus, erected on the site of Nero's

PLAN OF ROME
IN THE TIME OF TITUS
A.D. 39-81

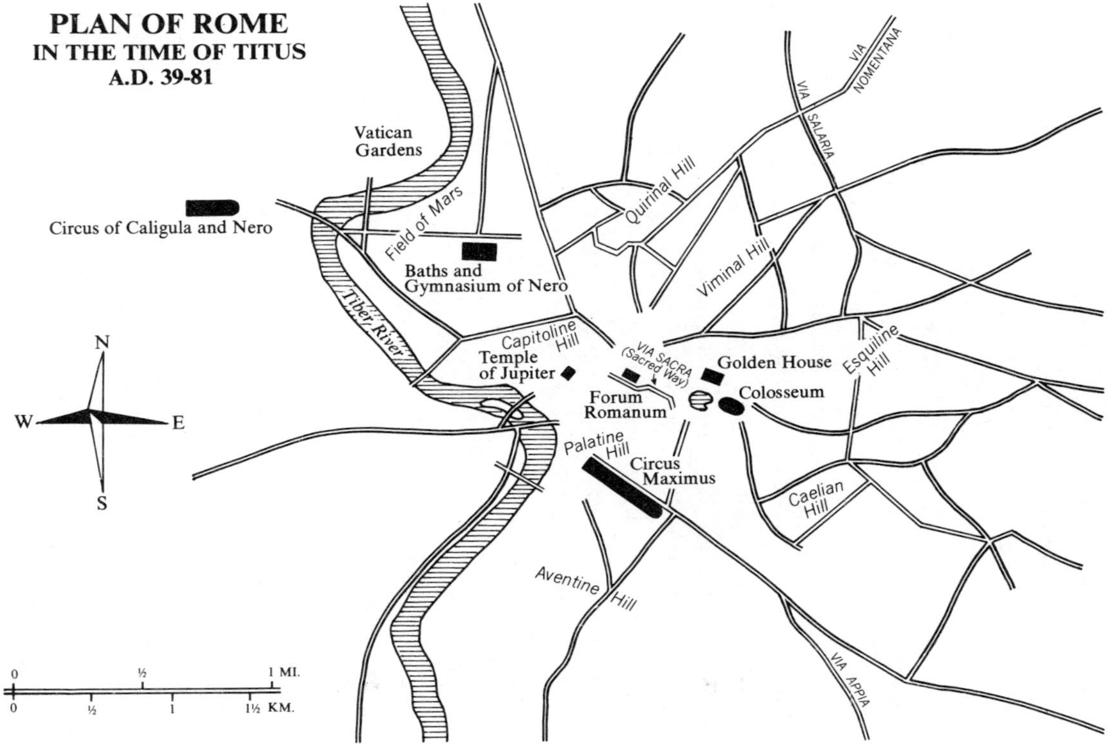

Vatican Gardens
Circus of Caligula and Nero
Field of Mars
Baths and Gymnasium of Nero
Tiber River
Capitoline Hill
Temple of Jupiter
VIA SACRA (Sacred Way)
Forum Romanum
Golden House
Colosseum
Palatine Hill
Circus Maximus
Aventine Hill
Caelian Hill
Esquiline Hill
Viminal Hill
Quirinal Hill
VIA SALARIA
VIA NOMENTANA
VIA APPIA
N
S
E
W
0
½
1 MI.
0
½
1
1½ KM.

Golden House. These public *thermae* were unique because red and gray granite was used in their construction for the first time. A great novelty at Rome in the first century, granite came from Egypt and was very expensive.

Titus' baths soon became crowded, for the Emperor allowed everyone, rich and poor, to use them. He even let others in when he was bathing there himself. Anyone could approach the Emperor. And he did his best to help them. Once, as Titus was entering the steam rooms, another bather called out something to him. "I've no time now," he replied. "Then don't be Emperor," the man shouted after him. "You're quite right," Titus replied, and interrupting his bath, listened to the stranger patiently.

He could be witty too. A gray-haired man once made a request which the Emperor, thinking it unreasonable, refused. Next day the same man was back again, this time with his hair dyed blond. "I've already refused your father," Titus quipped. He had not only inherited Vespasian's sense of humor, but his liking for simplicity. The Emperor lived without ostentation in Claudius' old palace on the Palatine, spending most of his time, as his father had, at Tertulla's farm in the Sabine hills.

Frugal with himself, Titus was extremely generous with others, and he was spending money lavishly to beautify Rome. Nero's Golden House had been torn down, his gardens became a public park, and the colossal frozen statue of him decorated the entrance to the circus that the Flavians, father and son, had been building for eight years at the end of the Sacred Way down which every procession rumbled into the Forum.

By the summer of 80 that great arena, begun by Vespasian,

was finished. Titus inaugurated it with a hundred consecutive days of games. Fifty thousand spectators filed daily into Rome's new recreation center for the events, but since the entrances corresponded to numbers stamped on their tickets, it was an easy walk for them through a numbered portal, up a broad staircase, to a numbered landing and a numbered seat.

Having found their places, the audience could settle down in comfort and marvel at the largest structure of its kind ever built. The Romans admired size, and the dimensions of the *Amphitheatrum Flavian* certainly inspired their respect—an elliptical building, a third of a mile long, and three stories high, its walls pierced by arches decorated with statues.

There were eighty entrances. One of them, closed to the public, led to a box reserved for Emperor Titus and his suite. The rest of the ringside was given over to the *populus romanus*, seated on different levels according to their rank. Closest to the arena floor, behind a protective wall, were the Senators and the diplomatic corps. Behind them, the first tiers of marble chairs were reserved for the army; the rows of stone seats above that for ordinary people; and the third section was allocated to women and slaves, who occupied wooden benches up under the gay, colored awning that served as a roof.

Posters announcing the programs in the *Amphitheatrum Flavian* were plastered up all over Rome for days before a performance. The games took place in the afternoon. After the Emperor, his Senators in purple-edged togas, and the foreign ambassadors in native costumes had taken their seats, the gladiators marched into the ring and stopped before the Imperial box to give their famous shout, "*Morituri te salutant!*" ("Those about to die salute you!"). The Emperor raised his hand to signal his permission, and there began what the Romans cynically called "games"—actually, the most brutal events ever staged, with animal pitted against animal, man against animal, or man against man.

Titus, who hated bloodshed, had decreed that these events be as merciful as possible. And everything went as he wished for a while. Gladitorial fights took place only between armed men—criminals, sentenced to die anyway. Blunt weapons were used, and the vanquished were usually spared. There were athletic competitions to watch, chariot races, and circus acts. Or the arena would be flooded, and on the artificial lake created, mock naval battles were staged. One would have thought that the *populus romanus* would have been satisfied. But no, they wanted to see blood flow—rivers of it. In spite of all that Titus could do, the "games" grew so brutal that the Flavian Amphitheater became the most blood-soaked building in the world.

Nine thousand animals were said to have been slaughtered there in three months. Driven by whips from cages in the basement, they were lifted by elevators to the arena floor and turned loose to fight one another—a lion against a bear, a leopard against an elephant, a tiger against a rhino—until there would be no more elephants left in North Africa, no more hippos in Nubia, or lions in Mesopotamia.

Still the thrill-hungry crowd demanded more, for centuries of warfare had made the Roman people callous to suffering. Animal blood no longer satisfied them. The spectators thirsted for human blood and bet their money on gladitorial fights to the death. Their favorite contest was between two men, one armed, the other carrying only a huge net in which he tried to entangle his opponent. The armed man would kill the unarmed, only to be deprived of his arms and dragged defenseless before a third man, heavily armed. So it went on, until the arena was covered with the dead. The corpses were then dragged away, sand raked over the blood, and the next event began.

But by then the Emperor Titus, revolted by this sickening butchery, refused any longer to attend the performances in his fine new Flavian Amphitheater.

31

DOMITIAN UNMASKED

Domitian was quick-tempered, spiteful, and cunning, but he draped his toga with such elegance and was so glib a talker that Julia—a shy, naive girl, given to romantic daydreams—had secretly loved her wicked uncle since childhood. But now as he came striding into the room, letting out a cry of annoyance, she stepped hastily back from the basin of water in which she was washing her hair.

"Domitianus, don't come here again in the daytime. What if Auntie hears of it?"

"How can she? Lying in bed since her stroke, hardly conscious."

"Besides, I'm washing my hair."

"What if you are? You look all right." He took a strand of Julia's long, black hair in his hand and pulled it until she squealed. Domitian grinned. He enjoyed hurting people. "Your hair is pretty, wet. It will dry fast enough on the pillow—"

"Hush!" Julia put her hand over his mouth. Then, turning to her ladies, she said primly, "Leave me alone with my uncle. We have matters to discuss."

"But your aunt said—" began Adriane in alarm.

Domitian scowled at her. "Begone, do you hear?" And as

the maid hesitated to disobey their mistress' orders never to leave Julia alone with a man, unchaperoned, he bellowed, "Go!"

Adriane bowed and went, the other maid following.

Domitian turned to Julia. "That will show them that when I want a kiss, I must have it at once."

He came closer, and as he took Julia in his arms and kissed her, Domitian thought how it had been all too easy. He was not a man who liked to spend a long time in wooing, but his seduction of Julia had been, due to necessity, unusually swift. The return to Judaea of Titus' Jewish mistress had frightened him. Titus was only forty-two. If he should marry now and have a son, what chance would a mere brother of the Emperor have then of gaining the throne? None, unless he could get Julia, the present heir apparent, with child.

It had not been hard to do. First, fatherly kisses. Then more tender kisses, and Julia was sobbing in her Uncle Domitian's arms, babbling about having always loved him. Soon, their lovemaking became more than just kisses. They were meeting in Paulita Flavius Sabinus' home secretly at night, once or twice a week, after the rest of her household was asleep.

Domitian was incapable of loving anyone. But the shy, inhibited Julia, who had been shut up for years in a gloomy old mansion with an invalid aunt, many servants, all elderly, and few friends, believing herself to be loved, began to bloom. A plump girl, she gave up sweets and lost several pounds. She learned to use rouge, powder, and perfume. But her tearful gratitude for her uncle's affections soon bored and, finally, irritated him to distraction. How long, Domitian began to wonder, must this ridiculous lovemaking go on?

After several months of it, Domitian was satiated. Having to make love to this stupid, silly girl was too high a price to pay, even to gain the throne! Sitting down beside her, he demanded roughly, "You went to the doctor yesterday. What did he say?"

"Oh, my dearest, darling Domitianus . . . that I'm pregnant!"

"Wonderful!" her uncle exclaimed. Then, trying not to show his elation too much, he forced himself to caress her.

Things were going splendidly. Right on schedule. An hour later, Domitian returned to his palatial home on the Aventine, looking so pleased with himself that his wife flew into a temper.

"So you've been to see Julia again!" Domitia cried. "Look here! It's the third time this week. I'm getting jealous. You're not beginning to enjoy making love to the girl, are you?"

She was a statuesque brunette with a thin-lipped mouth, wise blue eyes, and a heart as unable to feel or love any more than could Domitian. This hard-boiled, ambitious couple deserved each other. So now Domitia's husband took a cruel pleasure in adding to her distress. "If I've fallen in love with Julia, my dear, you've only yourself to blame." He shrugged. "Who's idea was it in the first place that I seduce her, then blackmail Titus into abdicating?"

"Mine, and I've gone along with it, haven't I? Only I'm surprised, my pet, that it's taken you so long to prove your virility, when half the children in Rome resemble you!"

"Oh, I haven't done so badly!"

"Domitianus, you don't mean . . . ?" His wife sprang to her feet, her eyes shining. "You wretch! You're almost licking your lips. Is Julia pregnant?"

"So she says."

"Splendid!" Beside herself with joy, already seeing herself the empress of Rome, Domitia began dancing wildly about the room. Surely, Domitian wouldn't run out on her now! Or could he? Knowing her husband only too well, Domitia suddenly stopped her happy dance, her smile faded, and she came and stood accusingly before him, hands on her hips. "You villain! You aren't thinking of double-crossing me, are you? Divorcing me to marry Julia?"

That being just what he intended doing, Domitian replied coldly, "My dear, have you considered what an empress of Rome you would make? The daughter of a discredited army officer. The former wife of a wine merchant–"

"Whom you murdered!" she shot back.

Domitian lost his temper. "When I met you, remember, my fine lady, you were nothing. And you'll go back to being nothing when it suits me. Yes, I intend to marry Julia. I would do more than that to become emperor."

"Even kill!" his wife muttered.

Domitian merely shrugged.

Now that he had gotten Julia with child, the next step was easy. Domitian had planned it all some time ago. The following morning he rode up Palatine Hill to Claudius' shabby, old palace, where he found Titus seated at a desk in his library.

"Why do you continue to live in this dump?" Domitian said to him, sitting down. "Too bad you didn't keep Nero's Golden House. Someday, this crumbling ruin will collapse on your head."

"Oh, I'm sentimental about it. Remember, this is where I lived as a boy, when I was Brittanicus' companion." Then leaning across his desk, Titus said genially, "I'm glad you've come to see me, Domitianus. I don't see much of you these days. What's on your mind?"

"I want to marry Julia."

Titus' face stiffened. He stared at his brother. "But you're already married. What about Domitia?"

"I'll divorce her."

The Emperor gasped in disbelief. "Domitianus, what nonsense are you saying! You didn't want Julia when I suggested that you marry her. Now you're willing to divorce your wife in order to get her. What's happened?"

"We're in love."

"How long has this been going on?"

"Several months. But we waited to tell you until Julia was pregnant. Now we'd like to get married."

"I'll never permit it."

Domitian's affable smile faded.

"I'm sorry you're taking it like this, Titus," he said, "because the news of Julia's illegitimate baby isn't going to read very well in the *Acta Diurna*, when that scandal sheet learns of it. And I'll certainly see that it does. I've no reputation to lose, but Julia has . . . My dear brother, hadn't you better change your mind? All this could be discreetly hushed up, without all Rome knowing about it, if I quietly divorced Domitia, married Julia, and you made me your heir—"

"So that's it!" Titus sprang to his feet. "You conniving scoundrel, get out! You've thought of everything, haven't you? Julia isn't a pretty girl. Not too bright and starved for affection. How could you be heartless enough as to have taken advantage of her? There's more behind this. What is it?"

Domitian never moved from his seat. "Simply, that I intend to become emperor, and before very long, that is, unless . . ." He smiled slyly. "I have a price, my dear brother. I can be bought off. Abdicate in my favor, and in return, I'm willing to marry Julia and make her baby legitimate."

Titus looked suddenly older. "Wait. Let me think."

The Emperor sat down with his hand cupped over his eyes. He sighed heavily a few times. Then taking his hand away, he looked up with scorn across the desk at Domitian.

"I've tried so hard to be a good brother and do all that I could for you. Is this to be my reward?" Titus asked, sadly. "Now I understand it all . . . what a contemptible person you are, Domitianus, and have been all along. You're trying to blackmail me into giving you the throne, aren't you? Well, you're not going to get away with it. Do you hear? You're not marrying Julia. I'm not abdicating in your favor. And I'm sending you out of Italy by force, as I should have done long ago."

"What about the child?"

"There won't be any. An abortion will fix that!"

"Suit yourself, Titus." Domitian rose and started toward the door. "I thought we could arrange all this between brothers, quietly, in a friendly manner. Now, I see that I shall have to use . . . well, other means . . ."

Titus knew what Domitian implied. And, for the first time, he was afraid of him.

32

WAR BETWEEN THE BROTHERS

It was August of 81 and Rome was swept that hot, unhealthy month by a severe epidemic of the plague. Several people in Paulita Flavius Sabinus' household died of the disease. Then Julia caught it. When he was told, Titus was overcome with remorse. He paced up and down his palace apartment, regretting his long neglect of the girl—due to the fact, Titus knew, that he had never believed that Julia *was* his daughter—and swearing to take her to live with him if she survived.

Julia's condition was aggravated by her recent abortion. It had left her very weak. She lay in bed, barely conscious. On visiting her sickroom, Titus wept at the sight that met his eyes. Julia smiled vaguely up at him, but she was not fully aware of who he was.

Titus turned to the doctor. "Any hope?"

"None, Caesar, she is sinking fast."

The Emperor nodded. He sat down by the bed and a half hour later the girl of seventeen, whose brief, unhappy life had been cut short by Domitian's ambitions, died in his arms.

There was a quiet funeral. Rome was told that Julia had

died of the plague. That she might have survived the attack, actually a mild one, except for her recent abortion, was known to only a few people. But Titus knew. And the morning after the funeral, he began the punishment of the man who had been the cause of Julia's death.

Tiberius Alexander was sent to hand the Emperor's brother his orders to leave Rome—not to take command of the Roman army on the Danube, but for Britain where he would serve under Agricola.

"In what capacity?" demanded Domitian.

"As a centurion," he was told.

A centurion? The Emperor's brother! Domitian, whose ego was colossal, flew into a rage and angrily left the room. His attendants were waiting outside in the hall. Domitian looked at them sharply. Had they overheard? Did they know that he had been humiliated?

Domitian was not a person to forgive a slight. No one could insult him and live. And never had he felt so belittled. He had expected to be exiled from Italy after what had happened to Julia, but never had he imagined that he would be shipped off to Britain to serve there as an officer over a small unit in the Roman army, a mere century (one hundred men). Well, he wasn't going. He would remain in Rome and fight for the throne. Other means having failed, only one way was left to him—murder!

He was no amateur killer. Domitian had done away with countless people. If it was necessary for him to get rid of someone, he removed them. When they were dead, he ceased to think about them. But murdering his brother, the Emperor, wouldn't be that easy. Titus had the complete loyalty of the Praetorian Guard. He was popular with the army. If any foul play was suspected, who would be the first person named? Himself. All Rome was aware of how much he coveted the throne. So Domitian knew that he must do away with Titus in such a way as not to arouse the slightest suspicion that he had any part in it.

A few days later, the Emperor was seated at his desk in the study of Claudius' old, crumbling palace on the Palatine, reading a letter from Agricola. His old friend and favorite general had written him that to protect Rome's province of Britannia against an invasion from the savage tribes of Caledonia to the north, the Picts, he was erecting two lines of defense forts. One of them had been built from the mouth of the Tyne to the Solway, a distance of seventy miles from sea to sea, and Agricola was now constructing another wall to the north of it from the Firth of Forth to the Clyde. Always interested in Britain from having lived there as a boy, Titus was bending over a map of the region, when the heavy ceiling over his desk and chair suddenly collapsed on his head.

His secretary, Quintus, cried out in alarm. Choking with the dust that filled the air, he and several others in the next room ran into the Emperor's study and to the spot where he had been sitting. They could not lift the massive beams off him or the thick blocks of concrete. So the men rushed from the apartment shouting for help. Guards and palace officials came running. But as the men worked frantically, trying to lift the fallen masonry, they shook their heads. "Under all that weight, the Emperor cannot possibly still be alive," they said.

Tiberius Alexander, who had been summoned, came hurrying to the rescue. He was horrified, for he loved Titus dearly. "Work harder! Harder!" the Emperor's chief of staff shouted at the diggers. Under his direction, the men obeyed; with the aid of shovels and axes, they managed to lift off the buried man some of the huge beams and heavy pieces of concrete. Finally, after a long effort, Titus was dragged out from under the great pile of rubble, unconscious and bleeding.

"Carry him to his bed," General Alexander ordered, "and send for the doctor." Lucius came. The Emperor was badly hurt, but he would live, the Imperial physician said, and as the news rapidly spread through the city all of Rome rejoiced, for no one wanted to see Domitian on the throne.

Titus was a strong man. Coming from sturdy Etruscan peasant stock, a week later he insisted upon going back to his desk. Letters from rich and poor, expressing their joy at the Emperor's lucky escape, came pouring in. There was even a note of sympathy from Domitian.

"Didn't I warn you that Claudius' old palace would someday fall on your head?" his brother wrote. "Now will you build yourself a new one?"

Going to a brazier, Titus burned his brother's letter, then for fear that poisoned ink had been used, washed his hands. He wanted nothing more to do with Domitian. The ceiling that had fallen on his head was no accident, he knew. His brother had probably arranged it. For some days before, workmen had been up on the roof of the palace repairing a leak, and Domitian had no doubt bribed them to saw in half some of the beams that held up the heavy concrete ceiling of his study.

When would his brother strike next?

More shaken by his near-fatal experience than he or anyone else realized, Titus caught a severe cold a week later, but, in spite of it, he decided to go for his usual weekend at his farm in Falacrina.

"Caesar, it's storming hard," Lucius, his doctor, protested. "This rain in Rome will be snow in the mountains, and you're too ill to travel in such foul weather. Please, if you insist upon going to Falacrina, let me go with you."

"No, Lucius, you'd be leaving too many sick people behind you in Rome. I'll send for you, if I need you," the Emperor replied. So, with only his secretary Quintus, his valet Julius, and a small escort of soldiers, he left for the Flavians' ancestral acres up the Tiber.

As the road climbed into the Sabine hills, the snow storm, unseasonable for September, increased in violence. Lying back shivering in his litter, feeling weaker and more ill every mile, Titus realized that this was no mere cold he had caught. Was it pneumonia? If so, would he die at forty-two? Titus had only reigned for two years. There was still so much that he wanted to do. For instance, to send a Roman fleet along the north coast of Caledonia in order to find out if Britain actually was an island, and to explore Hibernia (Ireland), that large tract of land to the west of Britain, out in the Atlantic Ocean. Titus thought how he had tried to be a good emperor, to rule wisely and well, with justice for all. Even the Christians had not been persecuted. To the best of his knowledge, he had but a single crime on his conscience.

Parting the curtains of his litter, Titus called his secretary, Quintus, to his side and said to him weakly, "I'm very ill . . . If I die, remember, there's only one thing in my whole life that I regret having done. Only one."

His retinue wondered, what did he mean?

They pushed on through the snow storm, although the

Emperor's condition was growing steadily worse, and by September 13, 81, the day that they reached Falacrina, pneumonia had made him a desperately sick man. Titus was running a high fever, he was delirious, and no longer knew where he was. Julius carried his master into the farmhouse to a ground-floor room, laid him down on the bed on which his father had died, and called Quintus.

The secretary came, alarm in his eyes, to look at the invalid. His short, painful breathing sounded through the house. "We must send to Rome for his doctor," Quintus exclaimed. Just then, they heard voices at the front door. "Someone has arrived," the secretary said. "I'll go and see who it is."

A short while later, Quintus was back accompanied by Domitian and a husky, red-haired young man. Domitian explained why he had come. "I heard that my brother was gravely ill, but in spite of it, had insisted upon going to Falacrina. Worried about Titus, I've followed him and brought with me a friend who is a doctor. I hope we can be of help. How is he?"

The red-haired young man came to Titus' bedside. His eyes were glazed, and although the Emperor appeared to look at him, he could no longer recognize anyone. After examining the sick man, Domitian's friend turned to Quintus and Julius. "It's pneumonia, but I think I can save him. That is, if you can get me the proper remedies. I shall need–" He named a list of medicines that could only be obtained in the town of Reate, several miles away.

"I'll go and fetch them!" Quintus offered, eagerly.

"You might as well go with him," the red-haired young man said to Julius. "I won't need you. And too many people in a sickroom are bad for a patient."

As soon as Quintus and Julius had ridden off to Reate and

left them alone, Domitian said to his "friend"—not a doctor, at all, but a hired thug—"Come! Let's get this thing over with—" Domitian placed his hands beneath Titus' shoulders, the younger man took his feet, and between them they lifted the Emperor from his bed and carried him, semiconscious, but still breathing, out of the house and dumped him into the snow.

Domitian laughed. "Well, that should bring down his fever!" Then, without even waiting for his brother to die, he galloped off to Rome, burst into the Praetorian barracks, and had himself proclaimed emperor.

A half hour later, when Quintus and Julius returned from Reate with the medicines, they thought the house strangely quiet. On going into the Emperor's ground-floor bedroom, the two men stopped short in amazement. Domitian was no longer there. And the bed was empty. Where was Titus?

Quintus and Julius looked everywhere. Finally, passing by a window, they gazed out in horror at a figure lying quietly in the snow. They stood numbed. They could not move. They could only stand there, staring before them, sick with fear at the thought of the future. What would happen to Rome now? And to the Empire?

For they knew that Titus was dead.

33

TWO WHO LOVED TITUS

BEGINNING WITH THE Via Appia built in 312 B.C., the construction of roads kept pace with the expanding Empire, until a network of fifty thousand miles of highways covered the Roman world. In mid-September of A.D. 81, government couriers galloped over them to inform the provinces that Titus had died and that his brother, Domitian, succeeded him as the eleventh Emperor of Rome.

It would take the news that there was a new Caesar on the throne a month to reach Judaea. Meanwhile, traveling there on a grain ship out of Ostia, bound for Egypt, was a man formerly high in the government, but now a fugitive—Tiberius Alexander.

Sailing in the Mediterranean was dangerous in late September. The shipping season ended for the winter by November, for boats were small and the lack of the compass compelled them to stay close to shore. So the *Salamis*, rather than cross directly to Egypt, had hugged the coastline to Greece, then skirted the bulge of Asia Minor down to Judaea, where the ship's captain was to drop Tiberius off at Caesarea.

After a rough journey in cramped quarters, he stood on the deck of the *Salamis* one morning, watching the shore of Judaea approaching with relief. Around him, the crew was busy with the sails, and Tiberius knew that not a sailor among them would change places with him—a man fleeing for his life. At times panic seized him still, as he remembered those tense weeks after Titus' death, when the late Emperor's friends had wondered if Domitian had murdered him? But Domitian was the Emperor now and such thoughts must not be spoken.

"I went to Falacrina, with my own doctor, and found Titus dying of pneumonia. To reduce his fever, we put him into a tub filled with snow. Perhaps, we did wrong, but it was well-intentioned," was Domitian's version of his brother's death. The truth of what had happened was very different, Tiberius had heard from Quintus and Julius. Sick at heart, they saw the man become Emperor who had carried out-of-doors his brother, desperately ill, but still breathing and possibly not beyond hope of recovery, and heartlessly left him to die of exposure in the snow.

Titus' funeral was magnificent, and Domitian was loud in his lamentations, but no sooner was he on the throne than he began the purge of all his brother's friends. Tiberius had only escaped death himself by slipping aboard the *Salamis* secretly one night and running away.

Now, as the ship entered the harbor of Caesarea, and the time came for him to land, General Alexander would gladly have gone on to Egypt and from there fled to India. But a certain woman was in Judaea. Tiberius knew how much she had meant to Titus. And he must find her.

The fortress of Machaerus is situated in Judaea among the desolate Moab Mountains, on the eastern shore of the Dead Sea. By the year 81, a crumbling castle was all that remained of Herod Antipas' stronghold, where his stepdaughter Salome had danced. Deserted for forty years, since Antipas' death in Gaul, the ruins of Machaerus were shunned by shepherds herding their flock on these barren heights swept by chill winds, for they feared the haunted castle in whose dungeons John the Baptist was beheaded. Yet, for over a year now, a woman had been living in the ruins, crippled by a fall and confined to a couch from which she could not move unless helped by her servant, Nicola.

One day in late October, a horseman came riding up the footpath from the Jordan Valley. A passerby was so rare a sight here that Berenice sent Nicola to find out who it could be.

Tiberius Alexander dismounted from his horse. And there were tears in the eyes of the tall, bearded man, who followed Nicola into the house and bent over the hand of the woman Titus had loved. At fifty-three, Berenice's hair was gray, her face scarred, but her body was still slim, her eyes dark and lustrous.

"Tiberius!" she exclaimed. "Such a happy surprise! What has brought you to Judaea?"

"You, my dear. I came to see you."

As she studied his face, Berenice's smile faded. "But you're so solemn, Tiberius, and so very tender toward me. You frighten me."

"Prepare yourself for terrible news."

She waited tense.

"Titus is dead."

Berenice stared at him, her expression blank. Slowly, she shook her head. "No! It cannot be. Titus is only forty-two. How can he be dead?"

"He is. From pneumonia," Tiberius replied. Why tell her more?

"Titus . . . dead?" gasped Berenice, looking like a person in a trance. It was as though her mind refused to accept what Tiberius said, because to do so would bring her a grief impossible to bear. She finally spoke. "It wasn't pneumonia, but the Lord who struck him down. He often takes a long time to strike. I warned Titus when he profaned the Temple that a god was still a god, even though worshipped by hostile people, and the God of Moses would punish him eventually for his act of impropriety." Bursting into wild sobbing then, she buried her face in her hands.

Tiberius put his arm around her. "My dear, I know the love there was between you. What can I say in comfort? Will it make your grief any easier to bear to know that Titus died as he would have wanted to die, where his father did, at the family homestead in Falacrina? He went to his farm, with a severe cold, and passed away soon after reaching there."

Berenice, staring blankly before her, pictured it all.

"On the way Titus told his attendants that he had tried to be a good emperor and, to the best of his knowledge, he had but a single crime on his conscience. What it was, of course, we don't know, but I believe the crime he referred to was that he had destroyed Jerusalem."

She nodded. "Yes, he always regretted it."

Those two, who had loved Titus, talked long after the sun had set. Then, after Tiberius returned to a village down by the Jordan to sleep, Berenice called Nicola to her and said, "Undress me and go. I would be alone with my grief."

During the night, the girl heard her mistress sobbing bitterly, and many times she called out Titus' name.

But the next morning when Tiberius returned to her mountain retreat, Berenice was composed enough to be able to tell him about the accident that crippled her and why she had come to Machaerus—to help the Queen of Armenia lay the ghost of a desert hermit, John the Baptist, whose death haunted her.

"I lived for several months with my cousin Salome and tried to convince her that no screams were coming from the dungeon. But her agitation increased. She kept hearing voices. So finally I was forced to write King Aristobulus of Armenia, my stepson, that his wife was going mad. He must come and take her home."

After the royal couple had returned to Armenia, leaving Berenice alone at Machaerus, disaster had come to her in an unexpected way. She who had survived the destruction of Pompeii was crippled suddenly one day when, coming out of Antipas' ruined castle, a termite-eaten step gave way and she fell down the stairs. Nicola carried her mistress to her bed, where she lay in agony until a doctor, secured with difficulty from a Jordan village miles away, could get to her.

"He told me that my hip was broken and I would never walk again." Berenice burst into tears. "So here you find me, Tiberius, confined forever to this wretched couch—"

"Not if I can get you to a good doctor," he replied. "I'm taking you down to Capernaum at once."

In the year A.D. 28, when Jesus was preaching and healing the sick by the Sea of Galilee, Berenice had been born at Tiberias in the palace of her father, Agrippa I of Judaea. So now her life had come full circle. For it was to Capernaum, eight miles up the shore of the lake from the town of Tiberias, that General Alexander brought Berenice to get medical aid, as the ill had come to seek Our Lord's help there fifty-three years before.

Situated at the north end of the Sea of Galilee, the town of Capernaum had changed little since Jesus stood in its synagogue and taught on the Sabbath day (Mark 1:21). Its inhabitants were mostly fishermen like Peter and Andrew, his brother, and it seemed to them only yesterday when Christ had set forth from there with his followers to celebrate the Passover in Jerusalem. The road from Damascus still led through the town along which Jesus and the Twelve walked on that last journey; and the custom house stood by the water's edge, where a man named Levi, who took the toll of the lake traffic, was called from his duties by a rabbi from Nazareth and asked by Him to become one of his disciples.

Now, a half century later, Levi–renamed Matthew (Gift of God) by Christ–had returned to Capernaum and, seated in a house on the Damascus road, he was trying to tell about his inspiring years with Jesus. Matthew's Gospel, the first in the New Testament, was written ten years or more after Mark's; but Mark's was in Greek for the Gentiles, while Matthew was writing his in Hebrew, mainly for the Jews.

Down the Damascus road a bit from Matthew's house, Berenice and Tiberius had found a modest dwelling, but the doctor they consulted gave them little encouragement. Berenice would always be a cripple.

Harder almost for her to bear than the pain she must endure was the news that came to them from Rome, where Domitian was venting his lifelong jealousy of his brother by destroying, now that Titus was gone, all that he had set out to do. By 84, a Roman fleet had sailed around the northern tip of Caledonia, establishing for the first time that Britain was an island, and the invasion of Hibernia (Ireland) was being planned, when Domitian recalled Agricola's army to Italy on the pretense that Hibernia was not worth the men and gold it would take to conquer it.

With Titus dead and seeing one of his most cherished projects abandoned, Berenice, no longer able to move except from her bed to a chair, sank into a melancholy from which nothing could rouse her. It was not only Titus she had lost, when he died, but the will to live.

A.D. 89, especially, was a bad year. Her brother, Agrippa, replaced by Domitian as governor of Egypt, had become a hermit living in the Sahara Desert, and when Tiberius Alexander passed away that summer, Berenice was left to face her last years alone.

They were not long in coming.

One day a traveler arrived in Capernaum suffering from the plague and died soon after. Before he was hardly buried, several local people came down with the contagious disease. In two weeks it had become an epidemic, completely out of control. All those who could abandoned everything and left Capernaum by foot, by donkey, or by cart, but Berenice was not able to escape, her litter bearers having fled with the others. She lay in bed paralyzed, ill with the plague and helpless, forgotten by everybody.

Alone, Berenice died.

Masked men entered the houses and gathered up the effects of the plague victims, threw them out into the street and burned them for fear they would spread the disease. The dead were too numerous for individual burials. Corpses were carried out of the houses, thrown into open two-wheeled carts, and driven off to a common grave. Death is no respecter of persons, and the body of a member of the royal Herod family of Judaea was treated like all the others, flung into a communal pit dug outside the walls of Capernaum.

But it was only Berenice's body they buried. Life had lost all meaning for her, and she had died years before, when Titus passed away.

34

THE LAST OF THE FLAVIANS

"WHO IS WITH the Emperor?" a page boy asked.

"No one," another replied. "Not even a fly."

The boys giggled. It was common talk at the palace how Domitian, when young, had learned to kill by catching flies and impaling them on a sharpened stylus, and from that progressed to murdering men.

By now the Emperor was thirty-eight and no longer the suave, foppish seducer idolized by Julia and countless other ladies. He had grown pot-bellied, lanky-legged, and increasingly effeminate; he perfumed himself and rouged his cheeks like a woman, and to hide his baldness, wore huge wigs which he had his hairdresser dye blond and sprinkle with gold dust.

Domitian had no real friends—unless you could call an ugly dwarf with a large, malformed head a friend. He took the dwarf with him everywhere, even to the Senate, where the pert little creature (hated in Rome) sat on the Emperor's lap. Domitian tried to outdo in extravagance all the Caesars before him. The Romans were entertained by endless gladiatorial fights and wild-beast hunts in the stadium that he built on the Campus Martius and, to the disgust of all decent people, even wrestling matches between women. Vespasian and Titus had let the followers of Jesus of Nazareth alone, but under Domitian they were persecuted again, and the Colosseum flowed with the blood of Christian martyrs as in the time of Nero.

Always interested in exotic beasts, Domitian kept various wild and tame animals in a huge enclosure on the Palatine. He had a favorite elephant on which he rode out to dinner in Rome and rode home afterwards. On gala occasions he would return from banquets, as Julius Caesar had, between lines of elephants holding torches in their trunks to light the way.

His guests were entertained by performing bears, seals trained to answer when called by name, and monkeys which were skilled tightrope walkers. Domitian still thought it amusing to frighten people. If one dined with him, he might be startled to find a lion or a leopard beside him at the dinner table, particularly if he had not been told that the animal was tame and perfectly house-trained.

One night, a number of Rome's leading citizens were invited to the palace. They were frozen with horror when they saw the banquet hall draped in black and miniature tombstones, with their names on them, before each place at the table. The Emperor's guests sat silent and trembling until the meal finally ended and they could escape to their homes. But an hour later, they were thrown into a fresh panic by the arrival of a messenger from the palace. What had he brought? Not a death warrant, but bags of gold, a gift from the Emperor.

Unhappily, Domitian did not always confine himself to intimidation. Inviting the people he planned to kill to dine with him, he would embrace them fondly, flatter them and shower them with presents, then pronounce the death sentence.

Rich men were put to death for their wealth and their property confiscated, for the eleventh emperor of Rome, who could have given Nero lessons in extravagance, was always in need of money. The lavish palace Domitian built on the Palatine, at the time when the public treasury was nearly empty, cost more than had Nero's Golden House. Each roof tile had to be overlayed with gold leaf.

He conducted little frontier wars from safe, comfortable quarters in Gaul and Germany, and returned home to stage magnificent triumphs and erect colossal statues in his honor. Finally, Domitian put up so many triumphal arches in Rome, decorated with four-horse chariots, that wags went out by night and wrote ENOUGH! on several of them.

Yet his reign lasted for fifteen years. After his brother Titus' exemplary two years on the throne, they were a return to the worst times under Tiberius, Caligula, and Nero. It was only a question of when and how some patriot would rid the world of him.

No one realized this more than the Emperor. He had killed so many people that Domitian lived in constant terror of a violent death. When he tore down Titus' old palace and built himself a lavish one that extended across the summit of the Palatine for an eighth of a mile, so great was his fear of a stab in the back that he lined the walls of its immense rooms with highly glazed tiles from Cappadocia, which shone like mirrors when polished and would reflect any possible assassin who might creep up on him. Domitian hardly took his eyes from these mirror-like stones, being only at ease when he could see what was happening behind his back.

The astrologer, Ascletarion, had predicted that the Emperor would be murdered on September 16, in the year A.D. 96, at the fifth hour. "How will *you* die?" Domitian asked him. "I'll be torn to pieces by dogs," the astrologer answered.

"Oh, no, you won't!" declared the Emperor. To prevent such a thing happening, he had Ascletarion killed and cremated so that no dog could get at him. But a high wind blew over the funeral pyre, and the astrologer's half-burned body was, as he had predicted, torn apart by dogs.

From that moment on, Domitian became an hysterical, conscience-stricken man, haunted, it was said, by apparitions of his brother Titus. He could no longer sleep. At night, he would jump out of bed, call for torches to be brought in and, lighting up the room, shout that he was in deadly peril.

On September 16, 96, an eclipse of the moon occurred, always a forewarning to the Romans of disaster. Ascletarion had predicted that the Emperor would die that day at five o'clock and, just before the hour, he asked, "What time is it?" To reassure him, his attendants told Domitian, "Six o'clock." Greatly relieved, he started out to his heated and perfumed swimming pool. But, as he was leaving his bedroom, his secretary, Parthenius, stopped the Emperor to say that a visitor wished urgently to speak with him, for he had discovered a plot against his life.

Dismissing his attendants, Domitian shut himself in alone with this freedman, Stephanus, an athlete with whom he sometimes wrestled in the gymnasium and so thought harmless. Actually, the man had been sent to kill him by Domitia, who had been warned that her husband intended to poison her.

Stephanus apologized for the bandage he wore on his left arm. "Just a slight injury I received . . ." he said. But under the bandage was hidden a dagger. Stephanus handed Domitian a fictitious list of conspirators, and stabbed him to death from behind, as he read it.

It was like the end of some horrible dream.

Domitian's colossal equestrian statue in the Forum was overturned by the happy Romans and destroyed; every reminder of the eleventh Emperor of Rome was torn down; and the Flavian dynasty, which had begun so well with Vespasian and Titus, came to a disgraceful end with Domitian after a brief twenty-seven years.

CHRONOLOGICAL TABLE

A.D.	
4	Death of Herod the Great.
27-29	Ministry of Jesus. Crucifixion.
37	Caligula, Emperor of Rome. Birth of Nero.
39	Titus Flavius Vespasianus born.
41	Murder of Caligula; accession of Claudius.
43	Romans invade Britain, under Aulus Plautius. Titus' father, Vespasian, head of the Augusta II Legion, second-in-command of the expedition. Londinium (London) founded. The Emperor Claudius arrives, stays only sixteen days, but long enough to claim he conquered Britain, and returns to Rome to stage a triumph.
47	Vespasian captures the British chieftain, Caratacus, and is given an ovation in Rome. Hopes to get the name of Britannicus. Instead, he is sent to Africa as governor and forced to leave his son, Titus, to be the companion of the Emperor's son.
48-49	Titus comes to the Palatine to live. Death of the Empress Messalina. Claudius marries his niece, Agrippina.
51	Birth of Domitian, Titus' brother, in Africa.
54	Poisoning of Claudius. Agrippina's son Nero proclaimed Emperor.

55 Nero does away with Claudius' son, Britannicus, and almost succeeds in killing Titus. Afraid of Nero, Titus flees to Germany and enters the army.

56 Titus' mother dies in Africa. His younger brother, Domitian, returns to Italy to be brought up by a family friend, Antonia Caenis.

58 Paul of Tarsus, a prisoner in Judaea, asks King Agrippa and his sister, Queen Berenice of Cilicia, to allow him to go to Rome and appeal to Nero. Arrival of Paul in Rome (59). Nero murders his mother.

61 Titus, transferred from Gemany, serves under Suetonius in Britain. Meets Agricola and takes part in the revolt of the British queen, Boudicca.

62 Titus returns to Rome and becomes a lawyer. Marries Tertulla, the daughter of Burrus, commander of the Emperor's bodyguard. Nero tries to seduce Tertulla. To escape fom him, Titus and his wife flee to Britain. Tertulla dies there.

63 To get his revenge on Nero, Titus comes back to Rome and marries Marcia, a friend of the Empress Poppaea. Encourages Nero to make a spectacle of himself on the stage. Vespasian made proconsul of Egypt. Titus meets two Jews in Rome, Agrippa II, King of Judaea, and Joseph ben Matthias.

64 Birth of Julia. Great Fire of Rome. Doing rescue work, Titus saves Paul of Tarsus from the flames. Persecution of the Christians. Titus goes with Paul to hear Peter preach and meets another disciple, Mark, who is writing the first account of Jesus and his work. Peter and Paul martyred. Mark flees to Egypt.

65 Titus joins the Piso Conspiracy. Their plot to overthrow Nero discovered. Titus exiled to Egypt, divorced by his wife. Death of Marcia.

66-67 Jews revolt against Rome. Nero sends Vespasian to Judaea to crush the uprising. Titus made second-in-command of the expedition. Siege of Jotapata. Galilee subdued. Titus meets King Agrippa's sister, Berenice, and falls in love with her.

68-69 Year of the Four Emperors. Nero commits suicide. Galba, Otho, and Vitellius briefly succeed him on the throne. Backed by the Army of the East, Vespasian returns to Rome to become Emperor, leaving Titus to continue the Jewish War.

70 Taking over his father's command, Titus besieges Jerusalem and destroys the Temple. After a five-months' siege Jerusalem surrenders.

71 Roman triumph of Vespasian and Titus. The Apostle Mark among the spectators. Berenice, Agrippa, and Joseph ben Matthias come to live in Rome. Joseph writes a history of the late war. Berenice becomes Titus' mistress. The Romans dislike her for being a Jewess and a foreigner. Domitian stirs up their resentment. Titus is forced to send Berenice away.

72 Building of the Colosseum, begun by Vespasian. Titus' Victory Arch and a Temple of Peace erected in the Forum to display the trophies brought back from Judaea.

73 Capture by the Romans of Masada. End of the Jewish revolt.

77-78 Agricola sent by Vespasian to complete the conquest of Britain. Subdues Wales and advances into Caledonia (Scotland). Publication of Pliny's *Natural History*, dedicated to Titus.

79 Death of Vespasian. Titus proclaimed Emperor. He sends for Berenice, but dares not marry her. Due to Domitian's intrigue, the Senate forces the Emperor to renounce Berenice again. She goes to Pompeii, to live with her sister,

Drusilla. Titus promises the Senate never to see his Jewish mistress again. Two months later, Vesuvius erupts and destroys the towns of Pompeii and Herculaneum. Death of Drusilla and her son. Leading the rescue teams, Titus finds Berenice among the survivors.

80 Work continues on the Baths of Titus, his Victory Arch, and the Colosseum. Berenice returns to Judaea. The Colosseum, begun by his father, dedicated by Titus.

81 Death of Julia. Murder of Titus; accession of Domitian.

83-85 Matthew writing his Gospel. A Roman fleet circumnavigates Britain. Agricola planning an expedition to Hibernia (Ireland), when he is recalled by Domitian.

86 Death of Berenice.

96 Assassination of Domitian. End of the Flavian Dynasty.

NOTES OF A RESEARCHER

Britain

"Claudius only came to Britain to get his wife, Messalina, some pearls. Where did they come from?" I asked Norman Cook, the curator of the Guildhall Museum in London.

"From any swift, clear-water stream, usually those in Wales," he replied. "Certainly, not from our polluted Thames."

My husband, Tom, and I had come to England to do research for this book and, seated in the curator's office, we were discussing that first London founded in A.D. 43 by the Roman invaders. When the boy Titus lived there, Londinium (as the Romans called it) lay mostly on the east bank of the Walbrook, a small stream flowing into the Thames between two hills. Leadenhall Market now covers the eastern one, Cornhill, while St. Paul's Cathedral stands on the western Ludgate.

"The Walbrook, which flowed through Roman London, survived above ground until the end of the Middle Ages," Cook told us, "but has vanished now under the Bank of England."

The site of Roman Londinium which later became the City of London, Britain's chief commercial center, was visible from the Guildhall Museum, and its curator pointed out to us where that earliest London had been, laid out around a Forum, beyond which, between London Bridge and the Tower, the Roman galleys lay moored in the Thames. For hundreds of years (until 1750), London had only one bridge over the river, renewed from time to time in wood, then stone, but always on the site of the first one built by Plautius' legionaries.

"That's the fourth London Bridge to span the Thames there," Norman Cook said of the nineteenth-century replacement, "but it's been sold—more is the pity!—and is to be shipped to Arizona." Then, changing a painful subject, he asked, "Would you like to see the wall that the Romans built around Londinium?"

Indeed we would, so he took Tom and myself on a tour of several bomb-damaged places, where sections of the old Roman wall were uncovered during World War II when a large part of the City of London was leveled by German bombs. Then he drove us through busy Leadenhall Market, once the location of the Roman Forum or market place, and still a market.

"Londinium remained a Roman town for nearly four centuries, almost as long as from Shakespeare's time to the present day," Cook reminded us. "Yet because of Boudicca, their little frontier settlement barely suvived its infancy."

An hour later, the three of us were on the Thames Embankment gazing at the bronze statue of the tall, red-haired, warrior queen of the Iceni, standing defiantly in a chariot on Westminster Bridge. Looking at her proud face, we were thankful that Boudicca had escaped the humiliation of having to walk in Suetonius' Roman triumph, for after her defeat in Britain, when he was trying to force her to pass under the yoke, she managed to drink some poison she secretly carried.

The Romans were courageous too, Cook said, for when Boudicca burned Claudius' London, instead of abandoning its ruins, they not only rebuilt their tiny settlement but doubled its size. The Walbrook, that had formed Londinium's western limits, soon divided the town into two as it expanded westward over the hill on which St. Paul's Cathedral would someday be built.

Londinium is still visible to any well-informed visitor to the City of London, Cook told us, for the Square Mile that is the financial capital of the British Empire was actually the little town laid out by the Romans two thousand years ago. Surrounded now by Greater London, a city within a city, it remains the exact size it was in Titus' day, enclosed by an invisible wall.

Having shown us Roman London, Norman Cook planned our trip to Colchester (Caratacus' Camulodunum) in Exeter. "I wish I could go with you and have some of those oysters from the Colne," he said. "People have been eating oysters there since Roman times."

We understood why, several days later, when Tom and I were in Colchester, lunching on oysters and freshly caught trout at the Red Lion Inn on High Street. High Street follows the original Roman road along the crest of the hill above the river Colne and, at the end of it, are the remains of the temple the Romans built to deify "poor Claudius." Only its vaults still exist, for in the eleventh century William the Conqueror leveled the ruins left by Boudicca's tribesmen and erected on the foundations of Claudius' temple a Norman castle. In the Second World War, the inhabitants of modern Colchester used these old Roman vaults as an air-raid shelter.

When they came to Britain, the Romans found there only winding Celtic trackways, but their skilled engineers soon linked Londinium with the rest of the newly conquered province by a network of military roads, which are mostly in use today. Our drive to Colchester was only the first of several excursions that Tom and I took along these Roman highways built shortly after the Conquest–Watling Street, that ran clear across England from Dover to Chester; Ermine Street, the main road to Lincoln and the north; and the Fosse Way from South Devon to Norfolk. Names, incidentally, not given them by the Romans, but by the Saxons. What the Romans called them, if anything, we do not know; but as the highways of ancient Italy all had Roman names, such as the Appian Way, the Flaminian Way, it is reasonable to suppose that the Roman roads in Britain had names too. For convenience they are called in this book by their Saxon names, as they are known in England today.

The most interesting of our trips was along Watling Street, the first road built by the Romans, to Rochester in Kent, where Plautius' legions crossed the Medway and Vespasian won for them their first victory over the Britons. Watling Street began at the Channel port of Rutupiae (Richborough) near Dover, where the invaders landed, and continued to Chester on the opposite coast, a distance of 180 miles.

Returning from Chester, we stopped in Verulamium (St. Albans), the town Boudicca sacked after burning Camulodunum and Londinium, and returned to London for nineteen miles along the original Watling Street that became the Edgeware Road on nearing the Marble Arch. It was exciting to read the passing street signs—"Watling Street"—and realize that we were on a road laid down two thousand years ago. A long section of Roman pavement is rarely to be found in England today, we were told by Ivan Margary of Sussex, an expert on Roman roads in Britain. The ancient paving stones lie so far beneath the modern macadamizing that the stretch between St. Albans and London is the longest in Britain.

As we approached the round-abouts, our driver would invariably say, "These weren't here then, of course. The Roman roads ran perfectly straight." Were they all of them as rough? We had Watling Street mostly to ourselves. Other motorists preferred the Speedway. As our car bumped along over the crumbling, two-lane pavement, we thought, who could blame them?

Jerusalem

Lewis Augur Curtis was a small, round, rosy-faced Victorian gentleman of seventy-five. I was ten years old, he was my grandfather, and I loved him dearly. Each morning we made a tour of his fifty-acre estate, Rose Hill—a big house painted a hideous shade of green, perched on a hill overlooking Long Island Sound. Gardeners doffed their caps and bowed respectfully as Grandfather and I passed grandly by.

They were happy ones, those growing-up years at Grandfather's Rose Hill, where with my parents I spent my childhood under the watchful eye of a St. Bernard dog named Bruno and a French governess. Being an only child, there were no other children to share Marie's attentions. There was a cook in the kitchen, a waitress to serve, and a coachman to drive us to the Episcopal Church on Sunday, where Grandfather passed the plate.

He had graduated from Columbia when it was a small college, and proud of having kept up his Latin and Greek, his library shelves were filled with velum-bound copies of the Classics. There being no television in those days, the evenings were long, and we sat in the library around an oil lamp while Mother sewed, Father smoked cigars, and Grandfather read aloud to us from Thackery, Dickens, and James Fenimore Cooper. Often it would be from the Jewish historian, Josephus, who had written of the Roman's sack of Jerusalem in A.D. 70. That is why, as a child, I became interested in Titus.

Travel was a rarity then but each year my spry, little, old grandfather went off alone, to visit such faraway places as Alaska, Africa, Australia, or South America. He rode on the Trans-Siberian Railway from Moscow to Vladivostok when that famous train had no dining car, passengers must provide their own food on a six-thousand-mile journey; and when I was twelve, he took my parents and myself with him to Judaea. The four of us stayed at King David's Hotel. "Built on the site of Titus' camp, when he attacked Jerusalem," Grandfather told us, and shortly after our arrival, equipped with the Bible and Josephus as guides, we set out to tour the Holy City.

Jerusalem is built on several hills. We drove first to the highest of them, Mount Moriah, on which David was commanded by an angel of the Lord to build a temple (Chronicles I, 21). After his death, Solomon erected the temple his father had intended to build. It was destroyed in 586 B.C. by Nebuchadnezzar, who carried off the Jews as captives and the Temple's chief treasures to Babylon.

When the Jews returned from their captivity, they rebuilt

their temple. Five centuries later, Herod enlarged it. The work, started in 20 B.C. was not completed until thirty-four years after the Crucifixion. Then, only five years after Herod's Temple was finished, Titus' soldiers burned it down—oddly enough on August 30, the anniversary of its burning by Nebuchadnezzar.

Now on the site stands the Mohammedans' Dome of the Rock, built in the seventeenth century, and all that exists of Herod's Second Temple is a section of its western wall. "It's called the Wailing Wall," our guide explained, "because the Jews come here to pray and lament, especially on August thirtieth, the day their Temple was burned, and mourn its loss."

The afternoon we were there, rows of men in side-curls and women in shawls stood facing the Wall, touching and kissing the stones as they recited their prayers.

Sunset that day found us on the summit of the Mount of Olives, from where Titus first looked down upon the city he was to destroy. In the walled Garden of Gethsemane below, our guide pointed out some gnarled olive trees. "They've been there," he assured us, "since the time of Christ."

How could that be, I thought, but did not ask. Hadn't Josephus written (and he was an eyewitness) that Titus had cut down all the trees for twelve miles around Jerusalem to make crosses and assault ladders? But standing under an ancient olive, Grandfather was saying to us, "You know? This could be the actual tree under which Jesus was arrested."

So why remind him of Josephus?

As a child, with Grandfather, I had seen a Jerusalem little changed since Biblical times, but it was a different place Tom and I found there when we visited Palestine in 1964.

The Romans had done a thorough job in A.D. 70 of obliterating Jerusalem. Then, about a half century later, along came the Roman Emperor Hadrian, who built a completely new city on the site of the town burned down by Titus, and renamed it Aelia Capitolina, Aelia being Hadrian's name. The Romans occupied the Holy City for two centuries. They were followed by the Moslem Arabs who were succeeded, in turn, by the Crusaders, the Mamelukes, and the Ottomans. Each conqueror destroyed the buildings and walls of the vanquished and erected their own. To find any traces of the Roman period seemed to us hopeless. Josephus makes it plain that Titus reduced the Jews' Holy City to ashes, and except for a part of the Temple wall, left nothing intact after the siege but Herod's palace.

Built upon the site of Solomon's in the western part of Jerusalem, where the Citadel is now, all that endures of Herod's palace is a square tower near the Jappa Gate. This Tower of David, as the Crusaders called it, is actually the Phasael Tower, one of the three fortified turrets of Herod's old palace—the Mariamme, Hippicus, and Phasael. After the Romans marched away, the Phasael Tower alone remained standing to serve as a barracks for the *Legio X. Fretensis* (the Tenth Legion) left by Titus to police the smoking ruins of Jerusalem.

The city that Christ knew had been leveled to the ground, the Jews either slain in the siege or carried off by the Romans into slavery, and for sixty years, until Hadrian rebuilt Jerusalem, the sole sign of life on these barren hillsides was this tower of Herod's palace that housed the *Legio X. Fretensis*.

Three years after the fall of Jerusalem, the only Jews holding out against the Romans were a small band of Zealots, who had taken refuge at Masada in a rock-fortress built by Herod the Great on the western shore of the Dead Sea. So in A.D. 73 the Tenth Legion marched away from this Phasael Tower to crush this last stubborn nest of rebels. But when they scaled Masada's heights and launched their confident assault, the Romans were met by only silence. The entire Jewish garrison, rather than surrender, had committed suicide.

Now all that remains in the Holy City to recall Masada, one of the most historic last stands in history, is this Phasael Tower. With the Wailing Wall, it is the last vestige of Herod's city—unfortunately, lost today amid the incongruous mixture of Israeli high-rises, fragrant Arab bazaars, and dense traffic that clogs the narrow streets of modern Jerusalem.

Pompeii and Herculaneum

"Remember that Vesuvius is by no means an extinct volcano," Professor Alfonso de Franciscis, the superintendent of antiquities at Pompeii, said to us. "There was an eruption, as recently as 1944, that I witnessed myself."

He was escorting the Desmonds through the museum at Pompeii, where plaster casts on display made very real to us the catastrophe that occurred there twenty centuries ago. We saw how the people of Pompeii had reacted in the face of danger; and, most distressing of all, how they had died. The postures of their bodies revealed a death, swift or slow, as the case had been.

Professor de Franciscis stopped before one group to say, "We found this woman and child lying outside what we now call the Porta di Sarno. Trying to escape by the east gate of the walled town, they must have been caught in a flow of lava, shortly after leaving the city."

Could this be Drusilla and her son, Tony? I remembered how Berenice had seen her sister and nephew swept away from her, and hoped it was, for the woman was lying with her arms about the boy as if asleep, her body suggesting a calm passing.

"Of course, you realize that you're not looking at actual people who perished at Pompeii," the museum curator explained, "but at a mold that has preserved the shape of their bodies. The lava hardened around the dead, making a shell in which their bodies slowly decomposed. A replica of it was obtained in the same way that a sculptor casts a statue, the shape of the victim leaving a space, which was filled with liquid plaster."

What could have brought home to us more vividly the last agonies of Pompeii than these plaster casts! For instance, a chained dog writhing with suffocation as the hot ashes piled up on him; his agony was painful for us to look at, even today.

Later, seated in his office, Professor de Franciscis told us how in the eighteenth century the buried cities of Pompeii and Herculaneum were found after two thousand years, and since then, have been gradually dug out and restored to what they were before the eruption. The commercial city of Pompeii was not discovered first, he said, but its neighbor, Herculaneum—a smaller, more residential place named from the fact that Hercules was the patron god of the town—and then it was stumbled upon purely by accident.

One day in 1709, while sinking a well, a workman in the town of Resina, four miles east of Naples, chanced to dig down into what had once been Herculaneum, destroyed with

Pompeii in the A.D. 79 eruption of Vesuvius. On examining the earth he removed, the well-digger found blocks of marble in it. Sculptors paid well for marble, and he hurried off to Naples to sell it.

News spread of the workman's find and Resina became a happy hunting ground for rich collectors, who adorned their villas with statues, columns, and frescoes from the age of Titus. But Herculaneum had hardly begun to be uncovered, when the treasure hunt there came to a halt. Resina was built on the rivers of petrified volcanic mud that had engulfed ancient Herculaneum, and since the buried city could not be reached without first demolishing the modern town, the inhabitants of Resina refused to allow any further digs.

So interest shifted to a site nine miles east on another flank of Vesuvius, where in December, 1754, repair work on a road had brought to light the remains of a house; and there started the uncovering of Herculaneum's more famous sister-city, Pompeii, which nothing has interrupted to this day.

"Pompei and Herculaneum are not yet entirely cleared," the Professor told us, "but the heavy blanket of pumice stone and ash, which caved in the roofs of Pompeii, were easier to shovel away than it was to hack into the thick crusts of mud lava that had flowed into the houses at Herculaneum and solidified, sealing everything there as if in plastic."

One wonders, when will it happen again? Pompeii and Herculaneum sit on an underground inferno. Under them, down in the bowels of the earth sleeps the fire, ever gathering pressure within Vesuvius, which, unleashed someday, may again erupt over the peaceful countryside and the cities that once more lie trustingly at its foot.

Waiting outside the excavations at Pompeii one afternoon

for transportation back to Naples, Tom and I stood watching a man who had finished building a house and making himself a garden. Now he was digging a well.

"It's hard work," the farmer exclaimed, showing us his calloused hands, for the ground was full of marble columns and fragments of statues, and it had been necessary for him to dig out and cart away "a great deal· of rubbish." He had spilt the columns into garden steps, and made use of most of the marble in building his house. "The rest of it I threw over that cliff into the sea–" He jerked a thumb at the Mediterranean.

While digging his cellar, the farmer had come upon an underground room with red plaster walls, painted all over with drunken, naked people dancing. "It took me several days to scrape off all those indecent pictures and cover the walls with cement," he told us.

The man continued digging and, from time to time, he would pick up a slab of marble and throw it over a wall into the sea. At my feet, a chicken began to peck away at a gold coin. Picking up the Roman *aureus*, I saw on its obverse side the head of the Emperor Titus.

"It's only an old coin and of no value," the peasant shrugged. "If you want the thing, take it."

I have it still.

Rome

I am an ardent coin collecter. I do not know why a piece of beat-up bronze, silver, or gold money, used long ago, has such a fascination for me, unless because of its association. I like to hold a Roman *denarius* in my hand and think that when the coin was struck Caesar had not yet been assassinated, or own a Tribute Penny and know that during Christ's lifetime it was new and shiny. So, shortly after our arrival in Rome, armed with a letter of introduction from the American Numismatic Society, I climbed the stairs leading to the rooms of their Roman counterparts to show my gold *aureus* acquired at Pompeii to Rome's Keeper of Coins.

"May I see your coinage minted by Claudius, Vespasian, and Titus?" I asked, and told him about the book I was writing.

Signor Poggi had a superb collection. He went to a cabinet, fetched several coins, and I was soon examining with delight a gold piece minted in A.D. 44 that bore the head of the Emperor Claudius. On its reverse or "tail" side was a strange-looking object few would have recognized, with *De Britt* inscribed above it. "Do you know what that is?" the Keeper of Coins asked me.

"It's the triumphal arch that Claudius built to commemorate his conquest of Britain," I replied. "It spanned the Corso until Pope Alexander II had it pulled down."

"Good girl! You've read up on Rome, I see." He picked up another. "And this one?"

"That's the coinage Vespasian issued to celebrate his son's victory over the Jews." On the obverse (front) side of the coin was Titus' head and, on the reverse, the figure of a Jewess seated under a palm tree in tears, symbolizing the humiliation of Judaea. I could scarcely believe it. To think I was holding in my hand money that Titus may have used to pay off his troops!

Looking at the coins before me, the short Flavian dynasty—plain, no-nonsense Vespasian, gentle Titus, and wicked Domitian—passed before my mind's eye.

"Domitian tried hard to immortalize himself," Signor Poggi

was saying. "The Roman year began in March, from which we get Quinctilis (fifth month) renamed July in honor of Julius Caesar, and Sextilis (the sixth) later August after Augustus. But we would still be calling our seventh and eighth months Germanic and Domitian, if Domitian, who named them after himself, had not been so universally hated that after his death, to forget him, they became merely November (ninth month) and December (the tenth)."

He was on very bad terms with his father and brother during his lifetime, but Domitian took great pains to have their memory honored, to increase his own prestige. He erected to his father a temple at the base of the Capitoline of which only three columns remain, and a mausoleum to the *gens Flavia* on the Malum Punicum (the present Via della Quatro Fontane), the street running down Quirinal Hill on which Vespasian lived when he first came to Rome.

This building containing the remains of the three Flavian emperors is said to have existed as late as the fourth century. There are no traces of it today. Nor of Vespasian's Temple of Peace in the Forum, containing the trophies of war his son brought back from Judaea, which was destroyed by lightning in the sixth century. But the Piazza Navona perfectly reproduces the shape and size of the stadium that Domitian erected on the Campus Martius, and the ruins of the Basilica Julia exist in the Forum, where Titus served as a lawyer. While, nearby, surviving more or less intact, are the two most celebrated monuments of his reign, the Arch of Titus and the Colosseum. To this day they continue to be the chief sights that every tourist to Rome wants to see.

"When the Colosseum falls, Rome will fall; when Rome falls, so will the world," is an old saying. Through the centuries Titus' great arena deteriorated and became a public quarry ruthlessly plundered by vandals, who stole its marble to construct other buildings. Some of the Colosseum's stones helped to build St. Peter's Cathedral. Yet, somehow, Titus' amphitheater survived and seemed to be indestructible. Not any more. When Tom and I went to visit it, we found its entrances barricaded and were told that the most popular tourist attraction in Rome was closed to visitors indefinitely.

"We're afraid of falling masonry," a guard explained. "Only this month, thirty forty-pound stones have come tumbling down, dislodged by the vibrations from the subway trains that thunder under the Colosseum at ten-minute intervals day and night."

Decay is also eating away at Titus' triumphal arch. But standing at the head of the Sacred Way, this single span of Pentelic marble—small in comparison to the huge bulk of most Roman arches—still dominates the Forum; and, so we were told, is hated by the Jews, who refuse to walk under the archway, for it is a perpetual reminder to them of the destruction of Jerusalem by the Romans.

Finished by Domitian after his brother's death, Titus' chief memorial is famous for two reliefs on its inner jambs. The one on the north shows Titus riding in a chariot driven by the goddess Roma; on the opposite relief, his exultant soldiers are carrying on their shoulders through Rome the most valuable of the Jewish spoils—the golden table for the shewbread loaves, the silver jubilee trumpets, and the seven-branched candlestick.

Before the Jews were driven off into exile by Nebuchadnezzar, two candelabra of pure gold had stood, one on each side, of the high altar in the Temple. But the Ark of the

Covenant disappeared in Babylon, and the Jews returned from their captivity with but a single candlestick for the Romans to steal.

What became of it? No one knows. It vanished along with the other Temple treasures when Rome was sacked in A.D. 455 by Genserich, King of the Vandals. One story is that the Jews of Rome, to save them from the Vandals, threw these sacred relics into the Tiber, where they lie sunk in the mud to this day. But it is more probable that they were taken by Genserich to Carthage, where the cherished objects remained for seventy-nine years. Then, on the defeat of the Vandals, the Byzantine general, Belisarius, took them to Constantinople. For, according to tradition, they were last seen in A.D. 534 being carried through the streets of that city. After which the Emperor Justinian, heeding the pleas of the Byzantine Jews, is said to have ordered the Temple treasures to be returned to Jerusalem. But, on the way, they were lost at sea.

Whether this is true or not is anyone's guess. But Tom and I left the Forum that day thinking how the Roman Empire had crumbled, yet the Jews were back in Judaea and an independent nation again. On the stones of the arch showing Titus' conquering army marching in triumph through the streets of Rome after Jerusalem's downfall, a tourist from Israel had scrawled two emblems—the Star of David and a V for victory. It is not always the strong who survive.

BIBLIOGRAPHY

ANCIENT SOURCES

Dio, Cassius (A.D. 150-235). *Roman History*. Translated by Herbert Baldwin Foster. Troy, N. Y.: Patraets, 1905.

The author, also known as Cassius Dion, was a Roman politician and historian of Nicaea, Bithynia. He was consul of Rome (A.D. 220-229), then governor of Africa and Dalmatia. Dio spent twenty-two years on this history of Rome, written in Greek, which covers the events from 68 B.C.-A.D. 54. To him, we owe the only account we possess of the invasion of Britain by Claudius.

Josephus, Flavius (A.D. 37-100).

Born in Jerusalem, Joseph ben Matthias (his real name) was governor of Galilee. In 66, during the Jewish revolt against Rome, he led the defense of Jotapata and was taken prisoner. Changing sides, Joseph was with Titus at the fall of Jerusalem, and returned with him to Rome. He adopted Vespasian's family name (Flavius) and became a Roman citizen. His books are:

Jewish Antiquities. Written in Aramaic. English edition by William Whiston. London: Thomas Tegg, 1825.

What became of Herod Antipas and his wife, Herodias, after John the Baptist was beheaded? The Bible says no more about them. It is in Josephus' history of the Jews we learn that Antipas and Herodias were exiled to Gaul by the Emperor Caligula, and Antipas' brother Agrippa and his wife Cypros (Berenice's parents) became the rulers of Judaea. Nor does the Bible make any further mention of Salome after the Baptist's death. It is her contemporary, Josephus, who tells us Salome's subsequent history.

A paragraph in the *Antiquities* mentions Jesus of Nazareth, the only reference to Christ outside of the New Testament. Most scholars, however, consider this paragraph apocryphal.

The Jewish War. Written in Aramaic. English translation by William Whiston. London: Thomas Tegg, 1830.

Josephus' history of the rebellion, published toward the end of Vespasian's reign and dedicated to Titus. The only account of the destruction of Jerusalem by the Romans in A.D. 70 that has come down to us is found in this book Josephus was commissioned to write by the Emperor. Who could do it better? He was with Titus during the siege and his eyewitness account of it is the authority from which all other writers have taken their material. Josephus also based his description of the Roman attack on Masada upon what the few survivors were able to tell him.

Autobiography. (Same as above.) Written by Josephus to defend himself against the charge that he brought about the rebellion. English translation by J.Thackery.

SECUNDUS, GAIUS PLINIUS, known as Pliny the Elder (A.D. 23-79). *Natural History*. English translation by H. Rackam. London: Bohn, 1755. 6 vols.

Pliny was born in Como, Italy. He served with the Roman cavalry in Africa and Germany, and was governor of Spain under Nero (70-72). Before that, he was on Titus' staff in Syria. Placed by Titus in command of the Roman fleet off Neapolis, Pliny saw Vesuvius erupt in August, 79, and died trying to observe the phenomenon too closely.

In the intervals between his official duties, this prolific man wrote books on military tactics, history, grammar, rhetoric, and science. His *Natural History* (an encyclopedia covering anthropology, zoology, geography, and mineralogy) is the only one of Pliny's works extant. Inspired by his friend Titus, Pliny's most famous book, published in 77, is dedicated to him.

TACITUS, CORNELIUS (A.D. 55-125). *The Complete Works of Tacitus*. Translated from the Latin by Alfred John Church. New York: Random House, 1942.

Tacitus was born at Interamna in Umbria. In 78 he married the daughter of Gnaeus Julius Agricola, governor of Britain. A writer, he also found time to hold several political jobs: quaester under Domitian (88); consul (97); and governor of Asia (112-116). As Tacitus said of himself, "My public career was launched under Vespasian, promoted by Titus, and still further advanced by Domitian." He wrote:

Germania. Translated by J. Anderson. Oxford, 1938. Tacitus' book on Germany is all we know about that country during the early Empire.

Life of Agricola. Translated by Ogilvie & Richmond. Oxford, 1967. This biography of Tacitus' father-in-law is invaluable for the light it casts on the Britons of that period.

Histories. English edition by W. A. Sponner. London, 1891.

Annals. English translation by Donald R. Dudley. New American Library, Mentor Series, 1966.

Tacitus' chief works are his *Histories*, an account of the Roman Empire from A.D. 68-70, and his *Annals*, covering the reign of Tiberius, the last years of Claudius, and the first years of Nero. Written two generations after the events, Tacitus obtained most of his information from the memoirs written by Nero's mother, Agrippina. But Titus was his close friend and patron. So naturally Tacitus blackened the reputation of all previous Emperors, and stressed the virtues of the Flavians, under whom he lived and wrote.

TRANQUILLUS, GAIUS SUETONIUS (A.D. 70-160). *The Lives of the Twelve Caesars.* Translated by Philemon Holland. Italy: Stamperia Valdonego, 1913.

Suetonius (as he is generally called) was a friend of the younger Pliny, whom he accompanied to Asia Minor in 112, when the latter became governor of Bithynia. Returning to Rome, Suetonius was first a lawyer, then private secretary to the Emperor Hadrian (119-121). Most of his work is lost, but Suetonius' *De Vita Caesarum*, which contains biographies of Julius Caesar and the eleven Emperors from Augustus to Domitian has survived almost intact. This book alone made him famous.

As Hadrian's secretary, Suetonius had access to the government archives, and since he liked to repeat scandalous stories, *The Lives of the Twelve Caesars* makes entertaining reading, even today.

SUGGESTED MODERN READING

Africa, Thomas W. *Rome of the Caesars.* London: John Wiley & Sons, 1955.

Asimov, Isaac. *The Roman Empire.* Boston: Houghton, Mifflin, 1967.

———. *The Shaping of England.* Boston: Houghton, Mifflin, 1969.

Assa, Janine. *The Great Roman Ladies.* New York: Grove Press, 1960.

Balsdon, J. P. *Life & Leisure in Ancient Rome.* London: Bodley Head, Ltd., 1969.

———. *Roman Women.* New York: John Day, 1963.

Brauer, George C. *Judaea Weeping.* (The Jewish struggle against Rome from Pompey to Masada.) New York: Crowell, 1970.

Brion, Marcel. *Pompeii and Herculaneum.* London: Elek Books, Ltd., 1960.

Burn, A. R. *Agricola and Roman Britain.* New York: Collier Books, 1962.

Butterfield, Roger. *Ancient Rome.* New York: Odyssey Press, 1964.

Carcopina, Jerome. *Daily Life in Ancient Rome.* New Haven: Yale University Press, 1940.

Collingwood, R. G. and Myers, J. N. *Roman Britain.* London: Oxford University Press, 1939.

Cornfield, Gaalyahu (ed.). *Daniel to Paul.* New York: Macmillan, 1962.

Deiss, Joseph Jay. *Herculaneum: Italy's Buried Treasure.* New York: Crowell, 1966.

Dudley, Donald R. *The Rebellion of Boudicca.* London: Routledge & Kegan, 1962.

———. *The World of Tacitus.* Boston: Little, Brown, 1968.

Durant, G. *Britain: Rome's Most Northernly Province.* London: Bell & Sons, 1949.

Ferrero, Guglielmo. *The Women of the Caesars.* New York: Century Co., 1911.

Feuchtwanger, Lion. *Josephus.* Translated by Edwin Muir. New York: Viking Press, 1933.

Fox, A. and Sorrell, Alan. *Roman Britain.* London: Lutterworth Press, 1968.

Furneaux, Rupert. *The Roman Seige of Jerusalem.* New York: David McKay, 1972.

Giannelli, Giulio (ed.). *The World of Rome.* Translated from the

Italian by Joan White. London: Macdonald, 1967.

Grant, Michael. *Nero: Emperor of Rome*. New York: American Heritage Press, 1970.

——. *The World of Rome*. Cleveland: World Publishing Co., 1969.

Graves, Robert. *Claudius, the God*. New York: Harrison Smith, 1935.

——. *I, Claudius*. New York: Grosset & Dunlap, 1934.

Gray, John. *A History of Jerusalem*. New York: Praeger, 1969.

Grimal, Pierre. *In Search of Ancient Italy*. London: Evans Bros., 1964.

Grimas, W. F. *The Excavations of Roman London*. New York: Praeger, 1968.

Hadas, Moses. *A History of Rome*. (Told by Roman historians.) New York: Doubleday, 1956.

Howard, Maitland. *Ancient Britons*. New York: Praeger, 1969.

Johnston, Mary. *Roman Life*. Glenview, Illinois: Scott, Foresman, 1957.

Keller, Werner. *The Bible as History*. New York: William Morrow, 1964.

Lissner, Ivan. *The Caesars*. Translated by J. Maxwell Brownjohn. New York: Putnam, 1958.

Liversidge, Joan. *Britain in the Roman Empire*. New York: Praeger, 1968.

MacKendrick, Paul. *The Mute Stones Speak*. New York: New American Library, 1960.

Maiuri, Amedeo. *Pompeii*. Novaro, Italy: Instituteo Geografico, 1970.

Massa, Aldo. *The World of Pompeii*. Geneva, Switzerland: Minerva, 1970.

Merrifield, Ralph. *The Roman City of London*. London: Ernest Benn, 1965.

——. *Roman London*. London: Cassell & Co., 1969.

Peach, L. du Barde. *Julius Caesar and Roman Britain*. Loughborough, England: Willis & Hepworth, 1959.

Perowne, Stewart. *The Later Herods*. London: Hodder & Stoughton, 1958.

——. *The Life and Times of Herod the Great*. New York: Abingdon Press, 1958.

Platmer, Samuel Ball. *The Topography and Monuments of Ancient Rome*. Boston: Allyn & Bacon, 1904.

Quennel, Peter. "The Colosseum." *Newsweek*, 1971.
Ronalds, Mary Teresa. *Nero*. New York: Doubleday, 1969.
Sandmel, Samuel. *Herod: Profile of a Tyrant*. Philadelphia: Lippincott, 1967.
Serviez, Jacques Roerges de. *The Roman Empresses*. Translated from the French by Boysee Molesworth. London: Walpole Press, 1899.
Sorrell, Alan. *Roman London*. London: Batsford, Ltd., 1969.
Webster, Graham. *The Roman Conquest of Britain*. London: Batsford, Ltd., 1966.
——. *The Roman Imperial Army*. London: W. & J. McKay, 1969.
Weigall, Arthur. *Nero: The Singing Emperor of Rome*. New York: Garden City Publishing Co., 1930.
Wheeler, Sir Mortimer, *Pompeii and Herculaneum*. London: Spring Books, 1970.
Williamson, G. A. *The World of Josephus*. Boston: Little, Brown, 1964.
Youngman, Bernard R. *The Lands and Peoples of the Living Bible*. New York: Hawthorn Books, 1959.

In French

Franciscis, Alfonso de. *Pompeii*. Paris: Grand Bateliere, 1970
Corneille, Pierre. *Tite et Bérénice*. (Drama). 1670.
Racine, Jean Baptiste. *Bérénice*. (Drama). 1670.

INDEX

ALICE CURTIS DESMOND is the author of twenty-one books, all of them based on her liking for travel and history. Much of her life has been spent in Europe, South America, and the Orient. She has visited Alaska, Scandinavia, Australia, New Zealand, South Africa, gone to Russia twice, and been three times around the world. The result of combining travel and firsthand research has been five books with Peruvian, Argentine, and Brazilian backgrounds, and two on Alaska. She has also written the biographies of seven famous women, including Marie Antoinette's daughter, Betsy Bonaparte, and Dolly Madison. Her most recent title was *Cleopatra's Children.*

One has only to read about Mrs. Desmond in *Who's Who in America* to realize how varied are her interests. She belongs to clubs of painters, photographers, and stamp collectors. Both Russell Sage College and Suffolk University have conferred upon Alice Curtis Desmond the honorary degree of Doctor of Letters. The wife of the late New York State Senator Thomas C. Desmond, she lives in Newburgh, New York.